The glea...
I held cup...ed in my
hand was a strange
find. It was a ball, a small globe of crystal. Within it was a tiny image—the image of a gryphon, the beast that was my own House symbol . . . I held it in the palm of my hand that I might study the gryphon closely. Now I could see that there were small flecks of crimson in the head to mark the eyes. And those flecks sparkled, almost as if they had life of their own.

I took it back to Riwal. When he saw it, there was vast amazement on his face. "This is a thing of Power," he said at last. "It will have many uses. It shall bind when the need is for binding; it shall open a door where there is want of a key; it shall be your fate, to lead you into strange places."

Andre
Norton

THE
CRYSTAL
GRYPHON

DAW BOOKS, INC.

DONALD A. WOLLHEIM, PUBLISHER

1301 Avenue of the Americas
New York, N. Y.   10019

To S.A.G.A.

(Swordsmen and Sorcerers Guild of America)
In recognition of their encouragement
in our chosen field of
Ensorcelling.

FIRST PRINTING, OCTOBER 1973

1 2 3 4 5 6 7 8 9

PRINTED IN U.S.A.

Here Begins the Adventure of Kerova, Sometime Lord-Heir in Ulusdale of High Hallack.

I was one born accursed in two ways. Firstly, my father was Ulric, Lord of Ulmsdale in the north. And of his stock there were told dire tales. My grandfather, Ulm the Horn Handed, he who led his people into this northside dale and chartered the sea-rovers who founded Ulmsport, had looted one of the places of the Old Ones, taking the treasure sealed within. All men knew that this was no ordinary treasure, for it glowed in the dark. And after that looting not only Ulm, but all those who had been with him on that fearsome venture, were visited by a painful sickness of body from which most of them died.

When I was born, my father was already in middle years. He had taken two ladies before my mother and had of them children. But the children had been either born dead or had quitted this world in their early years, sickly creatures one and all. He had sworn, however, to get him a true heir, and so he set aside his second lady in favor of my mother when it seemed as if he would get no son of her.

My mother's lineage also laid me under a curse. She was the Lady Tephana, daughter to Fortal of Paltendale, which lies farther to the northwest. There are those who even now make off-warding signs at dalesmen from those parts, saying that, when our folk moved thither to settle, there were still Old Ones, seeming like ourselves; and that our people—the Borderers—entered into a blood-mixing with these, the offspring therefrom being not altogether human.

Be that as it may, my father was desperate for an heir. And Tephana, lately widowed, had borne already a goodly child who was now in his second year—Hlymer. My father was willing to forego dowry, to close his ears to any rumor of mixed blood, and to welcome the lady with full honor. By all accounts I have heard, she was willing, even unto risking the curse laid on my father's family by their treasure theft.

My birthing came too early and under strange circumstances, for my mother was on her way to Gunnora's shrine to give offerings for a son and a safe delivery. When she was yet a day's journey away, her pains came on her very swiftly. There was no hall, not even a landsman's dwelling near enough, and a mighty storm was brewing. Thus her women and guards took her for shelter into a place they would have normally shunned, one of those strange and awesome remains of the Old Ones, the people of uncanny power who held the dales in the dim past before the first of our blood wandered up from the south.

This building was in good repair, as is often true of the constructions left by that unknown race. For the Old Ones seem to have used spells to bind stones together in such a way that even time cannot devour them, and thus some buildings look as if they were abandoned only yesterday. What purpose this one might have served none could guess. But there were carvings of men and women, or those who had such seeming, on the inner walls.

My mother's travail was hard, and her ladies feared that they might not save her. After I was born they half-wished that they had failed to, for asking to look upon the babe, she saw me full and gave a great cry, losing her senses and near her wits. She wandered in some mind maze for several weeks thereafter.

I was not as other children. My feet were not with toes, like unto human kind; rather they were small hoofs, split, covered with horn such as make up the nails upon fingers. In my face my eyebrows slanted above eyes that were the color of butter amber, the like of which are not seen in a human countenance. Thus, all gazing upon me knew that, though I seemed far stronger of wind and limb than my unfortunate half-brothers and sisters before me, in me the curse had taken another turning. I did not sicken and die, but thrived and grew.

But my mother would not look upon me, saying I was a demon changeling, implanted in her womb by some evil spell. When those about her brought me nigh, she became so disordered in her wits that they feared her state would be permanent. Soon she declared she had no true child but Hlymer —and later my sister Lisana, born a year after me, a fair little maid with no flaw. In her my mother took much pleasure.

As for me, I was not housed at Ulmsdale Keep, but sent out at nurse to one of the foresters. However, though my mother had so disowned me, my father was moved, not by any affection—for that I was never shown by those closest to me in blood—but rather by his pride of family, to see that my upbringing was equal to my birth. He gave me the name of Kerovan, which was that of a noted warrior of our House, and he saw that I was tutored in arms as became a youngling of station and shield, sending to me one Jago, a keepless man of good birth who had served my Lord as Master of Menie until he was disabled by a bad fall in the mountains.

Jago was a master of the arts of war, not only with the lesser skills that can be battered into any youngling with a strong body and keen eyes, but also those more subtle matters that deal with the ordering of bodies of men great and small. Crippled and tied to a way of living that was only a half-life for a once-active man, he set his brain to labor as he had once ordered his body. Always he searched for new lore of battle, and sometimes at night I would watch him with a strip of smoothed bark before him, patiently setting out in his labored and crooked script facts concerning the breaking of sieges, the ordering of assaults, and the like, droning on to me the while, emphasizing this point or that by a fierce dig into the bark with the knife he used for a pen.

Jago was far more widely traveled than most dalesmen, who perhaps in a whole lifetime know little beyond four or five dales outside their own birthplace. He had been overseas in his first youth, traveling with the Sulcar Traders, those dangerous sea-rovers, to such half-fabled lands as Karsten, Alizon, and Estcarp—though of the latter nation he said little, appearing uneasy when I besought him to tell of his travels in detail. All he would say was that it was a land where witch spells and ensorcellment were as common as corn in a field, and that all the women were witches and held themselves better and apart from men, so that it was a place where one kept one's eyes to oneself and walked very quietly and mum-tongued.

There was this which makes me remember Jago well and with gratitude. In his eyes I was apparently like any other youngling, and not a young monster. So when I was with him I could forget my differences from my fellows and rest content.

Thus Jago taught me the arts of war—or rather such as a dale heir should know. For in those days we did not know the meaning of real war, giving that name to our petty skirmishing between rival lords or against the Waste outlaws. And of those we saw many in the long winters when starvation and ill weather drove them against us to plunder our granaries and try to take our warm halls and garths. War wore a far grimmer face in later years, and men got full bellies of it. It was no longer a kind of game which was played by rules, as one moves pieces back and forth across a board on a winter's eve.

But if Jago was my sword tutor, the Wiseman Riwal showed me there were other paths of life in the world. It had always been held that only a woman could learn the ways of healing and perform the spells my people draw upon in their time of need in body and spirit. Thus Riwal was as strange to his fellows as I. He had a great thirst for knowledge, which was in him as a longing for bread might be in a starving man. At times he would go roving, not only in the forest country, but beyond, into the Waste itself. When he returned he would be burdened by a pack like any peddler who carried his own stock in trade.

Being kin to the Head Forester, he had taken without formal leave one of the cots nearby. This he made snug and tight by the work of his own hands, setting above its door a mask carved of stone, not in the likeness of our people. Men looked askance at Riwal, yes—but let any animal ail, or even a man keep his bed in sickness that could not be named—then he was summoned.

About his cot grew all manner of herbs, some of those long-known to every housewife in the dales. But others were brought from afar with masses of soil bundled up about their roots, and he set them out with care. Everything grew for Riwal, and the farmer who had a wish for the best of crops would go cap in hand at sowing time and ask the Wiseman to overlook his land and give advice.

Not only did he bring green life, but he also drew that which wings over our heads or pads on four feet. Birds and animals that were hurt or ailing came to him of their own wills. Or else he would carry them to his place gently and tend them until they were able once more to fend for themselves.

This was enough to set any man apart from his fellows. But it was also well known that Riwal went to the places of the Old Ones, that he tried to search out those secrets our blood had never known. And for that, men did fear him. Yet it was that which drew me to him first.

I was as keen-eared as any child who knows that others talk about him behind their hands. And I had heard the garbled stories of my birth, of that curse which lay upon the blood of Ulm, together with the hint that neither was my mother's House free of the taint of strange mixture. The proof of both was perhaps in my flesh and bone. I had only to look in the mirror of Jago's polished shield to see it for myself.

I went to Riwal, boldly perhaps in outward seeming, but with an inward chill that, young as I was, I fought to master. He was on his knees setting out some plants which had long, thin leaves sharply cut, like the heads of boar spears. He did not look up as I came to him, but rather spoke as if I had already spent the morning in his company.

"Dragon's Tongue, the Wisewomen call this." He had a soft voice with a small tremor, not quite a stammer. "It is said to seek out the putrid matter in unhealing wounds, even as a tongue might lick such hurts clean. We shall see, we shall see. But it is not to speak of plants that you stand here, Kerovan, is it, now?"

"It is not. Men say you know of the Old Ones."

He sat back on his heels to look me eye to eye.

"But not much. We can look and finger, search and study, but of their powers—those we cannot net or trap. One can only hope to brush up a crumb here and there, to speculate, to go on everseeking. They had vast knowledge—of building, of creating, of living—beyond our ken. We do not even know why they were near-gone from High Hallack when the first of our ancestors arrived. We did not push them out— no, already their keeps and temples, their Places of Power were emptied. Here and there, yes, a few lingered. And they may still be found in the Waste and beyond the Waste in that land we have not entered. But the most—they were gone, perhaps long before men, as we know them, arrived. Still—to seek what may still lie here—it is enough to fill a lifetime and yet not find a tenth of a tenth of it!"

In his sunbrowned face his eyes were alight with that same spark I had seen in Jago's when he spoke of a trick of swordplay or a clever ambush. Now Riwal studied me in turn.

"What seek you of the Old Ones?" he asked.

"Knowledge," I answered. "Knowledge of why I am as I

am—not man—yet neither—" I hesitated, for my pride would not let me voice what I had heard in whispers.

Riwal nodded. "Knowledge is what every man should seek, and knowledge of himself most of all. But such knowledge I cannot give you. Come."

He arose and started toward his dwelling with his swinging, woodsman's stride. Without further question I followed after. So I came into Riwal's treasure house.

I could only stand just within the door and stare at what lay about me, for never before had I seen such a crowding of things, each enough to catch the eye and demand closer attention. For in baskets and nests were wild animals, watching me with bright and wary eyes, yet seeming, in this place, to feel such safety that they did not hide in fear. There were shelves in plenty on the walls. And each length of roughly hewn, hardly smoothed board was crammed with a burden of clay pots, bundles of herbs and roots, and bits and fragments that could only have come from the places of the Old Ones.

There was a bed, and two stools were so crowded upon the hearth that they sat nearly in the fire. The rest of the dwelling was more suited for storage than for living. In the middle of the room Riwal stood with his fists planted upon his hips, his head turning from side to side as if he tried to sight some special thing among the wealth of objects.

I sniffed the air. There was a mingling of many odors. The aromatic scent of herbs warred with the musky smell of animals and the suggestion of cooking from a pot still hanging on the boil-chain in the fireplace. Yet it was not in any way an unclean or disgusting smell.

"You seek the Old Ones—look you here, then!" Riwal gestured to one shelf among the many.

I skirted two baskets with furry inhabitants and came closer to see what he would show me. There I found set-out fragments, one or two being whole, of small figures or masks —bits which in some instances Riwal had fitted together to form broken but recognizable figures.

Whether these indeed represented various beings among the Old Ones, or whether they had had life only in the imagination of their creators, no one might know. But that they had beauty, even when they tended toward the grotesque, I could see for myself.

There was a winged figure of a woman, alas lacking a head; and a man of humanoid proportions, save that from the forehead curled two curved horns. Yet the face below was noble, serene, as if he were a great lord by right of his spirit. There was a figure with webbed feet and hands, plainly meant to suggest a water dweller; and a small one of another woman, or at least a female, with long hair covering most of her body like a cloak. These Riwal had managed to restore in part. The rest were fragments: a head, crowned but noseless, the eyes empty pits; a delicate hand that bore an intricate ring of metal on both thumb and forefinger, those rings seemingly a part now of the hand, whose substance was not stone but a material I did not know.

I did not touch; I merely stood and looked. And in mo was born a longing to know more of these people. I could understand the never-ending hunger that kept Riwal searching, his patient attempts to restore the broken bits he found that he might see, guess, but perhaps never know—

So Riwal also became my teacher. I went with him to those places shunned by others, to search, to speculate; always hoping that some find might be a key that would open to us the doors of the past, or at least give us a small glimpse into it.

My father made visits to me month by month, and when I was in my tenth year, he spoke to me with authority. It was plain he was in some uneasiness of spirit when he did so. But I was not amazed that he was so open with me, for always he had treated me, not as a child, but as one who had good understanding. Now he was very sober, impressing me that this was of import.

"You are the only living son of my body," he began, almost as if he found it difficult to choose the words he must use. "By all the right of custom you shall sit in the High Seat at Ulmskeep after me." He paused then, so long I ventured to break into his musing, which I knew covered a troubled mind.

"There are those who see it differently." I did not make that a question, for I knew it to be a statement of fact.

He frowned. "Who has been saying so to you?"

"None. This I have guessed for myself."

His frown grew. "You have guessed the truth. I took Hlymer under my protection, as was fitting when his mother became Lady in Ulm. He has no right to be shield-raised to the High Seat at my death. That is for you. But they press me now to hand-fast Lisana with Rogear, who is cousin-kin to you."

I was quick enough to understand what he would tell me and yet loath to hear it. But I did not hesitate to bring it into the open myself.

"Thus Rogear might claim Ulmsdale by wife-right."

My father's hand went to his sword hilt and clenched there. He rose to his feet and strode back and forth, setting his feet heavily on the earth as if he needed some firm stance against attack.

"It is against custom, but they assault my ears with it day upon day, until I am well-nigh deafened beneath my own roof!"

I knew, with bitterness, that his "they" must be mainly that mother who would not call me son. But of that I did not speak.

He continued. "Therefore I make a marriage for you, Kerovan, an heir's marriage so that all men can see that I do not intend any such offense against you, but give you all right of blood and clan. This tenth day Nolon rides to Ithkrypt, carrying the proxy axe for your wedding. They tell me that the maid Joisan is a likely lass, lacking two years of your age, which is fitting. Safe-married, you cannot be set aside—though your bride will not come to you until perhaps the Year of the Fire Troll."

I counted in my mind—eight years then. I was well content. For marriage had no meaning for me then, save that my father deemed it of such importance. I wondered, but somehow I did not dare at that moment to ask, whether he would tell this Joisan, or her kinsmen who were arranging our match, what manner of lord she would meet on her true bride-day—that I was what I was. Inside I shrank, even in thought, from that meeting. But to a boy of my years that fatal day seemed very far away, and perhaps something might happen to make sure it would never occur.

I did not see Nolon set forth to play my role in axe marriage, for he rode out of Ulmkeep where I did not go. It was only two months later that my father came to me looking less unhappy, to tell me that Nolon had returned, and that I was indeed safely wed to a maid I had never seen, and probably would not see for at least eight more years.

I did not, thereafter, think much of the fact that I had a lady, being well-occupied with my studies and even more with the quests on which I went with Riwal. Though I was under the guardianship of Jago, he made no protest when I spent time with Riwal. Between those two came to be an odd companionship, in spite of their being so dissimilar in thought and deed.

As the years passed, that stiffness which had come from my tutor's old hurt grew worse, and he found it difficult to face me in open contest with sword or axe. But with the crossbow he was still a skilled marksman. And his reading of maps, his discussion of this or that battle plan, continued. Though I saw little use then for such matters in my own life, I paid him dutiful attention, and that was to be my salvation later.

But Riwal did not appear to age at all, and his long stride still carried him far distances without tiring. I learned early to match his energy. And, while my knowledge of plants was never as great as his, yet I found a kinship with birds and animals. I ceased to hunt for sport. And I took pleasure in the fact that his wild ones did not fear me.

Best of all, however, were our visits to the places of the Old Ones. Riwal prospected further and further over the borders of the Waste, seeking ever to find something intact from the ancient days. His greatest hope, as he confided in me, was to discover some book roll or rune record.

When I suggested that the reading of such could well be beyond his skill, for surely the Old Ones had not our tongue, he nodded in agreement. Still I felt he opposed that thought, sure that if he did find such, the Power itself would aid him to understand it.

It was in the Year of the Spitting Toad that I had been wed. As I came closer to manhood, the thought of that distant lady began now and then to trouble me oddly. There were two lads near my years in the foresters' hold, but from the first they had not been playmates, or later companions. Not only did rank separate us, but they had made me aware, from the beginning of my consciousness of the world about me, that my non-human appearance cut me off from easy friendships. I had given my friendship to only two men—Jago, old enough to be my father, and Riwal, who could have been an older brother (and how I sometimes wished that was the truth!).

But those forester lads went now to the autumn fair with lass-ribbons tied to the upper latches of their jerkins, whispering and laughing about the adventures those led them to. This brought to me the first strong foreboding that when it did at last come time to claim the Lady Joisan in person, she might find me as ill a sight as had my mother. What would happen when my wife came to Ulmsdale and I must go to bide with her? If she turned from me in open loathing—

Nightmares began to haunt my sleep, and Riwal at last spoke to me with the bluntness he could use upon occasion. When he demanded what ill thought rode me, I told him the truth, hoping against hope that he would speedily assure me that I saw monsters where there were only shadows, and that I had nothing to fear—though my good sense and experience argued on the side of disaster.

But he did not give me that reassurance. Instead he was silent for a space, looking down at his hands, which had been busied fitting together some of his image fragments, but now rested quiet on the table.

"There has ever been truth between us, Kerovan," he said at last. "To me who knows you well—above all others would I choose to walk in your company. But how can I promise you that this will turn to happiness? I can only wish you peace and—" he hesitated. "Once I walked a path that I thought might end in hand-fasting and I was happy for a little. But while you bear your differences to others openly, I bear mine within. Still, there they be. And the one with whom I would have shared Cup and Flame—she saw those differences, and they made her uneasy."

"But you were not already wed," I ventured, when he fell silent.

"No, I was not. And I had something else."

"That being?" I was quick to ask.

"This!" he spread out his hands in a gesture to encompass all that was about him under that roof.

"Then I shall have this also," I said. Marry I had, for the sake of custom and my father's peace of mind. What I had seen and heard of marriages among the dale lords did not set happiness high. Heirs and lords married to increase their holdings by a maid's dowry, to get a new heir for the line. If inclination and liking came afterward, that was happiness, but it certainly did not always follow so.

"Perhaps you can." Riwal nodded. "There is something I have long thought on. Perhaps this is the time to do it."

"Follow the Road!" I was on my feet, as eager as if he meant to set out upon that beckoning mystery this very moment. For a mystery it was, and beckon it did.

We had come across it on our last venture into the Waste, a road of such building as put any dale's effort to shame, making our roads seem like rough tracks fit only for beasts.

The end of the road we had chanced upon was just that, a sharp chopping-off of that carefully laid pavement, with nothing about the end to explain the why-for. The mystery began nearly on our doorstep, for that end point was less than a half day's journey from Riwal's cot. The road ran on back into the Waste, wide, straight, only a little cloaked here and there by the drift of windborne soil. To find its other end was a project we had indeed long held in mind. The suggestion that we set out on this journey quite pushed from my mind the thought of Joisan. She was just a name anyway, and any meeting between us was still years ahead, while the following of the road was here and now!

I was answerable to none but Jago for my actions. And this was the time of year when he made his annual trip to Ulmskeep, where he kept festival with old comrades-in-arms and reported to my father. Thus I was free to follow my own wishes, which in this case meant the road.

Here Begins the Adventure of Joisan, Maid of Ithkrypt in Ithdale of High Hallack.

I, Joisan of Ithkrypt, was wed at harvest time in the Year of the Spitting Toad. By rights that was not considered a year for new beginnings; but my uncle, Lord Cyart, had the stars read three times by Dame Lorlias of Norstead Abbey (she who was so learned in such matters that men and women traveled weary leagues to consult her), and her report was that my wedding was written as a thing needful to my own fortune. Not that I was aware of much more than the stir the question caused, for I was thereupon the center of long and tiring ceremonies that brought me close to tears for the very tiredness they laid upon me.

When one has no more than eight years, it is hard to judge what occupies most the thoughts and plans of those in the adult world. I can remember my wedding now mostly as a bright picture in which I had a part I could not understand.

I remember wearing a tabard stiff with gold-thread stitchery that caught up a pattern of fresh-water pearls (for which the streams of Ithdale are rightly famous). But I was more occupied at the time with keeping to Dame Math's stern warning that I must not spot or wrinkle my finery; that I must be prudent at the feast table lest I spill and so mar the handiwork of long and patient hours. The robe beneath was blue, which did not please me over-much as it is a color I do not fancy, liking better the dark, rich shades such as hue the autumn leaves. But blue is for a maiden bride, so it was mine to wear.

My new lord was not present to drink the Life Cup and light the House Candle with me hand to hand. In his place stood a man (seeming ancient to me, for his close-cropped beard was frost-rimmed with silver), as stern as my uncle in his look. His hand, I remember, bore a scar across the knuckles that had left a raised banding of flesh of which I

was acutely aware as he clasped my fingers in the ceremony.
And in the other hand he held a massive war axe that signi-
fied my true lord who was about to twine my destiny with
his—though that lord was at least a half-dozen years or
more away from being able to raise that axe.

"Lord Kerovan and Lady Joisan!" the guests shouted our
names together, the men unsheathing their knives of ceremony so that the torchlight flashed upon the blades, vowing
to uphold the truth of this marriage in the future, by virtue
of those same blades, if need be. My head had begun to ache
with the noise, and my excitement at being allowed to attend
a real feast was fast ebbing.

The elderly Lord Nolon, who stood proxy at the wedding,
shared a plate with me politely throughout the feast. But,
though he asked me with ceremony before making a choice
from all offered platters, I was in too much awe of him
to say "no" to what I liked not, and his choices were mainly
of that nature. So I nibbled at what my taste rebelled against
and longed for it to come to an end.

It did, much later, when the women with great merriment
laid me, wearing only my fine night shift, in the great, curtained bed. And the men, headed by my uncle, brought in
that awesome axe and bedded it beside me as if it were indeed my lord. That was my wedding, though afterward it
did not seem too strange, just one of those things difficult for
a child to understand, something to be dismissed to the back
of one's mind.

Only that axe, which was my partner in place of a flesh-
and-blood bridegroom, was a stark prophecy of what was to
come—not only to me but to all the country that was my
home: High Hallack of the many dales.

After the departure of Lord Nolon, life soon returned to
what I had always known, for by custom I would continue
to dwell under my birthroof until I was of a suitable age
for my lord to claim me.

There were some small changes. On high feast days I sat
at the left hand of my uncle and was addressed ceremoniously
by my new title of Lady of Ulmsdale. My feast-day tabard
also no longer bore only one House symbol, but two, being
divided in the center vertically with a ribbon of gold. To
the left, the leaping Gryphon of Ulmsdale was worked in
beads that glittered like gems. On the right was the familiar
Broken Sword of Harb, that mighty warrior who had founded
our line in High Hallack and given all his kin fame there-

after when he had defeated the dread Demon of Irr Waste with a broken blade.

On my name-day, or as near to that as travel conditions permitted, would come some gift sent by my Lord Kerovan, together with proper greetings. But Kerovan himself was never real to me.

Also, since my uncle's lady was dead, he looked to his sister Dame Math for the chatelaine's duties in Ithkrypt. She took over the ordering of my days, to secret sighs and stifled rebellion on my part. This and this and this must be learned, that I be a credit to my upbringing when I indeed went to order my lord's household. And those tasks, which grew with my years, induced in me sometimes a desire never to hear of Ulmsdale or its heir; a longing in all my being to be unwed and free. But from Dame Math and her sense of duty I had no escape.

I could not remember my uncle's lady at all. For some reason, though he lacked an heir, he made no move through the years to wed again. Perhaps, I sometimes thought, even he dared not think of lessening in any part Dame Math's authority. That she was an able chatelaine, bringing peace and comfort to all she had dominion over, could not be denied. She kept those about her in quiet, sobriety and good order.

In her long-ago youth (it was almost impossible to think of Dame Math as ever being a maid!) she had been axe-wed in the same fashion as I to a lord of the south. But before he could claim her, the news came that he had died of a wasting fever. Whether she thereafter regretted her loss, no one ever knew. After the interval of mourning she retired to the House of Dames at Norstead, an establishment much-revered for the learning and piety of its ladies. But the death of her brother's lady had occurred before she took vows of perpetual residence, and she had returned to the mistress's role at Ithkrypt. She wore ever the sober robe of Dame, and twice a year journeyed to Norsdale for a period of retreat. As I grew older, she took me with her.

My uncle's heir was still undecided, since he had made no binding declaration. He had a younger sister also—one Islaugha, who had married and had both son and daughter. But since that son was heir to his father's holding, he was provided for.

I was the daughter of his younger half-brother, but not being male, I could not inherit save by direct decree—the which my uncle had not uttered. My dowry was such to attract a husband, and my uncle, should he wish, had also the right—no, even duty, to name that husband heir, but only when he declared it so would it be binding.

I think Dame Math would have liked to see me in the House of Dames, had the marriage with Kerovan not been made. And it is the truth that I did find my visits there pleasant. I was born with an inquiring mind and somehow attracted the notice of Past-Abbess Malwinna. She was very old, but very, very wise. Having talked with me several times, she directed that I be given the right to study in the library of the House. The stories of the past which had always enchanted me were as nothing to the rolls of chronicles and travels, dale histories, and the like, that were on the shelves and in the storage boxes in that room.

But what held me most were the references to the Old Ones, those who had ruled this land before the first of the dalesmen came north. I knew well that such accounts as I found were not only fragmentary, but perhaps also distorted, for the larger numbers of the Old Ones had already withdrawn before our forefathers arrived. Those our ancestors had contact with were lesser beings, or perhaps only shadows, left as one would discard a threadbare cloak.

Some were evil as we judged evil, in that they were enemies to humankind—like the demon Harb had slain. There were still places that were filled with dark enchantment, so that any venturing unwisely into such could be enwebbed. Other such beings could grant prayers and gifts. Such was Gunnora— the Harvest Mother—to whom all women were loyal, and whose mysteries were as great in their way as the Worship of the Cleansing Flame to which the House of Dames was dedicated. I myself wore an amulet of Gunnora—her sheath of wheat entwined with ripened fruit.

Yet others seemed neither good nor ill, being removed from the standards of humankind. At times they manifested themselves capriciously, delivering good to one, evil to another, as if they weighed men on some scales of their own and thereafter dealt with them as they saw fit.

It was chancy to deal with any of the Old Ones save Gunnora. The accounts I found at Norstead were full of instances where humans had awakened from long slumber powers that never should have been disturbed. At times I would seek out Abbess Malwinna in her small garden and ask questions, to which she gave answers if she could. If she could not, she admitted her ignorance frankly. It was on my last such meeting with her that I found her sitting with a bowl upon her knee.

The bowl was of green stone, wrought so finely that the shadow of her fingers about it showed through the substance. It had no ornamentation but its beauty of line, and it was very beautiful indeed. Within was enough wine to cover the bottom and come a bit up the sides.

I knew it was wine, for the heady smell reached me. The warmth of her fingers about it was releasing the scent of the grape. She turned it slowly around and around, so the liquid washed back and forth, but she did not watch it. Instead she looked at me so searchingly that I felt discomfort, as if I had been found wanting in some necessary quality. I searched my conscience hurriedly for any fault I might recently have shown.

"It is long," she said, "since I have tried this, Joisan. But this morning I awoke with the need for doing so, and for you. In my youth I had the gift of farseeing—for gift it is, though some shrink from it. They are afraid of that which they cannot touch, see, taste, hear, or otherwise clearly perceive. It is a gift that cannot be controlled. Few who have it can summon it at will; they must wait until the time it draws them to action. But if you are willing, this day I can use it for you —for how much or how well, that I cannot tell."

I was excited, for of farseeing I had heard. The Wise-women could use it—or some of them could. But, as the Past-Abbess said, it was not a talent that could be sharpened for use and then put ready to hand like a man's sword or a woman's needle—it must be seized upon when it came, and there was no use in trying to control it. However, with my excitement there was also a tiny chill of fear. It was one thing to read, to listen to, stories of the Power. It was, I understood now, another to see it in action, and for one's own self. Yet at that moment I do not think even panic would have kept me from saying "yes" to her offer.

"Kneel before me, Joisan. Take this bowl within your two hands and hold it level and steady."

I did as she bade, cupping my palms, one on either side of the bowl, holding it as one might hold a firebranch that might be ignited at any moment. Then she leaned forward and touched the fingers of her right hand to my forehead.

"Look upon the wine; think of it as a picture—a picture—" Oddly enough her voice sounded farther and farther away. As I looked down into the bowl, I was no longer seeing only dark liquid. It was rather as if I hung suspended in the air above a wide, borderless expanse of darkness, a giant mirror with none of the brilliance a true mirror possesses.

There came a misting, a change on that surface. Tendrils of the mist became shadow forms. I saw a round ball that glinted and, entombed in that, a form familiar to me—that of a gryphon gleaming white.

At first the ball was very large, near filling the whole of the mirror. Then it shrank swiftly, and I saw it was fastened to a chain. The chain swung from a hand, so that the ball revolved. The gryphon in it sometimes faced me, sometimes faced away. But there grew in me the knowledge that this ball was of great importance.

It was very small now, for the hand that dangled it was also shrinking. The arm to which it was attached, and then the body belonging to the arm, appeared. Now a man stood there. His face was turned from me, hidden. He wore war mail, the hood drawn up about his throat. There was a battle sword girded to him, and over his shoulder I saw the arch of a crossbow. But he wore no House tabard, nothing to identify him, only that swinging ball. Then he left, tramping away as if he had been summoned elsewhere. The mirror was dark and empty; nor did any more shadows gather there.

Malwinna's hand fell from my forehead. As I raised my eyes to blink and blink again, I saw a woeful pallor on her face. So I quickly set aside the bowl and dared to take her hands within mine, striving to help her.

She smiled weakly. "It draws the strength—the more when one has little strength left. But it was laid on me to do this thing. Tell me, my daughter, what did you learn?"

"You did not see it, then?" I was surprised.

"No. It was not a farseeing for me, that I knew. It was yours only."

I told her what I had seen: the gryphon englobed and a man in battle dress holding it. And I ended, "The gryphon is the badge of the House of Ulm. Did I then see the Lord Kerovan to whom I am wed?"

"That may be so," she agreed. "But it is in my mind that the gryphon is that which is of the greatest importance to your future. If such ever comes to your hand, my daughter, do you guard it well. For it is also to be believed that this is a thing of the Old Ones and a focus of some power they once knew. Now, call Dame Alousan, for I have need of one of her strengthening cordials. But speak not of what we have done here this morning, for farseeing is a private thing and not to be talked of lightly."

I said naught to any of the Dames, nor to Math. And the Past-Abbess allowed them to believe that she was merely a little wearied, so they fussed about her, for she was greatly loved. No one paid any attention to me. I had taken the bowl with me into the guesting room and put it on the table there.

Though I continued to look into it now and again I saw nothing but the wine; no dark mirror, no shadows moving. Yet in my mind was so vivid a picture of the crystal gryphon that I could have painted it, had I any skill in limning, in every small detail. And I speculated as to what it might mean. The gryphon so enclosed had differences from the one that appeared as Ulm's badge. A gryphon by rights had the wings and forepart of an eagle: its front legs end in a bird of prey's strong talons. But the rear, the tail, the hind paws are those of a lion, one of the beasts known to the south alone. On its bird's head a lion's ears stand upright.

In the ancient learning the gryphon symbolizes gold: the warmth and majesty of the sun. Ofttimes in legends it is the guardian of hidden treasure.

Thus the gryphon is mainly pictured in red and gold, which are sun colors. Yet the one enclosed in the globe was the white of ice—a white gryphon.

Shortly after that farseeing, Dame Math and I returned home to Ithkrypt. But we did not remain there long. For in this Year of the Crowned Swan I had reached the age of fourteen, and Dame Math was already preparing my bride clothes and the furnishings I would take with me when Kerovan would send for me, as was the custom, in the next year or two.

So we went on to Trevamper, that town set at the meeting of highway and river where all merchants in the north show their wares upon occasion. Even the Sulcarmen, who are sea-rovers and seldom come far from wind and wave, travel to Trevamper. For there is the interior trade. And by chance we met there also my Aunt Islaugha, her son Toross, and her daughter Ynglida.

She came to pay a call on Dame Math, but I felt it was one of duty only and there was little liking between these sisters. However the Lady Islaugha presented a smiling face and spoke us fair, congratulating me on the fine marriage that had united me to the House of Ulm.

Yngilda pushed closer to me when our elders had turned their attention back to their own concerns, and I thought she stared rudely. She was a stout girl, bundled in rich clothing down which her braids rippled, their ends bound in ribbons hung with little silver bells meant to chime sweetly as she moved. Such a conceit did not suit her broad, flattish face, with its too-small mouth always pursed a little as if she chewed upon a spicy secret she debated over sharing.

"You have seen the likeness of your lord?" she asked almost abruptly.

I stirred uneasily under the probing of her eyes. I knew her then for unfriend, though why she should be so when we hardly knew each other, I could not guess.

"No." As always when such uneasiness with others was in me, I was wary. But the truth is better than any evasion which may later trip one up. And for the first time I wondered a little at a matter I had never considered before. Why had Kerovan not caused to be sent a likeness of himself? That such was done in axe marriages I knew.

"A pity." Her gaze seemed to have some manner of triumph in it now. "Look you here—this is my promised lord, Elvan of Rishdale." She brought out of her belt pocket an oblong of wood with a face painted on it. "He sent it with his bride gift two years ago."

The painted face was that of a man of middle years, no boy. And it was not a pleasant countenance to my thinking, but perhaps the limner had either not been skillful or had some reason not to flatter this Elvan. That Yngilda was proud of it was plain.

"He would seem a man of authority." I did the best I could in way of praise. My disliking for the pictured face grew stronger the longer I regarded it.

She took that, as I had hoped, as a compliment to her promised lord.

"Rishdale is an upper dale. They are wool people, and the trade is rich. Already my lord has sent me this, and this—" She patted an amber necklace which lay above her tabard and thrust her hand out to me that I might look upon a massive thumb ring of a serpent with eyes that were flecks of red gem-fire.

"The serpent is his House badge. This is his own ring, sent for a welcome gift. I go to him next harvest time."

"I wish you happy," I answered.

Her pale tongue swept out over her lower lip. Again she

was in two minds over some speech to make. At last she brought herself to it, bending her head even closer, while I had all I could do not to withdraw at her approach, for her close company did not please me.

"I would I could say the same to you, kinswoman."

I knew I should not encourage her now, yet something made me ask, "And why not, kinswoman?"

"We are not so far from Ulmsdale as you. We have heard —much." And she strove to give such a dire accent to that last word that she did indeed make an impression on me. For all my prudence and distrust, I could not now deny her this confidence.

"Much of what, kinswoman?" My tone made a challenge of that, one she was quick to note and that pleased her, I am sure.

"Of the curse, kinswoman. Did they not tell you that the Heir of Ulmsdale lies under a double cursing? Why, his own mother has refused to look upon his face since his birth hour. Have they not told you that?" she repeated with open relish. "Alack, that I should spoil your dreaming about a brave young lord. He is a monster thing, they say, sent to live apart because all men shrink from—"

"Yngilda!" That saying of her name was as sharp as a whip crack, and under it she flinched as if indeed some lash had bitten into her body. Dame Math stood over us, and it was plain in her face she had heard those words.

So open was her wrath that at that moment I knew Yngilda had indeed spoken the truth, or at least come so close to it as to shake my guardian. Only the truth could have aroused her ire so greatly.

She said no more, only eyed Yngilda menacingly until the girl edged back, her full cheeks blanching a little in her fright. She gave a kind of squeak and scrambled away. But I sat where I was and met Dame Math eye to eye. Within me the cold grew, setting me to shivering.

Cursed—a monster whom even his mother could not bear to look upon! By the Heart of Gunnora, what had they done to me, to give me in marriage to that? I could have screamed my terror aloud, but I did not. For in that much I kept my control. I only said slowly, forcing my voice to be level, determined to know the full of it here and now, "By the oath of the Flame you serve, Lady, tell me now the truth. Are her words that truth? Am I wed to one who is not like other men?" For I could not bring myself to say "monster."

I think up until that moment Dame Math might have covered with fair words. But now she sat beside me, her face grave, as the flush of anger faded.

"You are no longer a child, Joisan. Yes, I will give you what truth I know. It is true that Kerovan dwells apart from his kin, but he is not a monster. There is a curse laid on those of the House of Ulm, and his mother comes from the up-dales, from a family rumored to have inter-wed with Old Ones. Thus he has such blood within him. But he is not monstrous—of this Lord Cyart made sure before he would consent to the marriage."

"Yet he dwells apart from his kin. Is it true that his mother will not look upon him?" The cold within me was such now I could hardly control myself.

Still she was frank with me. "That is true because of the manner of his birthing, and she is a fool!" Then she told me an unusual tale of how the Lord of Ulm had taken wives and had no living heir because of the curse. How he wed a third time with a widow, and how she had been taken on the road before her time with birth pains and had borne her son within the walls of one of the Old Ones' buildings. And of how thereafter she had turned her face from him because she was so filled with fear that the babe was of the Old Ones' sending. But he was sound and no monster. His father swore to that by the Great Oath for which there can be no breaking.

Because she told it all so plainly, I believed her and was less shaken.

Then Dame Math added, "Joisan, be glad that you take a young lord. Yngilda, for all her prating, goes to one already wed once, a man old enough to be her father, and one who will have little patience with any youthful follies. She will find him far less indulgent to her whims and laziness than her mother, and she will perhaps rue the day she left her own keep for his.

"Kerovan by all accounts is one you will well company with—for he is learned in rune scrolls as well as in swordplay, which so occupies the minds and bodies of most men. He has a liking for searching out old things, such as you have also. Yes, you have much to think right in your wedding, and little to see of shadows. You are a maid of good mind and not easily shaken. Do not let the envious words of this foolish wench overset your reason. I swear, if you wish it, by the Flame—and you well know the meaning of such an oath for me—that I would not stand by without protest and see you wed to any monster!"

Knowing Dame Math, that reassurance was indeed all I needed. Yet during the days that followed I did think again and again of the strange upbringing Kerovan must have had. That a mother had turned her face from her child was hard to believe. Still, giving birth in a place of the Old Ones might have poisoned her mind against the cause of her pain and fear as she lay therein. And I knew well from my reading at the Abbey that many such places had malignant atmospheres that worked subtly upon mankind. She could well have fallen prey to such influences during her hours of labor.

For the rest of our stay in town my aunt and her daughter did not come near us. Perhaps Dame Math had made plain her views on what Yngilda had told me. I was well content not to see her full face, her pursed mouth, and her probing eyes again.

To most dalesmen the Waste is a fearsome place. Outlawed men were driven to refuge there, perhaps coming to regard it in time as they had their native dales. And there are hunters, wild as any outlaws in their own fashion, ranging it to bring back packloads of strange furs as well as lumps of pure metal congealed into odd shapes: not native ores, but substances that had been worked and then reduced to broken pieces.

Such lumps of metal were greatly prized, though smiths had to rework them with care. Swords and mail made from this metal were stronger, more resistant to weathering. On the other hand, sometimes it had fearsome properties, exploding in vast conflagrations to consume all nearby—as if some power had struck it. A metal-smith both yearned to use it for the promise of fine craftsmanship and feared that each piece he brought to the forge might be one of the cursed bits.

Those who found such metal and traded in it were notoriously close-mouthed about the source. Riwal believed that they mined, not the earth, but places of the Old Ones wherein some ancient and unbelievably horrible conflict had fused metal into these lumps. He had attempted to win the confidence of one Hagon, a trader, who had twice passed through our forest territory. But Hagon refused to talk.

So it was not only the broken-off road that beckoned us. There were other secrets to be uncovered. And I found this venture well to my liking.

We reached the broken-off end of the road by mid-morning and stood studying it before we set foot on its earth-drifted surface. It was indeed a puzzle, for that break was as clean-cut as if some giant swordsman had brought down his blade to sever the masonry. Yet, if some such action had occurred, where was the rest? For beyond the break there was not even a trace of old rubble to suggest it had ever run beyond this point. And why would any road come to such a purposeless ending? It may be true that the purposes of the Old Ones were not the same as those of men, and we cannot judge their actions by ours.

"How long ago since men walked here, Riwal?" I asked.

He shrugged. "Who knows? If it were *men* who did so. But if the road ends thus, the beginning may be of more interest."

We were riding the small, desert-bred horses used by Waste rovers, tough beasts with an inherited ability to go far on a minimum of drink and forage. And we led a third horse with our supplies in a pack. We went clothed as metal traders, so that any spying upon us could believe we were of the Waste ourselves. We traveled alert to sign and sound, for only he who is ever-watchful can hope to best the traps and dangers of such a land.

The Waste is not pure desert, though much is arid land with a scant covering of small, wind-beaten shrubs and sun-dried grass in ragged clumps. At times, dark copses of trees grow so thick they huddle trunk to trunk. And outcrops of stone stand like pillars.

Some of these had been worked, if not by man, then by creatures who used stone for monuments. But the pillars had been so scoured by years of winds that only traces of the working remained. Here a wall could be seen for a bit; there a pair of columns suggested a past building of some pride.

We passed such a place soon after we took to the road, but there was not enough left to explore. In the open there was silence, for this was a windless day. The clop-clop of our mounts' feet on the pavement seemed to echo, making far too loud a sound, so that I found myself looking from side to side, and now and then over my shoulder. The feeling grew stronger that we were being watched—by outlaws?

In spite of myself I found my hand straying ever in the direction of the sword hilt, ready to defend against attack. Yet when I glanced at Riwal, I saw him riding easy, though he also watched right and left.

"I feel"—I urged my mount closer to his—"that we are watched." Perhaps I humbled my pride to admit that, yet this was more his land than mine, and I relied on him.

"It is ever so—in the Waste," he returned.

"Outlaws?" My fingers closed about the hilt now.

"Perhaps. But more likely other things." His eyes did not quite meet mine, and I sensed he was at a loss to explain. Perhaps he, too, feared to display some weakness before me, a younger and less-tried venturer.

"It is the truth then that the Old Ones left guardians?"

"What man among us knows?" He countered my question with another. "This much is so: when one ventures into their ways, there is often this feeling of being watched. Yet it has never been with me more than just watching. If they left guardians, as you say, those are now too old and tired to do more than watch."

I found that hardly reassuring. And still I continued to watch—though nothing stirred out in that flat land across which the road hammered a straight and level path.

At nooning we drew to the side of the pavement, ate and drank, and gave our horses to drink also from the water skins we carried. There was no sun, and the sky over us was gray; still I could see no clouds gathering to threaten storm. But Riwal sniffed the air, his head up to the sky.

"We must seek shelter," he said, and there was urgency in his voice.

"I see no storm clouds."

"Storms come unheralded and swiftly in the Waste. There —"He had been surveying the countryside around, and now he pointed ahead to where there was a pile beside the road, perhaps another cluster of time-eroded ruin.

We pushed on, to discover that sight-distance was deceptive in this place. There was a haze that seemed to rise from the ground so that things appeared closer than they were. But at length we reached the spot he had appointed. And none too soon, for the sky was no longer the gray of a gloomy day, but had darkened now into twilight come hours too soon.

Chance had brought us to shelter. Though the ruins at the outset of the road had been so formless as to only suggest they had once had purpose, this ancient building was in better preservation. There was actually part of a room or hall among the jumble of stone blocks with a portion of roof over it. And into that we crowded both ourselves and our animals.

Now the wind blew, whirling up the grit, hurling it in marching columns to fill eyes, mouths, nostrils. We had to fight to gain the last few strides to cover. Once inside, when we turned to look out, it was to see a curtain of dust.

That did not last long. Overhead sounded the rumble of thunder as if an army with a siege train marched. And the lash of lightning followed with force enough to suggest it had struck not too far away. Then came rain—quickly beating down the dust, yet not clearing any path for our vision; rather providing a second curtain, this time of moisture, not grit.

Water ran in a stream across the pitted floor, so we crowded back into the farthest corner of the ruin. The horses whinnied and snuffled, rolling their eyes, as if they found this fury of nature frightening. But to me our corner gave an illusion of shelter, though I flinched when the lightning struck again.

Such fury deafened us. We were reduced to the point of simple endurance and we kept hold of the reins, lest our mounts break out into the storm. As they began to quiet, no longer tossing their heads or stamping, I relaxed a little.

The dark was close to that of true night, and we had no torch. So crowded were we that Riwal's shoulder rubbed mine whenever he moved even slightly, yet the rain was so tumultuous we could not have heard each other without shouting, which we did not do.

What had been the original purpose of the ruin? Built so beside the road, could it have been an inn? Or was it a guard post for some patrol? Or even a temple? As Riwal had said, who knew the purposes of the Old Ones?

With one hand I explored the wall. The surface of the stone was smooth, not pitted as the more exposed portions were. My fingers could detect no seam or joining, yet those blocks had been set together somehow. Suddenly—

Men sleep and dream. But I will swear any oath I did not sleep. And if I dreamed, then it was unlike any dream I had ever known.

I looked out upon the road, and there were those moving along it. Yet when I tried to see them through what appeared to be a mist, I could not. They remained but shapes, approximating men. Could they be men?

Though I could not see them clearly, their emotion flowed to me. They were all moving in one direction, and this was a retreat. There was a vast and overwhelming feeling of—no, it was not defeat, not as if some enemy had pressed them into this withdrawal, but rather that circumstances were against them. They seemed to long for what they left behind, with the longing of those torn from deep rooting.

Now I knew that they were not all alike or of one kind. Some as they passed gave to me their sense of regret, or loss, as clearly as if they had shouted it aloud in words I could understand. But others were less able to communicate in this fashion, though their emotions were none the less deep.

The main press of that strange and ghostly company was past. Now there was only a handful of stragglers, or of those who found it the hardest to leave. Did I or did I not hear the sound of weeping through the rain? If they did not weep in fact they wept in thought, and their sorrow tore at me so I could not look at them any longer, but covered my eyes with my hands and felt on my dusty cheeks tears of my own to match theirs.

"Kerovan!"

The shadow people were gone. And so was the force of the storm. Riwal's hand was heavy on my shoulder, as if he shook me awake from sleep.

"Kerovan!" There was a sharp demand in his voice, and I blinked at what I could see of him in the dusk.

"What is the matter?"

"You—you were crying out. What happened to you?"

I told him of the shadow people withdrawing in their sorrow.

"Perhaps you have the sight," he said gravely when I had done. "For that might well have happened when the Old Ones left this land. Have you ever tried farseeing or tested a talent for the Power?"

"Not I!" I was determined that I would not be cut off from my fellows by a second burden. Different I might be in body because of the curse laid on me before my birth, but I needed not add to that difference by striving to follow those paths trod by Wisewomen and a few men such as Riwal. And he did not urge me, after my quick denial. Such a way must be followed by one wholly willing; not by one led into it by another. It has its disciplines that are in some ways more severe than any warrior training, and its own laws.

After the storm the day lightened again, and we were able to set out at a brisk pace. The water still settled in pools and hollows, and we refilled our smaller water bag, letting the horses drink their fill before we moved on.

I wondered, when we rode that way, if I would have the sensation of the company of those I had seen in the vision or dream. But that was not so. And shortly I forgot the intensity of the emotion that I had shared with them. For that I was thankful.

The road, which had run so straight, made a wide curve heading toward the north and the greater unknown of the Waste. Now ahead we caught sight of heights making a dark blue line across the sky of evening, as if we headed for a mountain chain.

Here also the land was more hospitable. There were trees where before had been mostly shrubs and stretches of grassland. We came to where the road arched in a bridge over a stream of some size. And it was beside that running water that we camped for the night. In fact Riwal settled us, not on the bank of the stream, but on a bar which thrust out into it. The water was high from the storm, and there was flotsam carried with it, piled around the rocks edging that bar.

I eyed his choice with some disfavor. To my mind he had deliberately selected a site which would give us little room and which appeared dangerous from the sweep of water. He must have read my expression for he said, "This is chancy land, Kerovan. It is best to take the common precautions when within it—some uncommon ones too."

"Common precautions?"

He gestured at the stream. "Running water. That which is ill-disposed to us, if it be of the Power and not human, cannot cross running water. If we camp so, we have only one front to defend."

So reasoned, it was common sense. Thus I pushed rocks and pulled loose drift to clear a space between for us and the horses. Nor did Riwal deny us a fire made from the driest of the drift. The river was falling, but the current was still swift. It held life also, for I saw a dark shape of a length to suggest that the fish of this country were of a huge size, though I was teased by the disturbing suggestion that that shadow beneath the surface did not altogether resemble any fish I knew. I decided that in the Waste it was better not to probe too deeply into the unknown.

We set a watch, as we would in enemy country. At first, during my tour of duty, I was so uneasily alert that I found myself peopling each shadow with an intruder, until I took my fancies in hand and forced control over them.

Though the day had been sunless, we did not lack a moon. Its rays were particularly strong, making the landscape all black and silver—silver in the open, black in the shadows. There was life out there, for once I heard the drum of hoofs, and our horses nickered and tugged at their tethers, as if some of their wild kin had pounded by. Once I heard a distant, mournful cry, like the howl of a hunting wolf. And something very large with wings planed noiselessly over our camp as if to inspect us. Yet none of these were frightening in themselves, for all men know that there are wild horses in the Waste, and wolves run through the dales as well. And there are winged night-hunters everywhere.

No, it was not those sounds that disturbed me. It was what I did not hear. For I was as certain as if I could see it that out there in the black and silver land lurked something, or some-one, who watched and listened with the same intensity that I did. And whether it was of good or ill I could not guess.

Sun and morning banished such fancies. The land was open, empty, in the daylight. We crossed the hump of the bridge and headed on, while before us the mountains grew sharper to the sight.

By nooning we were in the foothills, which were ridges sharper than our dales, more like knife slashes in soil and rock. No longer was the road straight. It narrowed to a way along which two of us might still ride abreast, but no wider, and it twisted and curved, ran up and down, as if its makers had followed always the easiest route through this maze of heights. Here, too, the Old Ones had left their mark. Carved on the walls of rock were faces, some grotesque, some human-seeming and benign, and often bands of runes that Riwal busied himself to copy.

Though no one could read the script of the Old Ones, Riwal had hopes that someday he would be able to do so. We had dawdled so while he copied the runes that noon found us in a narrow vale where we took our rest under the chin of a vast face that protruded strongly from the parent cliff of which it had been carved.

I had studied it as we came up, finding in it something vaguely familiar, though what that was I could not say.

Oddly enough, though we were here surrounded by the work of those who had vanished, I felt free of that watching, as if whatever had been here once was long gone and had left no trace. And my spirits rose as they had not since the storm caught us.

"Why all these carvings?" I wondered. "The farther we go, the more they are clustered on the walls."

Riwal swallowed a mouthful of travel bread in order to answer. "Perhaps we now approach some place of importance; a shrine, even a city. I have gathered and sifted the stories of traders for years, yet I know of none who have come this way, into the foothills of the mountains."

That he was excited I could see, and I knew that he antici-pated some discovery that would be far greater than any he had made during his years of wandering in the Waste. He did not linger over his food, nor did I, for his enthusiasm grew to be mine also. We did not pause beneath that giant chin for long, but rode on.

The road continued to weave through the foothills, and the

carvings grew more complex. There were no more heads or faces. Now runes ran in complex patterns of lines and circles. Riwal reined in before one.

"The Great Star!" His awe was plain to see.

Surveying the complexity of that design, I could at last make out a basic five-point star. But the star was overlaid with a wealth of other curves and bits, so it took careful examination to make it out at all.

"The Great Star?" I asked.

Riwal had dismounted and gone to the rock face in which that pattern was so deeply chiseled, running his fingers along the lines as far up as he could reach, as if he wished to assure himself by touch that what his eyes reported was true.

"It is a way, that much we know, of calling upon one of the highest of the Powers," he said, "though all save the design has been lost to us. Never before have I seen it in so complex a setting. I must make a drawing of this!"

Straightway he brought out his horn of ink, tight-capped for journeying; his pen; and a fresh piece of parchment on which he began to copy the design. So lost was he in the task that I grew restless. At last I felt I could no longer just sit and watch his slow stroke upon stroke as he studied each part of the design to set it down.

"I shall ride on a little," I told him. He grunted some answer, intent upon his labors.

Ride on I did, and the road took a last turning—to the end!

Before me a flat rock face bore no sign of any gateway or door. The pavement ended flush with that cliff. I stared in disbelief at such an abrupt and seemingly meaningless finish to our quest. A road that began nowhere and ended thus—? What had led to its making? What could its purpose have been?

I dismounted and went to run my fingertips along the surface of the cliff. It was real, solid rock—the road ran to it and ended. I swung first to one side and then to the other, beyond the boundaries of the pavement, seeking some continuation, some reason. There were two pillars standing, one on either hand, as if they guarded some portal. But the portal did not exist!

I advanced to lay hand upon the left pillar, and, as I did so, at its foot I caught a glimpse of something. It was a faint glimmer, near-buried in the gravel. Straightway I was on my knees, using first my fingers and then the point of my knife, to loosen my find from a crack in which it had been half-buried.

The gleaming object I held cupped in my hand was a strange find. It was a ball, a small globe of crystal, a substance one might have thought would have been shattered among these harsh rocks long since. Yet it did not even bear a scratch upon its smooth surface.

Within it was a tiny image, so well-wrought as to be the masterpiece of some gem-cutter's art—the image of a gryphon, the beast that was my own House symbol. The creature had been posed with one eagle-clawed foot raised, its beak open as if it were about to utter some word of wisdom to which it bade me listen. Set in the globe directly above its head was a twisted loop of gold, as if it had once been so linked to a chain for wearing.

As I stood with it cupped in my hand, the glimmer of light that had led me to its discovery grew stronger. And I will swear that the crystal itself became warm, but only with such warmth as was pleasing.

I held it on the palm of my hand, level with my eyes, that I might study the gryphon closely. Now I could see that there were small flecks of crimson in the head to mark the eyes. And those flecks sparkled, even though there was no outer light to reflect within them, almost as if they had life of their own.

Long had I been familiar with all the broken bits on Riwal's shelves, but never before had such a thing been found intact —save for the broken loop at the top, and that, I saw, could be easily repaired. Perhaps I should offer it to Riwal. And yet as I felt its warmth against my flesh, saw the gryphon's stance of wisdom and warning within, I had the belief that this was meant for me alone and that its finding was not by mere chance but by the workings of some purpose beyond my knowledge. If it were true that my mother's House had inter-mated with Old Ones, then it could well be that some small portion of such blood in my own veins made me find the crystal globe familiar and pleasant.

I took it back to Riwal. When he saw it, there was vast amazement on his face.

"A treasure—and truly yours," he said slowly, as if he wished what he said were not so.

"I found it—but we share equally." I made myself be fair.

He shook his head. "Not this. Is it mere chance that brings a gryphon to one who wears that badge already?" Reaching forth, he touched the left breast of the jerkin above my mail, on which was discreetly set the small gryphon head I always wore.

He would not even take the globe into his hand, though he bent his head to study it closely.

"This is a thing of Power," he said at last. "Do you not feel the life in it?"

That I did. The warmth and well-being that spread from it was a fact I could not deny.

"It will have many uses." His voice was low, and I saw that his eyes were now closed, so he was not viewing it at all. "It shall bind when the need is for binding; it shall open a door where there is want of a key; it shall be your fate, to lead you into strange places."

Though he had never said he could farsee, in that moment I knew that he was gripped by a compelling force which enabled him to envision the future uses of the thing I had found. I wrapped it within a scrap of his parchment and stowed it against my flesh within my mail for the greatest safety that I could give it.

About the bare cliff Riwal was as puzzled as I. All the signs suggested a portal of some importance, yet there was no portal. And we had, in the end, to be content with what we had discovered and to begin the trek back from the Waste.

Never during that journey did Riwal ask to see the gryphon again, nor did I bring it forth. Yet there was no moment during the return that I was not aware of what I carried. And the two nights that we lay encamped on the return road, I had strange dreams, of which I could remember very little save that they left an urgency upon me to return to the only home I had ever known, because before me lay a task of importance.

Though I had little liking for Yngilda, I found her brother Toross unlike her. In the autumn of that year, soon after we returned to Ithkrypt, he came riding over the hills with a small escort, their swords all scabbarded with peace-strings, ready to take part in the fall hunt that would fill our winter larder after the kills were salted down.

Differing from his sister in body as well as in mind, he was a slender, well-set youth, his hair more red than the usual bronze of a dalesman. He possessed a quick wit and a gift of song that he used to advantage in the hall at night.

I heard Dame Math say to one of her women that that one, meaning Toross, could well carry a water horn through life to collect the tears of maids sighing after him. Yet he did nothing to provoke such admiration; never courted their notice, being as ready in riding and practice of arms as any of the men, and well-accepted by them.

But to me he was a friend such as I had not found before. He taught me the words of many songs and how to finger his own knee-harp. Now and then he would bring me a branch of brilliant leaves clipped at their autumn splendor, or some like trifle to delight the eye.

Not that he had much time for such pleasures, for this was a bustling time when there was much to be done for the ordering of supplies against the coming of cold days. We stewed some fruits and set them in jars with parchment tied firmly over the mouths; dried other such; brought forth heavy clothing and inspected it for the need of repairs.

More and more of this Dame Math left to my ordering, as she said that now I was so nigh in years to becoming the lady of my lord's household I must have the experience of such ways. I made mistakes, but I also learned much, because I had no mind to be shamed before strangers in another keep. And I felt more than a little pride when my uncle would notice with approval some dish of my contriving. He had a sweet tooth, and rose and violet sugars spun artfully into flowers were to him an amusing conceit with which to end a meal, and one of my greater triumphs.

Though I busied myself so by day, and even a little by lamplight in the evening when we dealt with the clothing, yet I could not altogether thrust out of mind some of the thoughts Yngilda had left with me. Thus I did something in secret that otherwise only a much younger maid would have thought on.

There was a well to the west in the dale that had a story about it—that if one went there when the full moon was reflected on its water surface and cast in a pin, then luck would follow. Thus, not quite believing, yet still drawn by some small hope that perhaps there *was* luck to be gained by this device, I stole away at moonrise (which was no small task in itself) and cut across the newly harvested fields to the well.

The night was chill, and I pulled high the hood of my cloak. Then I stood looking down at the silvered reflections in the water and I held out my pin, ready to drop it into the disk mirrored there. However, before I released it, the reflection appeared to shiver and change into something else. For a long moment I was sure that what I had seen there had been far different from the moon, more like a crystal ball. I must have dropped the pin without being aware, for suddenly there was a troubling of the water, and the vision, if vision it had been, was gone.

I was so startled that I forgot the small spell-rhyme I should have spoken at that moment. So my luck-bringing was for naught, and I laughed at my own action as I turned and ran from the well.

That there is ensorcellment and spell-laying in the world we all know. There are the Wisewomen who are learned in such, as well as others, such as the Past-Abbess, who have control over powers most men do not understand. One can evoke some of these powers if one has the gift and the training, but I had neither. Perhaps it is better not to dabble in such matters, Only—why at that moment had I seen again (if I had in truth seen it) that englobed gryphon?

Gryphon—beneath the folds of my cloak my fingers sought and found the outlines of that beast as it was stitched upon my tabard. It was the symbol of the House of Ulm, to which I was now bound by solemn oath. What was he like, my thoughts spun on, this unseen, unknown lord of mine? Why had he never sent to me such a likeness of himself as Yngilda carried? Monster—Yngilda had no reason to speak spiteful lies, there must lie some core of truth in what she had said to me. There was one way—

Gifts came yearly from Ulmsdale on my name-day. Suppose that when they were brought this year, I sought out the leader of the party bringing them, asked of him a boon to be carried to his lord: that we exchange our likenesses. I had my own picture, limned by uncle's scribe, who had such a talent. Yes, that was what I would do!

It seemed to me in that moment that perhaps the well had answered me by putting that thought into my head. So I sped, content, back to the hall, pleased that none there had marked my absence.

Now I set to work upon a project of my own. That was making a suitable case for the picture drawn on parchment. As deftly as I could, I mounted it on a piece of polished wood.

For it I then worked a small bag, the fore-part embroidered with the gryphon, the back with the broken sword. I hoped my lord could understand my subtle meaning: that I was dutifully looking forward to Ulmsdale; that Ithkrypt was my past, not my future. This I did in secret and in stolen moments of time, for I had no mind to let others know my plan. But I had no time to hide it one late afternoon when Toross came upon me without warning.

The mounted picture lay before me in the open, as I had been using it to measure. When he saw it he said sharply, "There is one here, kinswoman, who sees you well as you are. Whose hand limned this?"

"Archan, my uncle's scribe."

"And for whom have you had it limned?"

Again there was that sharp note in his voice, as if he had a right to demand such an answer from me. I was more than a little surprised, and also displeased, that he would use such a tone, where before he had been all courtesy and soft speeches.

"It is to be a surprise for my Lord Kerovan. Soon he will send my name-day gifts. This I shall return to him." I disliked having to spread my plan before him, yet his question had been too direct to evade.

"Your lord!" He turned his face a little from me. "One forgets these ties exist, Joisan. Do you ever think what it will mean to go among strangers, to a lord you have never seen?" Again that roughness in his speech, which I could not understand. I did not think it kind of him to seize so upon a hidden fear this way and drag it out before my eyes.

I put aside my needle, took up the picture and the unfinished case, and wrapped them in the cloth wherein I kept them, without answering him. I had no intention of saying "yes" or "no" to that question which he had no right to ask.

"Joisan—there is the right of bride-refusal!" The words burst from him as he stood there with his head still averted. His hands were laced upon his sword belt, and I saw his fingers tighten and press.

"To so dishonor his House and mine?" I returned. "Do you deem me such a nothing? What a poor opinion you carry of me, kinsman! What have I done to make you believe I would openly shame any man?"

"Man!" He swung around to face me now. There was a tautness to his mouth, an expression about his eyes I had never seen before. "Do you not know what they say of the heir of Ulmsdale? *Man*—what was your uncle thinking of when he agreed to such a match? Joisan, no one can hold a maid to such a bargain when she has been betrayed within its bonds! Be wise for yourself and think of refusal—now!"

I arose. In me anger grew warm. But it is in my nature that when I am most in ire I am also the most placid seeming outwardly. For which, perhaps, I should thank fortune, for many times has it given me good armor.

"Kinsman, you forget yourself. Such speech is unseemly, and I know shame that you could think me so poor a thing as to listen to it. You had better learn to guard your tongue." So saying I left him, not heeding his quick attempt to keep me there.

Then I climbed to my own small chamber and there stood by the northward window, gazing out into the dusk. I was shivering, but not with the cold; rather with that fear I thought I had overcome in the weeks since Yngilda had planted it in my mind.

Yngilda's spite, and now this strange outburst from Toross, who, I had not believed, could have said such a thing to me! The right of bride-refusal, yes, that existed. But the few times it had been invoked in the past had led to death feuds between the Houses so involved. Monster—Yngilda had said that. And now Toross—repeating the word "man" as if it could not be applied to my lord! Yet my uncle would not wish to use me ill, and surely he had considered very well the marriage proposal when it had first been made to him. I had also Dame Math's solemn oath.

I longed all at once for the garden of the Past-Abbess Malwinna. To her alone could I speak on this matter. Dame

Math's stand I already knew: that my lord was a victim of misfortune. This I could believe more readily than that he was in any way not a man. For after sworn oaths between my uncle and his father, such a thing could not be. And I heartened myself by such sensible council, pinning additional hope on my plan to send Kerovan the picture.

But thereafter I avoided Toross as much as I could, though he made special attempts several times to have private conversation with me. I could claim duties enough to keep me aloof, and claim them I speedily did. Then there came a day when he had private conversation with my uncle, and before the day's end he and his men rode out of Ithkrypt. Dame Math was summoned to my uncle, and thereafter Archan came to bring me also.

My uncle was scowling as I had seen him do at times when he was crossed in some matter. And that scowl was turned blackly on me as I entered.

"What is this boil of trouble you have started, wench?" His voice was only slightly below a roar, aimed at me when I was scarcely within the doorway. "Are you so light of word that you—"

Dame Math arose from her chair. Her face was as anger-cast as his, but she looked at him, not me.

"We shall have Joisan's word before you speak so!" Her lower tone cut across his. "Joisan, this day Toross came to your uncle and spoke of bride-refusal—"

It was my turn to interrupt; my anger also heated by such an accusation from my uncle, before he had asked my position in the matter.

"So did he speak to me also. I told him I would not listen; nor am I an oath-breaker! Or do you, who know me well, also believe that?"

Dame Math nodded. "It is as I thought. Has Joisan lived under your eyes for all these years without your knowing her for what she is? What said Toross to you, Joisan?"

"He seemed to think evil concerning my Lord Kerovan, and that I should use bride-refusal not to go to him. I told him what I thought of his shameful words and left him, nor would I have any private speech with him thereafter."

"Bride-refusal!" My uncle brought his fist down on the table with the thump of a war drum. "Is that youngling mad? To start a blood feud, not only with Ulmsdale, but half the north who would stand beside Ulric in such a matter! Why does he urge this?"

There was frost in Dame Math's eyes, a certain quirk to her lips which suggested that she was not altogether displeased at his asking that.

"I can think of two reasons, brother. One stemming from his own hot blood. The other placed in his mind by—"

"Enough! There is no need to list what may or may not have moved Toross to this folly. Now listen, girl," he swung on me again. "Ulric took oath that his heir was fit to be the lord of any woman. That his wife was disordered in her wits when the lad was born, that all men know. She so took such a dislike to the child she named him monster, which he is not. Also Ulric spoke with me privately upon a matter which has much to do with this, and which I tell you now, but you shall keep mum-mouthed about it hereafter—remember that, girl!"

"I shall so." I gave him my promise when he paused as if expecting that assurance from me.

"Well enough. Then listen—there is always something behind such wild tales when you hear them, so learn in the future to winnow the true from the false.

"The Lady Tephana, who is your lord's mother (and a fine mother she has been to him!), had an elder son Hlymer, by her first marriage. Since he got no lands from his father, she brought him with her to Ulmsdale. In addition she has had a daughter—Lisana—who is but one year younger than your lord.

"This daughter she has seen betrothed to one of her own House. And the daughter she dotes upon with all the affection to equal her distaste for Kerovan. Thus Ulric of Ulmsdale has reason to believe that within his own household lie seeds of trouble for his heir—for Hlymer makes common cause with Lisana's betrothed, and they see a lord to come who is not Kerovan. Ulric can make no move against them, for he has no proof. But because he would not see his son despoiled when he could no longer protect hm, he wished some strong tie for Kerovan, to unite him with a House that would support him when the time comes that he needs shields raised for him.

"Since no man can sit in the high seat of a keep who is not sound of body and mind, how better create doubt in possible supporters for a threatened heir than by bending rumor to one's use, spreading tales of 'monsters' and the like? You have seen what happens when such tales come into the hearing of those who do not guess what may lie behind their telling. Toross came to me with such a story—he is filled with it.

Since I am sworn not to reveal, save to the parties most deeply concerned, any of Ulric's fears for the future, I bade Toross ride forth if he could not hold his tongue. But that you might have listened to him—"

I shook my head. "It was he who came to me with it. But I had already heard such a tale in greater detail from his sister in Trevamper."

"So Math told me." The flush had faded from my uncle's face. Now I knew he was slightly ashamed of the way he had greeted me, not that he would ever say so. But such things had always been understood between us.

"You see, girl," he continued, "how far this story has spread. I do not think Ulric is altogether wise in not better ordering his household. But each man is lord in his own keep and needs must face his own shadows there. But know this— your wedded lord is such a man as you will be proud to hand-fast when the time comes—as it will soon now. Take no heed of these rumors, knowing their source and purpose."

"For which knowing I give thanks," I replied.

When Dame Math and I left his company together, she drew me apart into her own chamber and looked at me searchingly, as if by that steady gaze alone she could hunt out every unspoken thought within my mind.

"How chanced Toross to speak to you on this matter? He must have had some reason—one does not so easily break custom. You are a wedded lady, Joisan, not an unspoken-for maid who allows her eyes to stray this way or that."

So I told her of my plan. To my surprise she did not object nor seem to think what I was doing was beneath the dignity of my station. Instead she nodded briskly.

"What you do is fitting, Joisan. Perhaps we should have arranged such an exchange ourselves long ago. That would have broken such rumors. Had you had a picture of Kerovan in your belt-purse when Yngilda spoke to you, it would have answered well. So Toross was angered at what you did? It was past time when that youth should have returned to those who sent him to make trouble!" She was angry again, but not with me. Only what moved her now she did not explain.

So I finished the picture case, and Dame Math approved its making as an excellent example of my best needlecraft. Making all ready, I laid it away in my coffer against the arrival of the party from Ulmsdale.

They were several days late, and the party itself was different from the earlier ones, for the armsmen were older, and several of them bore old, healed wounds which would keep them from active field service. Their leader was crooked of back and walked with a lurch and a dip.

Besides a casket that he delivered with ceremony to me, he bore a message tube sealed with Ulric's symbol for my uncle and was straightway taken into private conversation with him, as if this were a matter of great import. I wondered if my summons to Ulmsdale had come at last. But the nature of the bearer was such that I could not accept that. My lord would have come himself as was right, and with a retinue to do me honor through those lands we must cross to his home.

Within the casket was a necklet of northern amber and gold beads, with a girdle to match. Truly a gift to show me prized. Yet I wished it had been just such a picture as I had ready to return to him. I knew that Dame Math would make opportunity to let me speak alone with this Jago who commanded the Ulmsdale force, that I might entrust him with my gift. But it appeared he had so much to say to my uncle there was little time for that, for he did not come out of the inner chamber until the hour for the evening meal.

I was glad he was seated beside me, for it gave me a chance to say that I would see him privately, that I had something to entrust to him. But he had a speech in return.

"Lady, you have had Ulmsdale's gift, but I have another for you from the hand of Lord Kerovan himself which he said to give to you privately—"

Within me I knew then a rise of excitement, for I could conceive of nothing save that we had been of one mind, and what Jago had for me was also a picture.

But it was not so. When Dame Math saw that we came together in a nook between the high seat and the wall, what he laid in my eager hand was not a flat packet, but a small, round one. Quickly I pulled away covering of soft wool to find that I held a crystal globe and within it a gryphon—even as I had seen it at the House of Dames! I nearly dropped it. For to have something of the Power touch into one's life so was a thing to hold in awe and fear. Set in its surface just above the gryphon's head was a ring of gold, and there was strung a chain so one could wear it as a pendant.

"A wondrous thing!" Somehow I found my tongue and hoped that I had not betrayed my first fear. For to no one could I explain the momentary panic I had felt. The more I studied it now, the clearer became its beauty, and I thought that it was truly a treasure, finer than any that had ever been sent to me in any casket of ceremony.

"Yes. My lord begs you accept of this, and perhaps wear it sometimes, that you may know his concern for you." That sounded like some set speech which he had memorized. And I decided swiftly to ask no questions of this man. Perhaps he was not too close to my lord after all.

"Tell my lord I take great joy in his gift." I found the formal words easier than I would have done a moment earlier. "It shall abide with me night and day that I may look upon it, not only for my pleasure in its beauty, but also because of his concern for me. In return," I hurriedly brought forth my own gift, "do you place this in my lord's hand. Ask of him, if he wills, to send its like to me when he may."

"Be sure that your wish is my command, Lady." Jago slipped it into his belt-purse. Before he could say more, if there was more to be said between us, there came one of my uncle's men to summon him again to that inner room, and I did not see him further that night.

Nor did we have more than formal speech together during the two remaining days that he was at Ithkrypt. I gave him ceremonious farewell when he rode forth, but by then all within the keep knew of the news that had come with the men from Ulmsdale.

By birth and inclination dalesmen are not sea-rovers. We have ports for trading set up along the coast, and there are villages of fisherfolk to be found there. But deep-sea ships do not sail under the flag of any dales lord. And those who trade from overseas, such as the Sulcarmen, are not of our blood and kin.

News from overseas is long old before it reaches us. But we had heard many times that the eastern lands were locked in a struggle for power between nation and nation. Now and then there was mention of a country, a city, or even some warlord or leader whose deeds reached us in such garbled form they were already well on the way to becoming a tale more fancy than fact.

Of late, however, there had been new ships nosing along our shores. The Sulcarmen had suffered some grievous defeat of their own two years since in the eastern waters. And so we had not the usual number of their traders coming for our woolen cloth, our wonder-metal from the Waste, our freshwater pearls. But these others had put in to haggle, driving hard bargains, and they seemed over-interested in our land.

Often when they had discharged a cargo, before taking on another, they would lie in harbor, and their crews would ride north and south as if exploring.

Our thoughts of war never encompassed more than the feuds between dale and dale, which could be dark and bloody at times, but which seldom involved more than a few score of men on either side. We had no king or overlord, which was our pride, but also in a manner our weakness, as was to be proven to us. Sometimes several lords would combine their forces to make a counter-raid on Waste outlaws or the like. But such alliances were always temporary. And, while there were several lords of greater following than others (mainly because they held richer and more populous dales), none could send out any rallying call all others would come to.

This must have been clear to those who spied and went—that we were feeble opponents, easy to overrun. However, they misread the temper of the dales, for a dalesman will fight fiercely for his freedom. And a dalesman's loyalty to his lord, who is like the head of his own family, is seldom shaken.

Since Ulmsport lay at the mouth of that dale, it had recently been visited by two ships of these newcomers. They called themselves men of Alizon and spoke arrogantly of the size and might of their overseas land. One of their men had been injured inland. His companion from the ship had been killed. The wounded man had been nursed by a Wisewoman. By her craft she could tell true from false. And, while he wandered in a fever, talking much, she listened. Later, after the coming of his comrades to bear him away, she had gone to Lord Ulric. He had listened carefully, knowing that she knew of what she spoke.

Lord Ulric was prudent and wise enough to see that there was that to it which might come to overshadow our whole land, as it did. Speedily he sent accounts of what had been learned to all the neighboring dales, as well as to Ithkrypt.

It seemed from the babbling of the wounded man that he was indeed a spy, the scout of an army soon to be landed on us. We realized that those of Alizon had decided that our rule was so feeble and weak in its nature they could overrun us at their pleasure, and this they moved to do.

Thus was the beginning of the great shadow on our world. But I nursed the crystal ball in my hand, uninterested in Alizon and its spies, sure that somehow the Lord Kerovan would do as I willed, and I would look upon the picture of a man who was no monster.

To my great surprise I discovered Jago had returned before Riwal and I came out of the Waste. His anger with me was such that, had I been younger, I think he would have cut a switch from the nearest willow and used it for my discipline. I saw that that anger was fed, not wholly from my supposedly ill-advised foray into the dubious territory, but also from something he had learned at Ulmskeep. Having spoken his mind hotly, he ordered me to listen, with such serious mien that I lost the defiance his berating had aroused.

On two occasions in the past I had been to Ulmskeep, both times when my mother was away visiting her kin. So it, and the lower part of the dale, was not unknown to me. Also on those times when my father had come to me, he had taken patience to make me aware of the spread of our lands, the needs of our people, those things that it was necessary for me to know when the day came for me to take his place.

But the news Jago brought I had not heard before. For the first time I learned of the invaders (though they were not termed so then, being outwardly visitors on leave from their ships at Ulmsport).

With what contempt they regarded us we quickly learned, for we are far from stupid—at least in that way. Dalesmen may insist too much upon their freedom, having a strong disliking for combining forces, save in time of immediate and pressing need. But we can sniff danger like wild things when it treads our land.

They had first come nosing into our ports, up river mouths, a year or so earlier. Then they had been very wary, circumspect, playing the roles of traders. Since the stuffs they had to offer in return for our native wool, metal, and pearls were new and caught the eye, they found a welcome. But they kept much to themselves, though they came ashore in twos and threes, never alone. Once ashore they did not linger in port, but journeyed inland on the pretext of seeking trade.

As strangers they were suspect, especially in those districts lying near the Waste, even though it was known that their origin was overseas. Men met them courteously and with guest right, but as they looked and listened, asked a question here, another there with discretion, so did others watch and listen. Soon my father, gathering reports, could see a pattern in their journeying which was not that of traders, but rather, to his mind, the action of scouts within new territory.

He sent privately to our near neighbors: Uppsdale, Fyndale (which they had visited under the pretext of the great fair held there), Flathingdale, and even to Vastdale, which also had its port of Jorby. With all these lords he was on good terms, for we had no feuds to separate us. And the lords were ready to listen and then set their own people to watching also.

What grew out of all this was the now-strong belief that my father had judged the situation rightly, and these overseas strangers were prowling our country for some purpose of their own, one meaning no good to the dales. It was soon to be decided whether or not the lords would make common cause and forbid new landings to any ship from Alizon.

However, to get the lords to make common cause on any matter was a task to which only a man with infinite patience might set himself. No lord would openly admit that he accepted the will of another. We had no leader who could draw the lords under one banner or to one mind in action. And this was to be our bane.

Now there were to assemble at Ulmskeep five of the northern lords to exchange their views upon the idea. They needed some excuse for such a gathering, however, for it must be a festival of a kind to keep people talking in such a way that the strangers might hear a false excuse. My father had found a cause in the first arming of his heir, bringing me now into the company of my peers as was only natural at my age.

So far I followed Jago. But at his flat statement that I was to be the apparent center for this gathering, I was startled. For so long had I accepted my lot apart from the keep and from the company of my kin, that this way of life seemed the only proper one to me.

"But—" I began in protest.

Jago drummed with fingertips upon the table. "No, he is right, Lord Ulric is. Too long have you been put aside from what is rightly yours. He needs must do this, not only to give cover to his speech with the lords, but for your own sake. He has learned the folly of the course he has followed these past years."

"The folly of—?" I was astounded that Jago spoke so of

my father, since he was so stoutly a liegeman of Ulric's as to think of him with the awe one approached an Old One.

"Yes, I say it—folly!" The word exploded a second time from his lips, as might a bolt from a crossbow. "There are those in his own household who would change matters." He hesitated, and I knew without words what he hinted at: that my mother favored my sister and her betrothed for the succession in Ulmsdale. I had never closed my ears to any rumor brought to the foresters' settlement, deeming I must know the worst.

"Look at you!" Jago was angry once more. "You are no monster! Yet the story spreads that Lord Ulric needs must keep you pent here in chains, so ill-looking a thing, so mind-damaged, that you are less than a man, even an animal!"

His heat struck a spark from me. So this was what was whispered of me in my own keep!

"You must show yourself as you are; be claimed before those whose borders march with Ulmsdale as the proper heir. Then none may rise to misname you later. This Lord Ulric now knows—for he has heard some whispering, even challenged those whisperers to their faces. And one or two were bold enough to tell him what they had heard."

I got up from the table which stood between us and went to Jago's great war-shield where it hung upon the wall. He spent long hours keeping it well-burnished so that it was like a mirror, even though the shape distorted my reflection.

"As long as I keep on my boots," I said then, "perhaps I will pass as humankind."

Those boots were cunningly made, being carefully shaped so my cloven hoofs appeared normal feet. When I went shod, no man might be aware of the truth. The boots had been devised by Jago himself and made from special leather my father sent.

Jago nodded. "Yes, you will go, and you will keep your boots on, youngling, so you can prove to every whisperer in the dales that your father sired a true heir, well able to take lord's oath. With weapons you are as good, perhaps even better, than those who are keep armsmen. And your wit is keen enough to make you careful."

Which was more praise than he had ever given me in our years together.

Thus mailed and armed (and most well-booted) I rode with Jago out of the exile which had been laid upon me and came at last to take up life in my father's keep. I did so with inner misgivings, having, as Jago pointed out, some store of wit, and well-surmising that I was far from welcome by some members of that household.

I had little chance to speak again with Riwal before I went —though I longed for him to offer to go with me, knowing at the same time that he never would. In our last meeting he looked at me in such a way that I felt he could somehow see into my mind and know all my uncertainties and fears.

"You have a long road to ride, Kerovan," he said.

"Only two days," I corrected him. "We but go to Ulmskeep."

Riwal shook his head. "You go farther, gryphon bearer, and into danger. Death stalks at your shoulder. You shall give, and, in giving, you shall get. The giving and the getting will be stained with blood and fire—"

I realized then that he was farseeing, and I longed to cover my ears, for it seemed to me that his very words would draw down upon me the grim future he saw.

"Death stalks at the heels of every man born," I summoned my courage to make answer. "If you can farsee, tell me what shield I can raise to defend myself."

"How can I?" he returned. "All future is fan-shaped, spreading out in many roads from this moment. If you make one choice, there is that road to follow; if you make another yet a second path, a third, a fourth—But no man can outstride or outfight the given pattern in the end. Yours lies before you. Walk with a forester's caution, Kerovan. And know this —you have that deep within you, if you learn to use it, that shall be greater than any shield or sword wrought by the most cunning of smiths."

"Tell me—" I began.

"No!" he half-turned from me. "So much may I say, but no more. I cannot farsee your choices, and no word of mine must influence you in their making. Go with the Peace." Then he raised his hand, and, between us in the air, he traced a sign. I half-started back, for his moving finger left a faint glimmering which was gone almost as quickly as I marked it. And I realized then that in some of his seeking Riwal must have been successful, for his sign was of the Power.

"Until we meet again then, comrade." I spoke friend-farewell.

He did not face me squarely, but stood, his hand still a little raised to me. I know now that he understood this was our last meeting and perhaps regretted it. But I was not cursed with that sight which can hurt far more than it shields. What man wishes to see into the future in truth when there are so many ills lying there in wait for us?

As we traveled to Ulmskeep, Jago talked steadily, and that this was of purpose, I shortly understood. He so made known to me the members of my father's household, giving each his character as he himself saw it, with unspoken shadings which allowed me to perceive that this one might be well-disposed, that one not. I think he saw me as a child fated to make some error that would bring about disaster and was doing what he could to give me some manner of protection against any outspoken folly.

My elder half-brother, who had come to Ulmskeep as a very young child, had, when he reached the age suitable for instruction in arms, been sent to our mother's kin. But within the past year he had returned, riding comrade-in-arms to our kinsman Rogear who was my sister's betrothed. I could well guess that he was to me an unfriend and with him I must be wary.

My mother had her followers among others at the keep, and Jago, with what delicacy he could summon, named those to me, giving short descriptions of each and of the positions they held. On the other hand my father's forces were in the greater number, and among those were the major officers— the Master of Armsmen, the marshal, and others.

It was a divided household, and such are full of pitfalls. Yet on the surface all seemed smooth. I listened carefully, asking some questions. Perhaps these explanations were Jago's idea; perhaps my father had suggested that I be so cautioned before I came to face friend and unfriend, that I might tell one from the other.

We rode into the keep at sunset, Jago having blown a signal with his approach horn so that we found the door guard drawn up to do us honor. I had marked the residence banners of Uppsdale and Flathingdale below our gryphon on the tower, and knew that two of those my father had summoned were already here. Thus, from the beginning, I would be under the eyes of the curious as well as those of the covertly hostile.

I must play my role well, seemingly unaware of any crosscurrent; bear myself modestly as became a candidate for arms, yet be far from a fool. Was I able to do this? I did not know.

The guards clanged swords together as we dismounted. My

father, wearing a loose robe of ceremony over his jerkin and breeches, came forth from the deep shadow of the main portal to the hall. I fell to one knee, holding out my sword by the point that he could lay fingers lightly on its hilt in acknowledgment.

Then he drew me to my feet in a half-embrace, and, with his hand still on my arm, brought me out of the open into the main hall where a feasting board had already been set up, and serving men and maids were busied spreading it across with strips of fair linen and setting out the plates and drinking horns.

There were two other men of early middle age, robes of ceremony about their shoulders. My father made me known to Lord Savron of Uppsdale and Wintof of Flathingdale. That they regarded me keenly I was well aware. But I was strengthened in my role by the knowledge that I made, in my mail and leather over-jerkin, no different appearance than their own sons might display. At this moment no man might raise the cry of monster. They accepted my proper deference as if this were an ordinary meeting and I had been absent from Ulmskeep for perhaps only an hour or two, not for all my life.

Since I was still considered but a boy and, by custom, of little importance, I was able speedily to withdraw from the company of my elders and go to that section of the barracks where the unmarried men of the household were quartered. In deference to my heirship, I was given a small room to myself—a very bare room in which there was a bed, narrow and hard, two stools, and a small table, far less comfortable than my room in the foresters' holding.

A serving lad brought in my saddle bags. I noted that he watched me with open curiosity when he thought I did not mark him, lingering to suggest that he bring me hot water for washing. When I agreed, I thought that he was determined to make the most of his chance to view the "monster" at close quarters and perhaps report his discoveries to his fellows.

I had laid aside my jerkin and mail by the time he returned, standing in my padded undercoat, sorting through my clothing for my best tabard with its gryphon symbol. He sidled in with a ewer from which steam arose, watching me as he placed it and a basin on the table, and twitched off a towel he had borne over one shoulder to lay beside it.

"If you need service, Lord Kerovan—"

I smoothed out the tabard. Now I deliberately unhooked my undercoat, letting it slide from my body, which was thus bared to the waist. Let him see I was not misshapen. As Jago said, if I clung to my boots, no man could miscall me.

"You may look me out a shirt—" I gestured toward my bags and then saw he was staring at me. What had he expected? Some horribly twisted body? I glanced down and saw what had become so much a part of me I had forgotten I still wore it—the crystal gryphon. Lifting its chain over my head, I laid it on the table as I washed and saw him eyeing it. Well enough, let him believe that I wore a talisman. Men did so. And one in the form of the symbol of my House was proper.

He found the shirt and held it for me as I redonned the gryphon. And he hooked my tabard, handed me my belt with its knife-of-pride before he left, doubtless with much to tell his fellows. But when he had gone, I drew the gryphon from hiding and held it in my hand.

As usual when I held it so, it had a gentle warmth. With that warmth came a sensation of peace and comfort, as if this thing, fashioned long before my first ancestor had ridden into the south dales, had waited all these centuries just to lie in my hand.

So far all had gone as it should. But before me still lay that ordeal from which my thoughts had shied since first I had known that I must come to Ulmsdale, the meeting with my mother. What could I say to her, or she to me? There lay between us that which no one could hope to bridge— not after all these years.

I stood there, cupping close the crystal ball and thinking of what I might do or say at a moment which could be put off no longer. Suddenly it was as if someone spoke aloud—yet it was only in my mind. I might have looked through a newly unshuttered window so that a landscape hitherto-hidden lay before me.

The scene was shadowed, and I knew it was not mine to ever walk that way, just as there could be no true meeting between us which would leave us more than strangers. Yet I felt no sense of loss, only as if a burden had been lifted from me, to leave me free. We had no ties; therefore I owed her no more than she willed me to. I would meet her as I would any lady of rank, paying her the deference of courtesy, asking nothing in return. In my hand the globe was warm and glowing. But a sound at the door made me slip that into hiding before I turned to face who stood there.

I am only slightly over middle height, being slender-boned and spare-fleshed. This youth was tall enough that I must raise my eyes to meet his. He was thick of neck and shoulder, wide of jaw. His hair was a mat of sandy curls so tight he must battle to lay it smooth with any comb. He had a half-grin on his thick lips. I had seen such an expression before among the armsmen when a barracks bully set about heckling some simpleton to impress his standing upon his fellows.

His tabard of state was wrought with fine needlework and stretched tightly over the barrel of his chest. And now he was running his fingers up and down its stiff fronting as if striving to draw attention to it.

Big as he was, he did not altogether fill the doorway, for there was a smaller and slighter figure beside him. I was for an instant startled. The oval of that face was like enough to mine to stamp us kinsmen, just as his darker hair was also mine. His expression was bland, nearly characterless, but I guessed that behind it lurked a sharp wit. Of the two I would deem him the more dangerous.

From the first I knew these for the enemy. Jago's descriptions fitted well. The giant was closer-kin to me than the other, for he was my half-brother Hlymer, while his companion was my sister's betrothed, my cousin Rogear.

"Greetings, kinsmen." I spoke first.

Hlymer did not lose his grin; it grew a little wider. "He is not furred or clawed, at least not as can be seen. I wonder in what manner his monster marking lies, Rogear." He spoke as if I were a thing and not able to hear or sense his meaning. But if he meant to arouse some sign of anger he could play upon, he was a fool. I had taken his measure early.

Whether he would have carried on along that theme if left alone I was not to know, because Rogear then answered, not Hlymer's comment, but my greeting, and courteously in kind, as if he never meant to do otherwise.

"And to you greeting, kinsman."

Hlymer had a high voice that some big men own and a slight hesitancy of speech. But Rogear's tone was warm and winning. Had I not known him to be what he was, I might have been deceived into believing that he had indeed sought me out to make me welcome.

They played my escort to the great hall. I did not know whether to count it as a relief or not when I saw that there were no chairs placed for ladies, that this meal at least was clearly intended only for the men. Undoubtedly my mother had chosen to keep to her own apartments. Since all knew the situation, none would comment on it.

I saw my father glance sharply at me now and then from his High Seat. My own place was down-table, between Hlymer and Rogear (though whether they had purposefully devised that or not, I did not know). If my father was not satisfied, there was little he could do without attracting unwelcome attention.

My companions' tricks began early. Hlymer urged me to empty my wine horn, implying that any moderation on my part marked me in that company. Rogear's smooth flow of talk was clearly designed to point up the fact that I was raw from some farmyard, without manners or wit. That neither accomplished their purposes must have galled. Hlymer grew sullen, scowling, muttering under his breath words I did not choose to hear. But Rogear showed no ill nature at the spoiling of whatever purpose he had in mind when we sat down.

In the end Hlymer was caught in his own trap—if he considered it a trap—and grew muddle-headed with drink, loud in his comments, until some of those around turned on him. They were young kinsmen of the visiting lords and, I think, frank in their desire for no trouble.

So began my life under my father's roof. Luckily I did not have to spend much time within the range of Hlymer and Rogear. My father used the fact of my introduction and comfirmation as his heir to keep me much with him, making me known to his neighbors, having me tutored in those details of the ceremony that occurred on the third day of the gathering.

I swore kin-oath before a formidable assemblage of dale lords, accepted my father's gift-sword, and so passed in an hour from the status of untried and unconsidered youth to that of man and my father's second in command. As such I was then admitted to the council concerning the men from Alizon.

Though all were agreed that there seemed to be some menace behind the coming of these men from overseas, there was sharp division as to how the situation was to be handled. In the end the conference broke, as such so often did in the dales, with no plan of action drawing us together after all.

Because of my new status in the household, I rode part way down the dale with the lord of Uppsdale to give him road-speed. On my way back my career as Heir of Ulmsdale was nearly finished before it had rightfully begun.

In courtesy to our guest, my sword was in peace-strings, and I had gone unmailed. But in the moment of danger I was warned. For there flashed into my mind such a sudden sensation of danger that I did not wait to loose the cords from my sword. Instead I plucked free my knife, at the same time throwing myself forward, so that the harsh hair of my mount's mane rasped my cheek and chin. There was the sharp crack of a bolt's passing, a burn across my shoulder—by so little I escaped death.

I knew the tricks the foresters used in savage infighting when the outlaws came raiding. So I threw my knife, to be answered with a choked cry from that man who had arisen between the rocks to sight on me a second time. Now I brought my sword around, charging a second man who had emerged, steel in hand. One of the battle-trained mount's hoofs crushed down, and the man was gone, screaming as he rolled across the ground.

We had made an important capture, we discovered, for though these two wore the dress of drifting laborers who make their way from dale to dale at harvest time, they were indeed the very invaders we had been discussing at such weary length. One was dead; the other badly injured. My father called the Wisewoman of the dale and had her attend him, and, light-headed with fever, he talked.

The purpose of their attack on me we did not learn. But there was much else of useful knowledge, and the threat lying over us grew darker. My father had me in with Jago and his trusted officers. Now he spoke his mind.

"I do not pretend to farseeing, but any man with wit in his head can understand that there is purpose and planning behind this. If we do not look ahead, we may—" He hesitated. "I do not know. New dangers mean new ways of dealing with them. We have always clung to the ways of our fathers—but will those serve us now? It may be that the day will soon come when we need friends to hold shields with us. I would draw to us now all assurances of those as we can.

"Therefore"—he smoothed out on the table around which we sat the map of the dalesside—"here is Uppsdale and the rest. To them we have already made clear what may come. Now let us warn the south—there we may first call upon Ithkrypt."

Ithkrypt and the lady Joisan. For long periods of time I had put her out of mind. Had the day now arrived when my father would order ours to be a marriage in fact? We had both reached an age when such were common.

I thought of my mother and the sister who had kept themselves stubbornly immured in their own apartments since I had come to Ulmskeep. Suddenly I knew that I would not have my Lady Joisan join them there as she would do if she came now. How could she help but be swayed by their attitude toward me? No, she must come willingly to me—or not at all!

But how could I make sure that she did so?

As that sudden warning of danger had saved my life, so again came an answer as clear and sharp as if spoken aloud.

Thus after my father had cautioned Jago as to what to say to Lord Cyart when he delivered the name-day gift to my lady, I spoke privately with my old tutor. I could not say why I had to do this; I did not want to; yet it was laid upon me as heavily as—a *geas*—is put upon some hero who cannot thereafter turn aside from it. I gave him the crystal gryphon, that he might put it in Lady Joisan's own hand. Perhaps it was my true bride-price. I would not know until that moment when we did indeed at long last stand face to face.

One difference did the news brought to my uncle from Ulmsdale make in my own plans for the future. It was decided that I would not be going there to join my lord this season as had been heretofore thought, but I must wait upon a more settled time. For if spies had been sent into Ulmsdale with such boldness, the enemies' forethrust might soon be delivered. My uncle sent such a message with Jago. There came no protest from Lord Ulric or Lord Kerovan in return, so he deemed they agreed. Thereafter he sat sober-faced, talking with his armsmen and with messengers he sent in turn to Trevamper and those dales where he had kinship or old friendship.

It was a time of spreading uneasiness. We harvested more closely that year than any time I could remember, plundering all the wild berries from the field bushes, taking nuts from the woods trees, laying up what manner of stores we could. It was as if some foreshadowing of the starving years to come already lay across the land.

And in the next summer my uncle ordered the planting increased, with more fields cleared and sown. The weather was as uncertain as the threatening future, for there were a number of storms of great severity. Twice the roads were washed out, and we were isolated until men could rebuild them.

We had only ragged scraps of news when some lord's messenger found his way to us. No more spies had come into Ulmsport. From the south there were rumors of strange ships that did not anchor openly in any dale port, but patroled the coast. Then these were seen no more for a space, and we took a little comfort in that.

It appeared that my uncle feared the worst, for he sent his marshal to Trevamper, to return with two loads of the strange metal from the Waste and a smith who straightway set about fashioning arms and repairing the old. Much to my astonishment, my uncle had him take my measurements and prepare for me a coat of mail.

When Dame Math protested, he stared at her moodily, for his good humor was long since fled.

"Peace, sister. I would give the same to you, save that I know you would not wear it. But listen well, both of you. I believe that we face darker days than we have ever known. If word comes that these invaders come in force, we may find ourselves beaten from dale to dale. Thus—"

Dame Math had drawn a deep breath then, her indignation fading, another emotion on her face, an expression I could not read.

"Cyart—have—have you had then—?" She did not finish, but her apprehension was such that fear uncoiled within me.

"Have I dreamed? Yes, Math—*once!*"

"Spirit of Flame shelter us!" Her hands went to the set of silver hoops slung together at her girdle. She turned them swiftly in her fingers, her lips shaping those formal prayers that were the support of those in the House of Dames.

"As it was promised"—he looked at her—"so have I dreamed—once."

"Twice more then to come." Her coifed head came up, her lips firm. "It is a pity that the Warning does not measure time."

"We are lucky, or perhaps cursed, to have it at all," he returned. "Is it better to know there is blackness ahead and so live in foreshadow? Or be ignorant and meet it unwarned? Of the two I choose the warning. We can hold Ithkrypt if they come by river or over the hill ways—perhaps." He shrugged. "You must be prepared at the worst to ride—not to the coast or southward—but to Norsdale, or even the Waste."

"Yet no one has yet come save spies."

"They will, Math. Have no doubt of that. They will come!"

When we were back in our own quarters I dared to ask a question. "What is this dream of which my lord speaks?"

She was standing by the window, gazing out in that blind way one does when one regards thoughts and not what lies beyond. At my words she turned her head.

"Dream—?" For a moment I thought she was not going to answer. Then she came away from the window, her fingers busy with her prayer hoops as if she drew comfort from them.

"It is our warning." Obviously she spoke reluctantly. "To those vowed to the Flame such things are—ah, well, I cannot gainsay that it happens, and it is not of our doing. A generation ago Lord Randor, our father, took under his protection a Wisewoman who had been accused of dealing with the Old Ones. She was a quiet woman who lived alone, seeking out none. But she had a gift of tending animals, and her sheep were the finest in the dale. There were those who envied her. And as my lord has said concerning ugly stories, malice can be spread by tongue and lip alone.

"After the way of her calling she went alone into the wild places seeking herbs and strange knowledge. But if she knew much others did not, she made no parade of it, or used it to the hurt of any. Only the poisoned talk turned the dale against her. They arose one night to take her flock and drive her forth.

"Lord Randor had been in Trevamper, and they thought him still there, or they would not have dared. As they set torch to her roof place, he and his men came riding. He used his own whip on those who meant her harm; set her under his shield for all men to see.

"She said then that she could not stay, for her peace, so broken, could not be reclaimed. But she asked to see our mother, who was heavy with child. And she laid her hands upon the Lady Alys' full belly, saying that she would have ease in the birthing—which was thankful hearing, for the lady had had one ill birth and a child dead of it, to her great sorrow.

"Then the Wisewoman said also that it would be a son, and he would have a gift. In times of great danger he would farsee by the means of dreaming. That with two such dreams he could take measures and escape whatever fate they foretold, but the third time would be ill.

"She went then from Ithkrypt and from the dale, and no man saw her go. But what she foretold came true, for our mother was safely delivered within a month of your uncle, the Lord Cyart. And your uncle did dream. The last time he dreamed, it was of the death of his lady, which happened when he was in the south and unable to come to her, though he killed a horse trying. So—if he dreams—we can believe."

Thus I learned to wear mail because my uncle dreamed. And he taught me also how to use a light sword that had been his as a boy. Though I was not too apt a pupil with that, I proved myself apt with the bow and won the title of marksman. In days to come I was to thank my uncle for such skills many times over—when it was too late for him to know that he had truly given me life by his forethought.

So passed the Year of the Moss Wife, which should have seen me with my Lord Kerovan in Ulmsdale. Sometimes I took into my hands the crystal gryphon and held it, thinking of my lord and wondering what manner of man he was. In spite of all my hopes, no messenger riding between Ulmsdale and Ithkrypt brought me the picture that I desired. At first that angered me a little; then I made excuses, thinking that perhaps they had no one in Ulmsdale with the art of limning out a face, for such talent is not widely given. And in the present chancy times he could not seek afar for something of such small importance.

Though we had stores in plenty, we used them sparingly that winter, scanting even on the Yule feast as had never been done in the past, for my uncle was ever on guard. He had his own scouts riding the frontiers of our dale and awaited all messengers impatiently.

The Month of the Ice Dragon passed, and that of the Snow Bird in the new year was well begun when the news we had awaited came from the lips of a man who had battled through drifts to come to us, so stiff with cold he had to be lifted from a horse that thereafter fell and did not rise again.

Southward was war. The invasion had begun, and it was of such a sort as to startle even those lords who had tried to foresee and prepare. These devils from overseas did not fight with sword and bow after the manner of the dales. They brought ashore from their ships great piles of metal in which men hid, as if in monsters' bellies. And these manmade monsters crawled ahead, shooting flames in great sweeps from their noses.

Men died in those flames or were crushed under the lumbering weight of the monsters. When the dalesmen retreated into their keeps, the monsters bore inward with their weight against the walls, bringing them down. Such a way of war was unknown, and flesh and blood could not stand against it.

Now that it was too late, the rallying call went forth. Those who lingered in their keeps to be eaten up one by one were the thick-headed and foolish ones. Others gathered into an army under the leadership of four of the southern lords. They had already cut off three of the monsters, which needed certain supplies to keep them running, and destroyed them. But our people had lost the coastline. So the invaders were pouring in more and more men, though their creeping monsters, happily, appeared not so numerous.

The summons came to the northern dales for men to build up a force to contain the invaders, to harass them and restrain them from picking off each dale in turn as one picks ripe plums from a tree.

Hard on the heels of that messenger came the first of the refugees, ones who had blood-claim on us. A party of armsmen escorted a litter and two women who rode, guided through the pass by one of my uncle's scouts—the Lady Islaugha, Yngilda, and, in the litter, delirious with the fever of a wound, Toross, all now landless and homeless, with naught but what they could carry on their persons.

Yngilda, wed and widowed within two years, stared at me almost witlessly, and had to be led by the hand to the fire, have a cup placed in her fingers, and ordered firmly to drink. She did not seem to know where she was or what had happened to her, save that she was engulfed by an unending nightmare. Nor could we thereafter ever get any coherent story from her as to how she had managed to escape her husband's keep, which was one of those the monsters had battered down.

Somehow, led by one of her lord's archers, she had made her way to the dale's camp and there met the Lady Islaugha, come to tend her son, who had been hurt in one of the attacks against the monsters.

Cut off from any safety in the south, they had turned for shelter to us. Dame Math speedily took over the nursing of Toross, while his mother never left him day or night if she could help.

My uncle was plainly caught between two demands—that of the army battering the invaders and his inborn wish to protect his own, which was the dalesman's heritage. But, because he had from the first argued that combination against the foe was our only hope, he chose the army.

He marshaled what forces he could without totally stripping the dale, leaving a small but well-trained troop to the command of Marshal Dagale. There was a thaw at the beginning of the Month of the Hawk and, taking advantage of that, he left.

I watched him alone from the gatetower (for Dame Math had been summoned to Toross, who had taken a turn for the worse), just as I had stood in the courtyard minutes earlier pouring the spiced journey drink from the war ewer into the horns of the men to wish them fair fortune. That ewer I still held. It was cunningly wrought in the form of a mounted warrior, the liquid pouring through the mouth of his horse. There was a slight drip from it into the snow. Red it was, like blood. Seeing it, I shivered and quickly smeared over the spot so that I might not see what could be a dark omen.

We kept Ithkrypt ever-prepared, not knowing—for no messengers came now—how went the war, only believing that it might come to us without warning. I wondered if my uncle had dreamed again, and what dire fortellings those dreams had brought him. That we might never know.

There was one more heavy snow, closing the pass, which gave us an illusion of safety while it lasted. But spring came early that year. And with the second thaw a messenger from my uncle arrived, mainly concerned with the necessity for keeping the dale as much a fortress as we could. He said little of what the army in the south had done, and his messenger had only gloom to spread. There were no real battles. Our men had to turn to the tactics of Waste outlaws, making quick raids on enemy supply lines and camps, to do all the damage they could.

He had one bit of news: that Lord Ulric of Ulmsdale had sent a party south under the command of Lord Kerovan, but he himself had been ill. It was now thought that Lord Kerovan might return to take control at Ulmsdale if the invading army forced a landing at Ulmsport as they had at Jorby and other points along the coast.

That night, when I was free of the many duties that now were mine, I took up the crystal gryphon, as I had not for a long time. I thought on him who had sent it to me. Where did he lie this night? Under the stars with his sword to hand, not knowing when the battle-horn might blow to arms? I wished him well with all my heart, though I knew so little of him.

There was warmth against my palm, and the globe glowed in the dusky room. It did not in that moment seem strange to me; rather it was comforting, easing for a moment my burdens.

The globe was no longer clear. I could not see the gryphon. Rather there was a swirling mist within it, forming shadows —shadows that were struggling men. One was ringed about, and they bore in upon him. I cried out at the sight, though none of it was clear. And I was afraid that this talisman from my lord had now shown me his death. I would have torn the chain from my neck and thrown the thing away; yet that I could not do. The globe cleared, and the gryphon watched me with its red eyes. Surely my imagination alone had worked that.

"There you are!" Yngilda's voice accused me. "Toross is very uneasy. They wish you to come."

She watched me, I thought, jealously. Since she had come from behind the curtain of shock that had hidden her on her arrival, she was once again Yngilda of Trevamper. Sometimes I needed all my control not to allow my tongue sharpness in return when she spoke so, as if she were mistress here and I a lazy serving maid.

Toross mended slowly. His fever had yielded to Dame Math's knowledge, but it left him very weak. We had discovered that sometimes I was able to coax him to eat or to keep him quiet when the need arose. For his sake I was willing to serve so. Yet lately I had come to dislike the way his hand clung to mine when I sat beside him and the strange way he looked at me and smiled, as if he had some claim on me that no one could deny.

This night I was impatient at such a summons, though I obeyed it, for I was still shaken by what I had seen, or imagined I had seen, in the globe. I willed myself not to believe that this had been a true farseeing. Though with men at desperate war, and my lord with them, I could well accept he was so struck down. At that moment I wished that I *did* have the farsight, or else that we had a Wisewoman with such skill. But Dame Math did not countenance the uses of that power.

That party of kinsmen had been only the first of the refugees to find their way hither. If my uncle had farseen that we might have to open our doors and supplies to such, he had not mentioned it. I wondered, marking each morn as I measured out the food for the day (which had become one of my more serious duties since Dame Math had the overseeing of the sick and wounded) whether we could eat even sparingly until harvest, if this continued.

For the most part the newcomers were lands-people, women and children, with a sprinkling of old or wounded men, few of them able to help us man any defense that might be needed. I had spoken with Dame Math and the marshal only the evening before, the three of us deciding that as soon as the weather lightened sufficiently, they would be sent on to the west, where there were dales untouched by war, even to the House of Dames at Norstead. We dared not keep the burden of useless hands here.

Now as I came into the chamber where Toross lay, I was trying to occupy my mind with plans for such an exodus, rather than allow myself to think of the shadows in the globe.

About that I could do nothing. I must consider what I could do.

He was braced up by pillows, and it seemed to me that he looked better than he had since they brought him here. If this was so, why had they sent for me? Such a question was actually on my lips when the Lady Islaugha arose from a stool by the bed and moved away, he holding out his hand in welcome to me.

She did not glance in my direction, but took up a tray, and with a hasty murmur left the room.

"Joisan, come here where I may truly look upon you!" His voice was stronger also. "There are shadows beneath your eyes; you drive yourself too hard, dear heart!"

I had come to the stool, but I did not sit. Instead I studied his face closely. It was thin and white, with lines set by suffering. But there was reason in his eyes, not the cloudiness of a fevered mind. And that uneasiness I had felt with him filled me.

"We all have duties in plenty here, Toross. I do no more or less than my share."

I spoke shortly, not knowing whether to comment on his using an endearment he had no right to give to me who was a wedded wife.

"Soon it will all be over," he said. "In Norstead the war and its ugliness cannot touch you—"

"Norstead? What mean you, Toross? Those who go to Norstead are the refugees. We cannot keep them here, our supplies will not allow it. But our own people do not go. Perhaps you will ride with them—"

As soon as I said that, I felt again a slight lightening of burden. Life in Ithkrypt would be easier without these kinsfolk ever at my side.

"But you shall go also." He said that as calmly as if there could be no question. "A maid has no place in a keep as good as besieged—"

Dame Math—surely she had not planned so behind my back? No, I knew her better. Then I lost that touch of panic—Toross had not the least authority over me. At my uncle's orders, or at Kerovan's, would I leave, but for no other.

"You forget, I am not a maid. My lord knows I am at Ithkrypt. He will come for me here. So I stay until that hour."

Toross' face flushed. "Joisan, do you not see? Why do you cling loyally to that one? He has not claimed you within the marriage term; that is already two months gone, is that not so? You can now give bride-refusal without any breaking of oaths. If he wanted you, would he not have come before this?"

"Through the ranks of the enemy, no doubt?" I countered. "Lord Kerovan leads his father's armsmen in the south. This is no time to say that the days of agreement be strictly kept. Nor do I break bond unless my lord himself says he does not want me!" Perhaps that was not quite so, for I had as much pride as any woman. But I wished Toross to understand, not to put into blunt words what could not be unsaid. If he went farther, it would end all friendship between us, and I had liked him.

"You are free if you wish it," he repeated stubbornly. "And if you are truthful, Joisan, you know that this is your wish. Surely that I—what I feel for you and have since first I saw you is plain. And you feel the same, if you will allow yourself to—"

"Untrue, Toross. What I tell you now is as strong as if I took Flame Oath—as I shall if you need that to make you understand. I am Lord Kerovan's wife and so I will remain as long as we live and he does not deny it. As a wife it is honor-breaking and unfitting that I listen to such words as you have just said. I cannot come to you again!"

I turned and ran, though I heard him stir and give a gasp of pain, then cry out my name. I did not look back, but came into the great hall. There was the Lady Islaugha ladling broth from a pot into a bowl, and I went to her swiftly.

"Your son needs you," I told her. "Do not ask me to go to him again."

She looked up at me, and I could see in her face that she knew what had happened and that she hated me furiously because I had turned from him. To her he was her heart's core, to which all must be allowed and given.

"You fool!" she spat at me.

"Not such a fool as I would be if I listened." That much of a retort I allowed myself, and then stood aside as, with the slopping bowl still in her hands, she hurried towards Toross' room.

I remained by the fire, stretching out my chilled hands to it. Was I a fool? What had I of Lord Kerovan to keep with me? A bauble of crystal—after eight years of marriage which was no marriage. Yet for me there had been no choice, and I did not regret what I had just done.

Kerovan:

It seemed that I could hardly remember a time when there had not been war, so quickly does a man become used to a state of constant alarm, peril, and hardship. When the news of the invasion came, my father made ready to march southward at the summons of those most beset. But before he could ride, he thought better of it for two reasons. He still believed that Ulmsport was now one of the goals of the enemy fleet, and he was not well. He had taken a rheum that did not leave him, and was subject to bouts of fever and chills that were not for an armsman in the field.

Thus it was that I led those who marched under the gryphon banner when we went to the aid of our kinsmen. Jago pled to ride with me, but his old hurt was not such as would allow it, and I went with Marshal Yrugo.

My half-brother and Rogear had returned to the dale of my mother's kin, as their true allegiance was to the lord there. I was not sorry to see them ride before I left. While there had never been an open break, nor had Hlymer, after the first few days of my coming to Ulmsdale, sought to provoke me, yet I remained uneasy in their company, knowing they were no friends.

In fact I had lain but little in Ulmskeep in those days; rather moving about the dale, staying in Ulmsport, collecting information for my father while he was confined to his bed. And in this I served two purposes: not only to act as his eyes and ears, but to learn more of this land and its people where, if fortune favored, I would some day govern.

At first I was met by covert hostility, even a degree of fear, and I knew Jago's warnings had deep roots; the rumors of my strangeness had been used to cause a stir. But those who saw me during my casting up and down the dale, who reported to me, or took my orders, soon were as relaxed in my presence as they would be with any marshal or master. Jago told me after a space that those who had been in such contact now cried down any mutterings, saying that anyone with two eyes in his head could see I was no different in any manner from the next lord's heir.

My half-brother had already done some disservice to any cause he might have wished to foster by his own defects of character. I had marked him as a bully on our first meeting, and that he was. To his mind no one of lesser rank had any wit or feelings and could be safely used as a man uses a tool. No, not quite, for the expert workman has a respect for a good tool and treats it carefully.

On the other hand Hlymer was able with weapons, and, for all his bulk, he was an expert swordsman with great endurance. He had a long reach, which put him to advantage over a slighter opponent such as myself. And I do not think in those days I would have cared to meet him in a duel.

He had a certain following within the household whom he relished parading before me now and then. I never went out of my way to attach any man to me, keeping to the circumspect role that I had taken when warned by Jago. Having been reared to find my company mainly in myself, I knew none of those small openings for friendship that could have led to companionship. I was not feared; nor was I loved. Always I was one apart.

I sometimes wondered during those days what my life might have been had not the invasion come. Jago, returning from his mission to Ithkrypt, had sought me out privately and put in my hand an embroidered case less than the length of my palm, made to contain a picture. He told me that my lady begged such of me in return.

Giving him my thanks, I waited until he was gone before I slipped the wooden-backed portrait out into the light and studied the face. I do not know what I expected—save I had hoped, perhaps oddly, that Joisan was no great beauty. A fair face might make her the more unhappy to come to such a one as I was after being flattered and courted. There are certain types of beauty that attract men even against their wills.

What I looked upon now was the countenance of a girl, unmarked as yet, I thought, by any great sorrow or emotion. It was a thin face, with the eyes over-large in it. And those eyes were a shade that was neither green nor blue, but a mixture of both, unless he who had limned that picture had erred.

I believed that he did not, for I think he had not flattered her. She must be here as she was in life. No, she was no beauty, yet the face was one I remembered, even when I did not look upon it. Her hair, like my own, was darker than usual, for the dalesmen tend to be fair and ruddy. It was the brown of certain leaves in autumn, a brown with a red undernote.

Her face was wider at the brow than the chin, coming to a point there, and she had not been painted smiling, but looking outward with sober interest.

So this was Joisan. I think that holding her portrait so and looking upon it made me realize in truth and sharply, for the first time, that here was one to whom my life was bound and from whom I could not escape. Still that seemed an odd way to regard this thin, unsmiling girl—as if in some manner she threatened to curb my freedom. The thought made me a little ashamed, so I hurriedly slipped the picture back into its case and thrust it into my belt-pouch to get it both out of sight and out of mind.

Jago had told me she wished one in return. Her desire was natural. But even if I desired—which somehow I did not—to honor her request, there was no way of doing so. I knew no one in the dale who had the talent for liming. And somehow I did not want to ask any questions to discover such a one. So to my lady's first asked boon I made no reply. And in the passing days, each with a new burden of learning or peril, I forgot it—because I wanted to, perhaps.

But the picture remained in my pouch. Now and then I would look upon its casing, even start to slide out the picture, yet I never did. It was as if such looking might lead me to action I would later regret.

By all custom Joisan herself should have come to me before the end of the year. But custom was set aside by the rumors of war. And the next season found me fighting in the south.

Fighting—no, I could not claim to so much! My forester training made me no hero of battles, but rather one of those who skulked and sniffed about the enemy's line of march, picking up scraps of information to be fed back to our own war camp.

The early disasters, when keep after keep along the coast had fallen to the metal monsters of Alizon, had at last battered us into the need of making a firm alliance among ourselves. That came very late. In the first place, the enemy, showing an ability to farsee and outguess us that was almost as superior to ours as their weapons were, had removed through murder several of the great southern lords who had personal popularity enough to serve as rallying points for our soldiers.

There were three remaining who were lucky or cautious enough to have escaped that weeding out. They formed a council of some authority. Thus we were able to present a more united front and we stopped suffering defeat after defeat, but used the country as another weapon, following the way of battle of Waste outlaws who believe in quick strikes and retreats without losing too many of their men.

The Year of the Fire Troll had seen the actual beginning of the invasion. We were well into the Year of the Leopard before we had our first small successes. Yet about those we dared not be proud. We had lost so much more than any gain, save slamming the invaders back into the sea again, would mean. The whole of the southern coast was theirs, and into three ports poured ever-fresh masses of men. It would seem, though, that their supply of such fearsome weapons as they had used in the first assaults—those metal monsters— was limited. Otherwise we could not have withstood them as long as we did, or made our retreat north and west any more than the disorganized scramble of a terrified rabble.

We took prisoners, and from some of those learned that the weapons we had come to fear the most were not truly of Alizon at all, but had been supplied by another people now engaged in war on the eastern continent where Alizon lay. And the reason for the invasion here was to prepare the way in time for these mightier strangers.

The men of Alizon, for all their arrogance, seemed fearful of these others whose weapons they had early used, and they threatened us with some terrible vengeance when the strangers had finished their own present struggle and turned their full attention on us.

But our lords decided that a fear in the future might be forgotten now. It was our duty to defend the dales with all we had, and hope we could indeed drive the invaders back into the waves. Privately I think none of us in those days was sure that we were not living in the last hours of our kind. Still no one spoke of surrender. For their usage of captives was such that death seemed more friendly.

I had returned from one of my scouts when I found a messenger from the battle leader of this portion of the country —Lord Imgry—awaiting me with an urgent summons. Bone-weary and hungry, I took a fresh mount and grabbed a round of dried-out journey bread, without even a lick of cheese to soften it, to gnaw on while I rode.

The messenger informed me that a warning of import had been flashed overland by the torch-and-shield method, and at its coming he had been sent to fetch me.

At least our system of placing men in the heights to use a torch against the bright reflection of a shield to signal had in part speeded up the alerts across country. But how I could be involved in such a message I could not guess. At that moment I was so achingly tired my wits were also sluggish.

Of the lords who comprised our war council, Lord Imgry was the least approachable. He was ever aloof. Still his planning was subtle and clever, and to him we owed most of our small successes. His appearance mirrored what seemed to be his inner nature. His face wore a cold expression. I do not think I ever saw him smile. He used men as tools, but did not waste them, and his care for his followers (as long as they served his purposes) was known. He saw there was food for their bellies and shelter if possible, and he shared any hardships in the field. Yet he had no close tie with anyone in his camp, nor, I believed, with any of the other lords either.

Imgry was respected, feared, and followed willingly by many. That he was ever loved I could not believe.

Now, as I came into his camp, a little dizzy from lack of sleep, long hours of riding, and too little food, I tried not to stagger as I dismounted. It was a point of honor to face Imgry with the same impassive front as he himself always presented under the most harrowing conditions.

He was not as old perhaps as my father, but he was a man one could never conceive of as having been truly young. From his cradle he must have been scheming and planning, if not for his own advancement (which I suspected), then for the advancement of some situation about him. There was a fire in the landsman's rude cottage where he had his headquarters, and he stood before it, gazing into the flames as if there lay some scroll for his absorbed reading.

The men of his menie were camped outside. Only his armsman sat on a low stool polishing a battle helm with a dirty rag. A pot hung on its chain over the flames, and from it came a scent to bring juices into my mouth, though in other days I might have thought such a stew poor enough fare.

He turned his head as I shut the door behind me, to regard me with that sharp, measuring look that was one of his principal weapons against his own kind. Tired and worn as I was, I stiffened my will and went to meet him firmly.

"Kerovan of Ulmsdale." He did not make a question of that, rather a statement.

I raised my gloved hand in half-salute as I would to any of the lords commanding.

"Herewith."

"You are late."

"I was on scout. I rode from camp at your message," I returned levelly.

"So. And how went your scout?"

As tersely as I could, I told him what my handful of men and I had seen.

"So they advance along the Calder, do they? Yes, the rivers make them roads. But it is of Ulmsdale that I would speak. So far they have only landed in the south. But now Jorby has fallen—"

I tried to remember where Jorby might lie. But I was so tired it was hard to form any map picture in my mind. Jorby was port for Vastdale.

"Vastdale?" I asked.

Lord Imgry shrugged. "If it has not yet fallen it cannot hold out. But with Jorby in their hands they can edge farther north. And Ulmsport is only beyond the Cape of Black Winds. If they can strike in there and land a large enough force, they will come down from the north and crack us like a marax shell in a cook's chopper!"

This was enough to push aside the heavy burden of my fatigue. The force I had brought south with me was a small one, but every man in it had been a grievous loss to Ulmsdale. And since then there had been five deaths among our number, and three so sorely wounded they could not raise weapons now, if ever. If the enemy invaded at Ulmsport, I knew that my father and his people would not retreat, but neither could they hope to hold for long against the odds those of Alizon would throw against them. It would mean the ruinous end of all I had known.

As he spoke, Lord Imgry took a bowl from the table, scooping into it with a long-handled ladle some of the simmering stew. He put the steaming bowl back on the table and made a gesture.

"Eat. You look as if you would be the better for it."

There was little grace about that invitation, but I did not need much urging. His armsman rose and pushed his stool

over for me. On that I collapsed rather than sat, reaching
for the bowl, too hot yet to dip into, but, having shed my
riding gloves, I warmed my chilled hands by cupping them
about its sides.

"I have had no news out of Ulmsdale for—" How long had
it been? One day in my mind slid into another. It seemed that
I had always been tired, hungry, cold, under the shadow of
fear—and this had gone on forever.

"It would be wise for you to ride north." Imgry had gone
back to the fire, not turning his head toward me as he spoke.
"We cannot spare you any force of men, not more than one
armsman—"

It rasped my pride that he would deem me fearful of traveling without an escort. I thought that my services as scout
must have proved that I could manage such a ride without
detaching any force save myself from his company.

"I can go alone," I said shortly. And began sipping at the
stew, drinking it from the bowl since there was no spoon offered me. It was heartening and I relished it.

He made no protest. "Well enough. You should ride with
the morn. I shall send a messenger to your men, and you can
remain here."

I spent the rest of the night wrapped in my cloak on the
floor of the house. And I did indeed ride with the first light,
two journey cakes in a travel pouch, and a fresh mount that
Lord Imgry's armsman brought to me. His lord did not bid
me farewell, nor did he leave me good-speed wishes.

The way north could not be straight, and not always could
I follow any road if I would make speed, taking mainly sheep
tracks and old cattle paths. There were times when I dismounted and led my horse, working a way along steep dale
walls.

I carried a fire touch with me and could have had a fire to
warm and brighten the nights I sheltered in some shepherd's
hut, but I did not. For this was wild country, and we had already heard rumors that the wolves of the Waste were raiding inland, finding rich pickings in the dales where the fighting
men had gone. For my mail and weapons, my mount, I would
be target enough to draw such.

Mainly I spent the nights in dales, at keeps where I was
kept talking late by the leaders of pitiful garrisons to supply
the latest news, or in inns where the villagers were not so
openly demanding but none the less eager to hear.

On the fifth day, well after nooning, I saw the Giant's Fist, that beacon crag of my own homedale. There were clouds over-head, and the wind was chill. I thought it well to speed my pace. The rough traveling was wearing on my horse, and I had been trying to favor him. But if I dropped down to the trader's road, I would lose time now, so I kept to the pasture trails.

Not that that saved me. They must have had their watchers in the crags ready for me to walk into a trap. And walk into it I did, leading my plodding horse, just at the boundaries of Ulmsdale.

There was no warning given me as there had been that other time when death had lain in ambush. So I went to what might have been slaughter with the helplessness of a sheep at butchering time.

The land here was made for such a deed, as I had to come along a narrow path on the edge of a drop. My horse threw up its head and nickered. But the alert was too late. A crashing blow between my shoulders made me loose the reins and totter forward. Then, for a moment of pure horror, I was falling out and down.

Darkness about me—dark and pain that ebbed and flowed with every breath I drew. I could not think, only feel. Yet some instinct or need to survive set me scrabbling feebly with my hands. And that urge worked also in my darkened mind, so that even though I could not think coherently, I was dimly aware that I was lying face-down, my head and shoulders lower than the rest of me, jammed in among bushes.

I believe that my fall must have ended in a slide and that those bushes saved my life by halting my progress down to the rocks at the foot of the drop. If my attackers were watching me from above, they must have thought I had fallen to my death, or they certainly would have made a way down to finish me with a handy rock.

Of such facts I was not then aware, only of my pain of body and a dim need to better my position. I was crawling before I was conscious of what I must do. And my struggles led to another slide and more dark.

The second time I recovered my senses it was because of water, ice cold with the chill of a hill spring as it washed against my cheek. Sputtering, choking, I jerked up my head, trying to roll away from that flood. A moment later I was head-down once more, lapping at the water, its coldness adding to my shivering chill, but still clearing my head, ordering my thoughts.

How long I had lain in my first fall I did not know, but it

was dark now, and that dusk was not a figment of my weakened brain I was sure. The moon was rising, unusually bright and clear. I pulled myself up to a sitting position.

It had not been Waste outlaws who had attacked me, or they would have come to plunder my mail and weapons and so finished me off. The thought awoke a horror in me. Had Lord Imgry's suggestion already come to a terrible conclusion here? Had the invaders moved in to occupy Ulmsdale, and had one of their scout parties met me?

Yet that attack had so much of an ambush about it, had been delivered in so stealthy a fashion, that I could not believe it had been launched by the enemies I had faced in the south. No, there was something too secret in it.

I began to explore my body for hurts and thought I was lucky that no bones seemed to be broken. That I was badly bruised and had a lump on my head was the worst. Perhaps my mail and the bushes in which I had landed had protected me from worse injury. But I was shaking from shock and chill, and found when I tried to drag myself to my feet I could not stand, but had to drop down again, clutching at a rocky spur to steady myself.

There was no sign of my horse. Had it been taken by those who had thrown me over? Where were they now? The thought that they might be searching for me made me fumble to draw sword and lay it, bare-bladed, across my knee. I was not too far from the keep. If I could get to my feet and get on I would reach the first of the pasture fields. But every movement racked me so with pain that my breath hissed between my teeth, and I had to bite down upon my lower lip until I tasted my own blood before I could steady myself.

I had been much-favored by fortune in escaping with my life. But I was in no manner able to defend myself now. Therefore, until I got back a measure of strength, I had to move slowly and with all caution.

What I heard were the usual night sounds—birds, animals, such as were nocturnal in their lives. There was no wind, and the night seemed to me abnormally still, as if waiting. Waiting for what—or whom?

Now and then I shifted position, each time testing my muscles and limbs. At last I was able to struggle to my feet and keep that position, in spite of the fact that the ground heaved under me. The quiet, except for the continued murmur of the water, continued. Surely no one could come near without revealing himself.

I essayed a step or two, planting my boots firmly on the rocking ground, looking ahead for hand-holds to keep me upright. Then I saw a wall, the moon making its stones brightly silver. Toward this I headed and then along it, pausing ever to listen.

Soon I reached a section without cover, and there I went to my hands and knees, creeping along the stones, still alert to all around me.

Some distance away sheep grazed, and that peaceful sight was reassuring. Had there been raiders in the dale, certainly this field would have been swept bare. Or were those real sheep? The wintertime tales of the landsmen came to mind, of phantom sheep and cattle coming to join the real. And of how on certain nights or misty mornings, no herder could get the same count twice of his flock. If that were the case, then he could not, above all, return them to the fold; for to pen the real and the phantom together was to give the phantom power over the real.

I pushed aside such fancies and concentrated on the labor at hand: to win the end of the field and the wall. And then to head for the keep.

When I did reach the end of the wall I could look directly at the keep where it stood on its spur base jutting out over the road to Ulmsport. In the moonlight it was clear and bright, light enough to let me see the lord's standard on its tower pole.

That did not seem to be as it should. And then, as if to make all plain, there came a light wind from the east, lifting the edge of what hung on the pole, pulling out to display the standard widely if only for a long moment—but enough to let me see.

I do not know whether I uttered any sound or not. But within me there was a cry. For only one reason would a lord's banner ever hang at night, tattered, in such ragged strips. And that was to signify death!

Ulmsdale's banner slashed, which meant that my father was—

I caught at the wall against the weakness that strove to bring me to my knees.

Ulric of Ulmsdale was dead. Knowing that, I could guess, or thought I could, why there had been an ambush set up in the hills. They must have been expecting me. Though if my father's death had been sent as a message, it had missed me on the way. Those who wanted to prevent my arrival must have had men at every southern entrance to the dale to make sure of me.

To proceed now might well be to walk into dire danger which I was not yet prepared to face. I must make sure of my path before I ventured along it.

Though I had willed Toross and his kinswomen to be out of Ithkrypt, their going was not so easily accomplished, for Toross still kept to his bed. Nor could I suggest that he be taken away by litter. But I did avoid his chamber. That I had garnered the ill will of Islaugha and Yngilda went without saying. Luckily there were duties enough to keep me out of their way.

In riding skirt, with a packet of cheese and bread for my nooning, I rode with an armsman in the morning, inspecting the fields; visiting our outposts in the hills. I wore mail now and that sword my uncle had given me, and none raised their voices to say such a guise did not become me, for these were times when each turned hand to what must be done.

A sickness had come upon us without warning, bringing fever and chills and deep, racking coughs. By some favor of the Flame I escaped the worst of this, and so into my hands came more and more authority. For Dame Math was one of the early stricken. And, while she also left her bed among the first, she was plainly weakened, though she attended to her duties with little care for herself.

Marshal Dagale was also among the sick, and during those days his men turned to me for orders. We manned the lookout posts as best we might and tried also to get in the crops. It was a hard season, for there was much to be done and few on their feet for the doing of it. Days and nights were lost to me in a general sea of weariness from which there was no rest.

All who could labor, did. Even the little children dropped seeds into the waiting furrows left by plows their mothers guided. But we could only do so much, planting less than the year before. By midsummer day, instead of celebrating by a feast, I rather selected those who must leave us for Norsdale and saw them off, mainly afoot, for we could not spare mounts.

Toross did not go with them. His hurt had mended now enough so he could get about, and I hoped he would have the courtesy to leave. But he did not. Rather he fell into companionship with Dagale, acting as his second in command when the Marshal once again took up his duties.

I was never happy during those weeks. Though Toross did not seek me out, yet I felt his eyes ever upon me, his will like an invisible cord striving to draw me as he wished. I could only hope that my will to resist was as strong. I liked Toross for himself, as I had from our first meeting. In those days he had had a gaiety of temper that was in contrast to the somber life I had always known. He was gentle and considerate and talked amusingly. His face was comely, and he knew well how to make himself agreeable in company. I had seen the eyes of the maids in the household follow him and had also felt his charm.

His wound had sobered him somewhat. Still he lightened our hearts in those days, and I did not deny that he had much to give. But his quiet confidence that I would go to him, yield —that I could not understand.

I know that dalesmen look upon women as possessions, perhaps to be wooed and indulged for a season, and then, once won, to be a part of the household like hawk, hound, or horse. We are bartered by our kin for our dowry rights, for alliances between dales. And in such matters we have no voice to oppose what we may fear or hate.

For a woman to set herself up in opposition to any alliance made for her is to suggest she may have some commerce with a dark power. And if accused of that she can be in dire danger, even from those to whom she has the closest blood ties. But this does not make it an easy portion to swallow.

My way had been relatively easy in such matters—until now. First, Dame Math was a woman of presence and spirit, one of the Dames who had the respect of men and a place of her own in the dales. Her brother had made her the head of his household and deferred to her, taking her counsel in many matters.

Being discreet, she had worked within the frame of custom, not in open opposition to it. She had seen to it that I learned much that was forbidden or deemed unnecessary for most maids. I could read and write, having been tutored at the House of Dames. And I had not been set to small tasks elsewhere when she and Lord Cyart conferred about important matters, but had been encouraged to listen. Dame Math sometimes thereafter quizzed me as to the decision I might have made on this matter or that, always impressing on me that such knowledge was needful for a lady of a keep.

My uncle had taken obedience to his decrees as his right, but in addition he had often explained the reason for them, not given orders only, though he had a hasty temper and could be sharp. But as I grew older, he asked my will in small matters, and allowed me to have it.

I knew that there was speculation among the dalesmen concerning me. I had heritage from my father, but not in land, as he was second son and half-brother to Cyart. Cyart could, by custom, name me heir, even though I was a girl, but the choice could also fall on Toross because of his sex.

Until the southland had been overrun, Toross had been heir in the direct line to his father's dale. Now he was as lacking in lordship as any second or third son. And his continued assumption that I would come to him was, a small nagging doubt told me, perhaps not because he was moon-struck with my person (for I had no such vanity) but that he might so have a double claim upon Cyart as heir-to-be.

Perhaps I did him wrong in that, but that this thought moved in Islaugha I am sure. It made her try to veil her dislike of me and strive rather to throw us together and foster a closer relationship. I began to feel much as a hare coursed by two hounds during those summer days, and clung closer and closer to duties I could use as a screen.

The leaving of the first refugee party at midsummer was a relief, though not as great a one as I had hoped for. I had an additional worry concerning Dame Math. Though she kept to her tasks, I was well aware that she tired very easily; that beneath her coif her face grew thinner, her skin more transparent. She often kept her hands clasped tight about her prayer hoops now, and, in spite of that tight grip, her fingers shook in a way she could not control.

I spent all the time I could with her, between us a question that neither of us, I believe, wanted to ask or answer. But she talked more than she had in all the years before, as if she had a very short time left in which to impart to me so much. The lore of healing and herbs I already knew a little, since that had been a part of her lessons since my childhood. Besides that she spoke of other things, some of it strange hearing, and so I learned much of what perhaps was seldom shared between one generation and the next.

That we lived in a haunted land we all knew, for a person need only turn head from one side to another to sight some remnant of the Old Ones. There were old dangers that could be stirred into life by the unwary—that, too, all knew. Children were warned against straying—venturing into places where there was an odd stillness, more like waiting than abandonment.

I was drawn into the edge of a secret that was not of my seeking, nor of Dame Math's save that duty, by which she ordered her life, urged it on her. The Flame to which the Dames gave homage was not of the Power as the Old Ones knew it. And at most times those who professed the Flame shunned what lay in the hills, invoking their own source of Power against the alien one. But it seemed that even one of the House of Dames could be driven in times of stress to seek aid elsewhere.

She came to me early one morning, her poor face even more worn and haggard as she stood plucking nervously at her prayer hoops, gazing over my head at the wall as if she did not want to meet my eyes.

"Joisan, all is not well with Cyart—"

"You have had a message?" I wondered why I had not heard the way horn. In those days such were always used between friend and friend on the approach to any keep.

"None by word of mouth, or in runes," she answered slowly. "I have it here." She allowed the hoops to dangle from her belt-chain and lifted her thin fingers to smooth the band across her forehead.

"A dream?" Did Math share that strange heritage?

"Not as clear as a dream. But I know ill has come to him, somewhere, somehow. I would go to the moon-well—"

"It is not night, and neither is it the time of the full moon," I reminded her.

"But water from that well can be used—Joisan, this I must do. But—but I do not think I can go alone—that far—"

She swayed and put her hand to the wall to steady herself. I hurried to her, and her weight came against me so I had trouble guiding her to a stool.

"I must go—I must!" Her voice rose, and there was in it an undercurrent of alarm that frightened me. When one who has always been rock-firm becomes unstable, it is as if the very walls are about to topple.

"You shall. Can you ride?"

There were beads of moisture showing on her upper lip. Looking at her straightly in that moment I saw that Dame Math had become an old woman. As if overnight all the weight of years had crushed down upon her, which was as frightening as her unsteadiness.

Some of her former determination stiffened her shoulders, brought her head upright again.

"I must. Get me one of the ponies, Joisan."

Leaning on me heavily, she came out into the courtyard, and I sent a stable boy running for a pony: those placid, ambling beasts we kept mainly for the carrying of supplies. By the time he returned, Dame Math was as one who has sipped a reviving cordial. She mounted without too much difficulty, and I led the pony across the fields to that very well where I had once slipped in the nighttime to ask a question of my own.

If any marked our going, they left us alone. The hour was early enough so that I think most were still at their morning food. As I tramped beside the pony, I felt the pinch of hunger at my own middle.

"Cyart—" Dame Math's voice was hardly above a whisper, yet it was as if she called and hoped to have an answer to her calling. I had never thought much about the tie between those two, but the ring of that name, uttered in her voice, told me much at that hour. For all their outward matter-of-fact dealing with each other there was deep feeling too.

We came to the well. When I had been there at night before, I had not seen clearly those traces by which others had often times sought out a sign of the Power that was said to be there. There were well-worn stones rimming in the well, and beyond those, bushes. To the bushes things were tied. Some were merely scraps of ribbon, color lost through the action of wind and weather. Others were crudely fashioned of straw or twig—manikins or stick horses, sheep—all twirling and bobbling within sight of the water, perhaps set there to signify the desire of the petitioners.

I helped Dame Math from the pony's back, guiding her forward a step or two until she pulled free from my aid and walked as might one who needed no help. With her goal in sight, a semblance of strength flowed back into her.

From a deep skirt pocket she brought forth a bowl no larger than could be fitted into the hollow of her hand. It was of silver, well-burnished. And I remembered that silver was supposed to be the favorite metal of the Old Ones, just as opals, pearls, jade, and amber were their jewels.

She gestured me to stand beside her and pointed to a plant that grew at the lip of the well itself. It had wide leaves of dark green veined with white, and I did not remember ever seeing its like before.

"Take a leaf," she told me, "and with it dip to fill this bowl."

The leaf, pinched, gave forth a pleasant aroma, and it seemed to twist almost of its own will into a cup, so I might spoon water into the bowl. The water in the well was very high, its surface only a little below the level of its stone rim. Three times did I dip and pour before she said, "Enough!"

She held the bowl between her hands and raised it, blowing gently on the liquid within so it was riffled by her breath.

"It is not water of the Ninth Wave, which is the best of all for this purpose, but it will do."

She ceased to puff, and the water was smooth. Over it she gave me one of those compelling looks that had always brought my obedience.

"Think of Cyart! Hold him as a picture in your mind."

I tried to draw a mind picture of my uncle as last I had looked upon him, when he had drunk the stirrup cup of my pouring before riding south. I was surprised that the months between had dulled my memory so quickly, because I found it hard to recall him with any clarity. Yet I had known him all my life long.

"There is that about you"—Dame Math looked at me narrowly—"which gainsays this. What do you have on you, Joisan, which obstructs the Power?"

What did I have about me? My hand went to my bosom where the crystal gryphon lay in hiding. Reluctantly, urged to this by the stern eyes of Dame Math, I brought forth the globe.

"Hang it over there!"

Such was her authority that I obeyed her, looping the chain near one of those straw people lashed to a branch. She watched and then turned her gaze again to the bowl.

"Think of Cyart!" she demanded once again.

Now it was as if a door opened and I could see him, clear in every detail.

"Brother!" I heard Dame Math cry out. Then there were no more words, only a desolate sound. She stared down into the small bowl, her face very bleak and old.

"So be it." She took one step and then another, turned over the bowl and let the water splash back into the well. "So be it!"

Harsh, startlingly clear, a sound tore the morning air, the alarm gong from the keep tower! That which we had feared for so long had come upon us—the enemy was in sight!

The pony whinnied and jerked at its tether, so I reached for the reins. As I struggled to control the frightened animal, the gong continued to beat. Its heavy ring sounded in echoes from the hills like the thunder of a rising storm. I saw Dame Math hold out the bowl as if offering it to some unseen presence, allowing it to drop into the well. Then she came to me.

The need for action was like youth poured into her frail body. Yet her face was one knowing hope no longer, looking forward into a night without end.

"Cyart has dreamed his final dream," she said, as she mounted the sweating pony. Of him she did not speak again; perhaps because she could not. For a moment or two I wondered what she had seen in the bowl. Then the alarm shook everything from my mind save the fact that we must discover what was happening at the keep.

The news was ill indeed, and Dagale broke it to us as he marshaled his men for what all knew could be no defense, only a desperate attempt to buy time for the rest of us. The invaders were coming upriver, the easiest road to us from the coast. They had boats, our scouts reported, that were not sailed or oared, but still moved steadily against the current. And we of Ithkrypt had little time.

We had long ago decided that to remain in the keep and to be battered out of it was deadly folly. It was better for those who could not fight to take to the hills and struggle westward. So we had even rehearsed such retreats.

At the first boom of the gong, the herdsmen had been on the move, and the women and children also, riding ponies or tramping away with their bundles, heading west. I went swiftly to my chamber, pulled on with haste my mail coat and my sword, and took up my heavy cloak and the saddle bags in which I had packed what I could. Yngilda was gone, garments thrown on the floor, her portion of our chamber looking as if it had already been plundered.

I sped down the hall to the short stairs and up to Dame Math's room. She sat there in her high-backed chair, resting across her knees something I had never seen in her hands before, a staff, or wand. It was ivory white, and along its surface were carven runes.

"Dame—your cloak—your bag—" I looked about me for those that we were to have ever-ready. But her chamber was as it had always been; there was no sign she meant to quit it.

"We must be off!" I hoped she was not so weak she could

not rise and go. I could aid her, to be sure, but I had not the strength to carry her forth.

She shook her head very slowly. Now I saw her breath came in gasps, as if she could not draw enough air into her laboring lungs.

"Go—" A whispering voice came with visible effort from her. "Go—at—once—Joisan!"

"I cannot leave you here. Dagale will fight to cover our going. But he will not hold the keep. You know what has been decided."

"I know—and—" She raised the wand. "For long I have followed the Flame and put aside all that I once knew. But when hope is gone and the heart also, then may one fight as best one can. I do now what I must do, and in the doing perhaps I may avenge Cyart and those who rode with him." As she spoke, her voice grew stronger word by word, and she straightened in her chair, though she made no effort to rise from it.

"We must go!" I put my hand on her shoulder. Under my touch she was firm and hard, and I knew that, unwilling, I could not force her from her seat.

"You must go, Joisan. For you are young, and there may still be a future before you. Leave me. This is the last command I shall lay upon you. Leave me to my own reckoning with those who will come—at their peril!"

She closed her eyes, and her lips moved to shape words I could not hear, as if she prayed. But she did not turn her prayer hoops, only kept tight hold on the wand. That moved as if it had the power to do so of itself. Its point dropped to the floor and there scratched back and forth busily as if sketching runes, yet it left no marks one could see.

I knew that her will was such she could not now be stirred. Nor did she look up to bid me any farewell when I spoke one to her. It was as if she had withdrawn into some far place and she had forgotten my existence.

Loath to go, I lingered in the doorway, wondering if I could summon men and have her carried out by force, sure she was not now responsible in word or deed. Perhaps she read my thought in my hesitancy, for her eyes opened wide once again, and in her loose grip the wand turned, pointed to me as a spear might be aimed.

"Fool—in this hour I die—I have read it. Leave me pride of House, girl, and let me do what I can to make the enemy sorry he ever came to Ithkrypt. A blood-debt he already owes me, and that I shall claim! It will not be a bad ending for one of the House of the Broken Sword. See you do as well when your own time is upon you, Joisan."

The wand twirled as it pointed to me. And I went, nor could I do otherwise, for this was like a *geas* laid upon me. A will and power greater than my own controlled me utterly.

"Joisan!" The gong no longer beat from the watchtower, so I heard that call of my name. "Joisan, where are you?"

I stumbled down the steps and saw Toross standing there, his war hood laced in place, only a portion of his face visible.

"What are you waiting for?" His voice was angry and he strode forward, seized me by the shoulder and dragged me toward the door. "You must mount and ride—as if the night friends themselves were upon us—as well they may be!"

"Dame Math—she will not come—"

He glanced at the stair and then at me, shaking his head.

"Then she must stay! We have no time. Already Dagale is at arms on the river bank. They—they are like a river in flood themselves! And they have weapons that can slay at a greater distance than any bolt or arrow can fly. Come—"

He pulled me over the doorsill of the great hall and into the open. There was a horse there, a second by the gate. He half-threw me into the saddle.

"Ride!"

"And you?"

"To the river, where else? We shall fall back when we get the shield signal that our people are in the upper pass. Even as we planned."

He slapped my mount upon the flank so that the nervous beast made a great bound forward and I gave all my attention to bringing it once more under control.

I could hear far-off shouting, together with other sounds that crackled, unlike any weapon I could imagine. By the time I had my horse again under control, I could see that Toross was riding in the opposite direction toward the river. I was tempted to head after him, only there I would have been far more of a hindrance than a help. To encourage those who fled, to keep them going, was my part of the battle. Once in the rougher ground of the heights, we would split apart into smaller bands, each under the guide of some herder or forester and so, hopefully, win our way westward to whatever manner of safety would be found in High Hallack now.

But before I came to the point where the trail I followed left the dale bottom a stab of memory caught me. The crystal

gryphon—I had left it snared on the bush beside the well!
And I had to have it. I swung my mount's head around, sending him across a field of ripe grain, not caring now that he
trampled the crop. There was the darker ring of trees marking the well-site. I could pick up the gryphon, angle in a different direction, and lose very little time.

Taking heed of nothing but the trees around the well and
what I had to find there, I rode for it and slid from the
saddle almost before the horse came to a full halt. But I had
enough good sense to throw my reins over a bush.

I pushed through the screen of growth, setting jogging
and waving many of those tokens netted there. The gryphon—
yes! A moment later it was in my hand, safe again. How
could I ever have been so foolish as to let it go from me? I
could not slip the chain over my mail coif and hood, but I
loosened the fastening at my throat long enough to thrust my
treasure well within.

Still tugging at the lacings to make them fast, I started for
my horse. There was a loud nicker, but I was too full of relief
at finding the gryphon to pay the heed I should have to that.
So I walked straight into danger as heedlessly as the dim
witted.

They must have seen me ride up and set their trap in a
short time, favored by the fact that I was so intent upon the
bauble that had brought me here. As I reached for the reins
of my horse, they rose about me with a skill suggesting this
was not the first time they had played such a game. Out of
nowhere spun a loop that fell neatly over my shoulders and
was jerked expertly tight, pinning my arms fast. I was captive,
through my own folly, to those of Alizon.

So my father was dead, and I had been left for dead. Who now ruled in Ulmskeep? Jago—my mind fastened on the only friend I might now find within those walls ahead. During the months I had spent here as my father's deputy, I had acceptance but no following to which I might look now for backing. But I must somehow learn what had happened.

I drew into a screen of brush at the fence corner. The night wind was chill, and I shivered, being unable to stop that trembling of my body any effort produced. The keep would be closed at this hour except for—

Now I could think more clearly. Perhaps the shock of seeing the tattered banner had cleared my head. There was the Escape Way—

I do not know what brought our forefathers up from the south. They left no records, only a curious silence concerning the reason for their migration. But the fortifications they built here, their way of life, hinted that they had lived in a state of peril. For the petty warrings they engaged in here after their coming could never have been so severe as to necessitate the precautions they used.

They did not have to fight against the Old Ones for the dales. Why then the keeps—one strong one built in each dale —with those secret exit points known only to each lord and his direct heir? As if each need look forward to some time of special danger when such a bolt-hole would be in need.

Therefore, Ulmskeep had an entrance open to me, my father having shown it to me secretly late one night. I had a way into the heart of what might now be enemy territory and, if I were to learn anything, that I must take. There was this also—I licked my lips tasting blood, a sorry drink for me —there was this: perhaps the last place they would search for me would be within that grim building with its tattered, drooping banner.

I took my bearings from the keep and began to move with more surety now that I had a goal in mind, though I did not relinquish any of my care not to be seen. It was some distance I must go, working my way carefully from wall to wall, from one bit of cover to the next. There were lights in the keep windows and in those of the village. One by one those winked out as I kept on at a snail's pace, for I had schooled myself to patience, knowing that haste might betray me.

A barking dog at a farmhouse, well up-slope, kept me frozen with a pounding heart until a man shouted angrily and the brute was still. So it took me some time to reach the place I hunted.

Ulmsdale was freer of those relics of the Old Ones than most of the northern dales. In fact it was only here, in the shadow of the Giant's Fist, that there were signs any had found their way into this valley before the coming of my own race. And the monument to the past was not an impressive one—merely a platform leveled among the stones of these heights, for what purpose no man might say.

The only remarkable thing about this smoothed stretch of stone was that deep-carven in it was that creature from which the first lord of Ulmsdale had taken his symbol—a gryphon. Even in this uncertain light the lines of the creature's body were clear enough to give me the bearings I needed.

So guided, I scrambled up the slope a little farther, my bruised, stiff body protesting every action, until I found that place in the wall of the valley where care had been taken generations ago to set stones about a cunningly concealed break.

I edged past those into a dark pocket. Until that moment I had not realized the difficulties of this path without a light. Drawing my sword, I used it to sound out walls and footing, trying to remember as clearly as I could what lay before me now.

All too soon the sword met empty space, and I had found my destination. I sheathed my blade and crouched to feel about with my bare hands. Yes, this was the lip of the vent down which I must go. I considered the descent. In the first place the boots fashioned to hide my feet were built only for ordinary service. I distrusted them when I had to use toe holds in the dark. In fact I was not even sure my hoofed feet would serve there, but at least they would be better free. So I wrested off my boots and fastened them to my belt.

The substance of my hoofs was not affected by the chill of the stone, seeming not to have the sensitivity of flesh, and somehow with my feet free I felt secure enough to swing over and test beneath me for footholds. I need not have worried; my hoofs settled well into each and, heartened, I began the descent. I could not recall how deep I must go. In fact when my father had brought me hither we had not climbed this; he had only shown it to me from below.

Thus I went down into the dark, and the space seemed to be endless. It was not. A reaching hoof touched solid surface, and very cautiously I placed the other hoof beside it. Now—a light—

Fumbling in my pouch, I brought out my strike-light, keeping it ready in one hand while I felt along the wall with the other. My fingers caught at a knob of wood. I snapped the light, and the torch flared, dazzling me with sudden illumination.

Not stopping to put on my boots, for I relished more and more the freedom of my hoofs, hitherto so cramped by concealment, I started along a downward-sloping way which would bring me under the dale-floor to the keep. It was a long way and, I think, more than half of it was a natural fault, perhaps the bed of some stream diverted by nature or man. The roof was low, and in several places I went to hands and knees to pass.

But here I did not have to fear discovery, and I made the fastest pace I could over the sand and gravel. The slope went sharply downward for a space; then it leveled out, and I knew that I was now in the valley. The keep could not be too far ahead.

My torch shone on a break in the wall of the passage, crude steps going up at a steep angle—though the passage kept on—into a sea-cave of which my father had told me. I thus had two ways of escape.

I began to climb, knowing this stair was a long one. It went up not only through the crag on which the keep was built, but within the wall of that to my father's own chamber. Halfway up I paused and rubbed out the torch on the wall. Now I needed both hands for the holds here, and there were peepholes along the way where light might betray me.

The first of these was in the barracks. A cresset burned low against the far wall, leaving the room much-shadowed. There were some men asleep here, but only a handful.

I climbed again and looked now into the great hall from a position somewhere behind my father's high seat. There was a fire on the hearth which was never allowed to go out. A serving-man nodded on a bench near it and two hounds were curled up there—nothing else. This was normal enough at this hour.

The end of the passage was before me, and I could no longer put off reaching it—though I dreaded what might lie ahead.

Men freely use the word "love" to cover both light emotions, such as affection and liking, and viler ones such as lust, or strong attachments that last through life. I had never been one to use it at all—for my life in youth had been devoid of much emotion—fear, awe, respect were more real to me than "love." I did not "love" my father. In the days that I had spent with him after he had given me public acknowledgment, I respected him and was loyally attached to his service.

Yet there always stood between us the manner of my upbringing; that I had been hidden away. Though he had come to see me during those years, had brought me small gifts such as boys delight in, had provided well for me, yet I had always sensed in him an uneasiness when we were together. I could not tell if that came from his reaction to my deformity, or whether he reproached himself for his treatment of me and yet could not bring himself to defy my mother's feelings to name me openly son. I knew only, from very early years, that our relationship was not akin to that of other fathers and sons. And for a long time I thought that the fault was mine, so I was ashamed and guilty in his presence.

Thus we built a wall stone by stone, each adding to it, and we could not break it down. Which was a great loss, I know, for Ulric of Ulmsdale was such a man as I could have "loved," had that emotion ever been allowed to grow in me. Now as I went to his chamber through the dark of this hidden way, I felt a sense of loss such as had never emptied me before. As if I had once stood at the door of a room filled with all the good things of this world and yet had been prevented from entering in.

My hand was on the latch of the panel that opened inward, concealed by the back of the huge, curtained bed. I inched this open, listening. Almost I swung it shut again, for I heard voices and saw the gleam of lamplight. But I remembered that so well-concealed was this way, that unless I crawled around the bed to boldly confront the speakers, they would not know of my presence. And certainly this was a chance to learn exactly what might be going on. Thus I squeezed through the door and edged around the head of the bed, the stiff, embroidered folds of the curtains providing excellent cover, until I found a slit to let me see as well as hear.

There were four in the room, two using for a seat the long chest against the wall; one on a stool; and the last in the high-backed chair in which my father had sat when I bid him farewell.

Hlymer and Rogear. On the stool a girl. I caught my breath, for her face—leaving out those points of difference that were due to her sex—could have been my own! And on the chair—I had no doubt that for the first time in my life I was looking upon the Lady Tephana.

She wore the ashen gray robes of a widow, but she had thrown back the concealing veil, though the folds of it still covered her hair. Her face was so youthful she could have been her daughter's elder sister by only a year or two. There was nothing in her features of Hlymer. By her cast of countenance I was indeed her son.

I felt no emotion, only curiosity, as I looked at her. Since I had reached the age of understanding, I had been aware that for all purposes of living, I was motherless, and I had accepted that fact. She had not even kin-tie to me as I watched her now.

She was speaking swiftly. Her hands, long-fingered, and with a beauty that drew the eyes, flashed in and out in quick gestures as she spoke. But what I saw and resented, was that on her thumb was the gleam of my father's signet, which only the ruler in Ulmsdale had the right to wear and which should have weighted my own forefinger at this moment.

"They are fools! And because they are fools, should we be also? When the news comes that Kerovan has been killed in the south, then Lisana will be heir, and her lord"— she nodded to Rogear—"will command here in her name. I tell you that these invaders offer good terms. They need Ulmsport, but they do not want to fight for it. A fight will gain nothing for us, for we cannot hold long against what they can land. Who gains by death and destruction? The terms are generous; we save this valley by such bargaining—"

"Willingly will I be Lisana's lord and Ulmsdale's," Rogear answered, as she paused for breath. "As to the rest—" He shook his head. "That is another matter. It is easy to make a bargain. To keep it does not always suit the one in power. We can open gates but not close them again thereafter. They know just how weak we are."

"Weak? Are we? Say you that, Rogear?" Lady Tephana gazed at him directly. "Foolish boy, do you then discount the inherited might of our kin? I do not believe that these invaders have met their like before."

He was still smiling, that small, secret smile which had always led me to think that he carried within him some belief in himself that far outreached what others saw in him. It was as if he could draw upon some secret weapon as devastating in its way as those the invaders had earlier sent against us.

"So, my dear lady, you think to invoke *those?* But take second thoughts or even third upon that subject. What may answer comes at its own whim and may not easily be controlled if it takes its own road. We are kinsmen, but we are not truly of the blood."

I saw her face flush, and she pointed her finger at him. "Do you dare to speak so to *me*, Rogear!" Her voice rose higher.

"I am not your late lord, my dear lady." If she threatened him with that gesture, he did not show it. "His line was already cursed, remember, thus making him easily malleable to anything pertaining to *them*. I have the same countermeasures bred in me that you have. I cannot be so easily shaped and ordered. Though even your lord escaped you in the end, did he not? He named his body-heir in spite of your spells and potions—"

Her face changed in a subtle way that made me suddenly queasy, as if something had sickened my inner spirit. There was evil in this room. I could smell it; see it sweep in to fill that vessel waiting to hold it—that form of woman I refused to believe had ever given me life.

"What did you deal with, my dear lady, in that shrine when you bore my so-detested cousin, I wonder?" Rogear continued, still smiling, though Hlymer drew away along the bench as if he expected his mother to loose some blast in which he did not want to be caught. "What bargain did you make—or was it made before my cousin's birth? Did you cast a spell to bring Ulmsdale's lord to your bed as your husband? For you have had long dealings with *them*, and not with those on the White Path either. No, do not try that on me. Do you think I ever come here unprotected?"

Her pointing finger had been drawing swift lines. Just as Riwal, when he bade me farewell, had gestured in the air, and as I had seen thereafter a faint gleam of light marking the symbol he had traced in blessing, so did her finger leave behind a marking, or pattern. The marking was smoky-dark. Still it could be seen in the subdued light of the chamber, as if its darkness had the evil, black quality.

Rogear's hand was up before his face. He held it palm-out, and all those hand lines that we bear from birth and that are said by the Wisewomen to foretell our futures stood out on his flesh as if they had been traced in red. Behind that hand he still smiled faintly.

I heard a short, bitten-off cry from the Lady Tephana, and her hand dropped back into her lap. On her thumb the ring looked dull, as if its honest fire had been eaten out by what she had done moments earlier. I longed to free it from her flesh.

"Yes," Rogear continued, "you are not the only one, my dear lady, to go seeking strong allies in hidden places. It is born into us to have a taste for such matters. Now, having made sure that we are equally matched, let us return to the matter at hand. Your amiable son—" He paused and nodded slightly at Hlymer, though Hlymer looked anything but amiable. He sat hunched-over, darting glances first at his mother and then at Rogear, as if he feared one and had begun to hate the other.

"Since your amiable son has rid us of the other barrier standing in the way of possession of Ulmsdale, we must indeed make our plans. But I do not altogether agree that we should deal with the invaders."

"And why not?" she demanded. "Do you fear them? You, who have that"—she nodded to his hand—"to stand to your defense?"

"No, I do not fear them personally. But neither do I intend to give tamely into their hands any advantage. I believe, my dear lady, that you can indeed summon thunder from the hills to counteract any treachery that they might plan. But that which can be so summoned will not take note of selective destruction, and I do not propose to lose Ulmsdale in defending it."

"You will lose it anyway then." For the first time Lisana broke silence. "Also, dear Rogear"—there was little liking in her voice as she named him so—"we are not yet hand-fasted. Are you not a little beforehand in naming yourself lord here?"

She spoke coolly, and regarded him straight-eyed, measuringly, as if they were not betrothed but, rather, opponents at a gamingboard.

"True spoken, my sweeting," he agreed amiably. Had I been Lisana I would not have found that amiability pleasing, though. "Do you intend to be lord as well as lady here?"

"I intend not to be any piece in your gaming, Rogear," she returned swiftly, and there was no sign of uneasiness in her.

He stared at her as one who studied some new and perhaps unaccountable thing. I thought I saw his eyes narrow a fraction. And then he looked not to her but to her mother.

"Congratulations, my dear lady. So you have made sure of your power this way also."

"Naturally. Did you expect any less?" She laughed. Then he echoed that laughter.

"Indeed not, my dear lady. Ah, what a happy household we shall be. I can see many amusing evenings before us, trying this spell and that, testing each other's defenses."

"There will be no evenings at all," growled Hlymer, "unless we unite upon what is to be done to hold Ulmsdale. And I see little chance of that where the great lords have failed. Ulmsport is open—they need only to bring up a goodly force and land. The keep can hold out for a day, mayhap two—but—" He shrugged. "You have heard all the tales; we shall end like the rest."

"I wonder." Rogear had lost that shadow-smile. He glanced from Lady Tephana to Lisana and back again. "What if they cannot land? Wind and wave, wind and wave—"

Lady Tephana was intent, regarding him in the same searching way he had earlier looked upon Lisana.

"That takes the Power."

"Which you have in part, and my sweeting"—he nodded to the girl—"has in part, and to which I can add. Wind and wave have this advantage also. It will seem a natural catastrophe and one they will not fault us for. We shall be blameless. Follow in part your suggestion, my dear lady, but do not treat, only seem to treat. Then wind and wave—"

She moistened her lips with tongue tip. "It is a mighty summoning."

"Perhaps one beyond your powers?"

"Not so!" She was quick to answer. "But it will take the three of us truly united to do such a thing, and we must have life force to draw upon."

He shrugged. "It is a pity that we cleared the path so well of your lord's devoted followers. Hate can feed such a force, and we could have used their hatred. That grumbler Jago, for example."

"He drew steel on me!" Hlymer shrilled. "As if a broken man could touch me!"

"A broken man, no," Rogear agreed. "Had he been the man he once was—well, I do not know, brother-to-be. At any rate there are others to lend us life force. If we decide—"

Lisana had lost her cool withdrawal. I saw her eyes shine with an avid hunger.

"We will!" she cried out. "Oh, we will!"

For the first time Rogear showed a faint shadow of uneasiness, and he spoke to the Lady Tephana rather than to her daughter.

"Best curb your witchling, my dear lady. Some rush where prudence walks with double care."

Lisana was on her feet so suddenly, her stool spun away as her skirts caught it.

"Do not lesson me, Rogear! Look to your own Power, if you have as much as you claim!"

"We shall all look to our Power," Lady Tephana replied. "But such a plan takes preparation, and that we must turn to now." She arose, and Hlymer went quickly to her side, offering his arm in clumsy courtesy. It was almost, I thought, as if he would rather be in her company than Rogear's. Lisana followed, and Rogear was left alone.

My hand went to my sword hilt. What I had heard here filled me with horror, though it explained much. That these were working with Dark Power was plain, and they were not fresh come to such dealings either. That they—or at least the Lady Tephana (for never again in my mind did I think of her as my mother)—were old in such work, they had admitted. If my father had been ensorcelled, as Rogear had hinted, that explained much, and I could now forgive him all. The wall was broken—too late for me to tell him so.

What they would enter upon now was some great summoning of the Power. Perhaps it could save Ulmsdale—for their own purposes. But dared I set my own love of country against them? If they aroused some of the ancient forces of this brooding land against the enemy successfully, then, even though I hated them, still I must count them allies at this moment. So I watched Rogear go out from that chamber, and I did not challenge him.

There was one thought only in my mind. I had no idea what might be the consequences of the act they spoke of. In spite of the signs set on me at birth, I had none of the talent those three appeared to possess. There was only one in this land now from whom I could seek enlightenment, to learn whether I must let them do this to keep the dale free, or else turn what I could set against them to ensure that they fail. Which was the greater danger—the summoning of the Power or allowing the invaders foothold here? I could not judge, but perhaps Riwal, with his learning in those matters, might.

There was nothing in my father's keep now but a trap, and the sooner I was out of it the better, not only for my own safety, but perhaps for the future safety of the dale itself. However, as I went, I cherished in my mind those words concerning Jago. That Hlymer had forced him to a fight I did not doubt. And someday he would account to me for that.

By the time I reached the gryphon-marked stone on the hillside, the night was far-advanced. Weariness added to the pain of bruises and of my aching head, yet I was driven by time. The sooner I reached Riwal the better. To do so on foot would be a lengthy journey, and hunger gnawed at me.

How I might have fared had I not met the trader, I do not know. But as I skulked along the dale rim, I came upon one of those traces, not really a road, but in the summer seasons were used by hunters and traders—especially those bound for the Waste.

I had taken to cover when I heard the clip-clop of hoofs on the stone outcrop that comprised part of the trail, since I was fairly sure that, even if he who came were not an enemy, he might report me where it would do the least good. Only when I saw the manner of man who rode one rough-coated pony and led another, was I a little easier.

He did not pass, but halted directly opposite the thicket wherein I had taken cover and raised a peeled branch he carried in his hand. Not quite a staff, nor yet a whip, for it was too thick for that.

"Lord Kerovan—" He did not raise his voice. In fact he spoke in a low tone, yet the words carried clearly to where I lay.

He wore the leather and rough wool of a poor traveler. Now he pushed back his hood as if in revealing himself fully he would make himself known to me. Yet I did not recall seeing his face before.

Unlike most of the traders he was clean-jawed, his skin showing little beard-marking. And his features had a slightly strange cast, not quite those of a dalesman. His hair was clipped short and stood out from his skull very thickly, more

like the fur of an animal pelt than any hair I had ever seen.
Also it was brindled in color, neither gray nor brown nor
black, but a mixture of those colors.

"Lord Kerovan!" He repeated my name and this time he
beckoned with his wand.

I could not resist that gesture. Whether I would or no, I
had to go to him, rising to my feet and pushing through
the bushes that I might show myself to one who might be
a deadly enemy.

Captive to Alizon! All those tales of dark horror that the refugees told made me expect to be surrounded by demons as I was jerked farther into the open by the rope that bound my arms to my body. Still, these were only men, save that there was that in their faces which made my mouth go dry with fear. A quick death can be faced, but there are other things—

They spoke among themselves, laughing, and their tongue was strange. He who seemed leader among them came to me and pulled at the still-loose neck-thongs of my mail, bringing off my hood so my hair, loosened by his roughness, spilled out across my shoulders. He stroked that, and I longed for a dagger in my hand. But they were careful to make fast their noose, and I had no chance.

Thus they brought me back to Ithkrypt, or nearly there. Before we entered the courtyard where the enemy clustered, there was a flash of light from the tower, followed by a thunderous sound. Then, my head ringing from the fearful noise, near-shaken to the ground, I saw such a thing as I would not have believed. Ithkrypt's walls began to sway; great gaps appeared between the blocks of which they were built. And the walls toppled outward, catching and crushing many of the enemy, while a choking dust arose.

I heard screams and cries through that cloud, and I tried to run. But fortune was against me, for the end of the rope that bound me kept me helplessly anchored.

Had this been the work of those monsters the invaders commanded? I was sure not, for they would not so have killed their own men.

Dame Math! But how had she done this? I was dumbstruck by the evidence of such Power as I believed only one of the Old Ones could conjure; the Old Ones or some Wisewoman who had had dealings with the forbidden. Wisewoman—Dame—such were opposed. But before she had surrendered her will to the Flame and the Sisterhood that paid it homage, what else had Math been? At any rate the blood-price she had taken here was worthy of our House, as she had promised. In spite of my own fear I rejoiced that this was so. Valiant had our men always been. My own father had fallen facing five Waste outlaws, taking four of them with him. And now these from overseas would know that our women could fight also!

But this was my only chance to get away. I tugged against the rope. The murk of the dust was clearing, enough to show what held me prisoner. He who had led me here lay with the rope about his own waist, and he was face-down, a broken hunk of stone between his shoulders.

I thought him dead, and that made me more frenzied in my attempt to free myself. For to be bound to a dead man was the last horror. Yet the cord held, and I was as well-tethered as a horse at an inn door.

So they found me when they came reeling out of the rubble of Ithkrypt and pounding up from the river. Of our men there were no signs, save for three bodies we had passed on our way here. I could only believe that Dagale's force had paid for our escape time with their lives.

Only for a short space were the enemy so disorganized. I regretted bitterly that we could not have taken advantage of that; wreaked more damage among them while they were shocked by what happened. Now I did not doubt that any prisoners they might take would pay for this unexpected slaughter. Such fear rode me as to freeze my body, half-stupify my mind.

Dame Math had had the best of it. She had gone to her death, yes, but in a fitting manner. It was plain I would not be allowed such an ending, though they did not strike me down when they came upon me still bound to my captor. Instead they slashed through the rope and dragged me with them out of the ruin of Ithkrypt down to the river where there was a group of officers.

One among them had the speech of the dales, though he mouthed words gutturally. I was still so deafened by that terrible blast that I could hardly hear him. When I did not reply to his questions, he slapped my face viciously, one side and then the other.

Tears of pain spilled from my eyes and I knew shame that these should see them. I summoned what small pride was left me and tried to face them squarely and with my head up, as became a daughter of my House.

"What—was—there?" He thrust his face close to mine, and his breath was foul. He had a brush of beard on his chin, and his cheeks above that were splotched with red, his nose veined and swollen. His eyes were keen and cruel, and he was not, I was sure, a stupid man.

There was no need to conceal what I thought I knew, perhaps more reason to say it, since even these invaders must know that High Hallack held many secrets, most of them not to be plumbed by humankind.

"The Power," I said.

I think he read in my face that I spoke a truth I believed. One of his companions asked a question in that other tongue, and he made answer, though he did not look from me to the questioner. A moment later came his second demand.

"Where is the witch?"

Again I told him the truth. Though we did not use that term, I understood his meaning.

"She was within."

"Well enough." Now he did turn away and make his report to the others, and they spoke for some time among themselves.

I felt very weak and tired and wished I could drop to the ground. My head hurt still, as if the assault of sound upon my ears had injured something far inside my skull, and the despair of my captivity was a leaden cloak about me. Yet I held as well as I could to my resolve to keep my pride.

He faced me again, this time looking me up and down searchingly. In his beard his thick lips grinned in some ways like those men who had first taken me.

"You are no farm wench, not with mail on your back. I am thinking we have caught us a prize. But more of that later."

So I was allowed a respite, for at his orders I was left on the river bank, where their boats clustered and men were still leaping ashore. To my eyes they seemed as many as the stalks of grain in the fields, and there was no end to them. How could our small force have hoped to halt them even for an instant, any more than a single pebble might halt the flow of a spring flood.

There I also saw what had happened to our men. Some had fallen in battle. Those were the lucky ones. For the rest—no, I shall try to hold the doors of memory against what happened to them. I believed now the invaders were not humans but demons.

I think they took pains for me to see all this in order to break me. But in that they judged me wrong, for it stiffened rather than bent me to any will of theirs. It is not how a man dies, but how he bears that final act that has meaning. And the same is true for a woman of the dales. In me grew a coldness like the steel from the Waste, twice-forged and stronger than any other thing in our world. I swore that Dame Math was right, and I must contrive to make my own passing count against the enemy.

But it seemed they now forgot me. I was still bound, and they made the rope fast to one of the boat-chains. Men came and looked at me from time to time as if I were a prisoned beast. Their hands were on my hair and my face, and they jabbered at me in their own tongue, doubtless warning of much I would certainly rue. But none did more than that. It was coming night, and they had set up a line of campfires and were driving in sheep and cattle, slaughtering some of them.

A mounted party had gone down-dale in pursuit of our people. I besought the Flame that those fleeing had won the rugged land where their guides could lead them by routes only dalesmen knew.

Once I saw a small party return, heard women screaming for a while, and knew that some of our people had been run down. I tried to close my ears, shut off thought. This was that place of Outer Darkness come to earth, that place to which evil crawls and from which it issues forth again—and to that evil there is no end.

I tried to plan my own ending before they could turn to me for amusement. The river—could I hurl myself into the waters there? If I could edge along the chain to which my rope had been tied, surely there was a chance.

Toross—dully I wondered what had become of him. I had not seen his body with those others. Perhaps he had escaped at the last. If so, I could still find a small, unfrozen part in me that wished him well. Oddly at that thought his face was vivid in my mind, as sharp as if he stood before my eyes. Within my mail and under my jerkin something was warm.

The gryphon. That unlucky bauble which had doomed me to this state. The gryphon was growing ever warmer, almost like a brand laid to my skin. From it flooded not only that heat, but something else, a strength, a belief in myself against all the evidence that reason provided for my outer eye and ear. It was like some calm voice assuring me that there was a way out, and that my delivery was at hand, though I knew this could not be.

Fear became a small, far-off thing, easy to put aside. My sight was more acute, my hearing keener. My hearing—!

Even through the clamor of the camp I detected that sound. There was something coming—down-river!

How I knew this, I could not have told. But I knew I must be ready. Perhaps I was only dazed by fatigue, by my fear and despair. Yet I was as certain of this rescue as I was that I still lived and breathed.

"Joisan!" A thread of whisper, but to my alerted ears so near a shout, I feared all the camp might hear it.

I was afraid to answer aloud, but I turned my head a fraction in the direction from which they had come, hoping the gesture would signal my recognition.

"Edge—this—way—" The words came from the river. "If —you—can—"

Tortuous and slow were my efforts to obey. I kept watch on all about me, my back to where that voice whispered, lest I somehow betray this hope. Now I felt wet hands reach up to mine, the swing of a knife against the rope. That fell away, my stiffened hands were caught and held; my rescuer was half in the water.

"Slip over!" he ordered.

I wore mail and the dragging skirt. I could not hope to swim so burdened. Yet it would be better to meet death cleanly. Now I waited as a party of the invaders tramped along the path. They did not glance in my direction. Then I rolled over and down into the water, felt hands catch and drag me even as I gulped air and went under.

We were in the grip of the current where the stream ran the swiftest, and my struggles would not surface me for long. I choked and thought this was the end. Still that other fought for me, with what poor aid I could give. We came against a rock where he clung and held my head above the flood.

His face was close to mine, and it was no surprise to see that Toross held me so.

"Let me go. You have given me clean death, kinsman. For that I thank you—"

"I give you life!" he replied, and there was stark determination in his face. "Hold you here, Joisan!" He set my hands to the rock and I held. He crawled and pulled himself up into the air, and then by main force, for I had little strength left, dragged me up beside him.

By fortune we had come across the river into rough

pastureland, downstream from the ruins of Ithkrypt, and between us and the western hills was now the full invader force. Toross was shivering, and I saw he had stripped to his linen undershirt, his mail gone. There was a raw slash across his cheek where blood welled.

"Up!" He caught my arm, pulling at me. My long skirt, so water-soaked, was like a trap about my legs, and the mail was a deadweight upon me. But I stumbled forward, unable to believe that we had actually achieved this much and that the alarm for my escape had not yet sounded.

Thus we reached some rocks and fell, rather than dropped, behind them. I fumbled with the lacings of my mail, wanting to be rid of that, but Toross caught my hands.

"No, you may need that yet. We are far from out of the dragon's jaws."

Of that I needed no reminding. I had no weapon, and, as far as I could see, Toross carried none except the knife. Perhaps he had found a sword too weighty for that swim. We were reduced to that single blade and perhaps stones snatched from the ground if we were cornered.

"We must take the hills." In the growing dark he gestured up-slope. "And try to work our way around those butchers to join our people. But we had better wait for full dark."

Something in me urged action, to get as far from those fires, the noise across the river, as we could. Yet what he said made sense. To draw upon one's patience was a new ordeal, I now discovered.

"How—how did you come alive from the river battle?" I asked.

He touched that slash on his face, which had now clotted again, giving him a bloody mask to wear. "I took this in the last charge. It stunned me enough to make them think me dead. When I realized that I must be dead to escape, I played that part. Then I got away—but I saw them bring you from Ithkrypt. What happened there, Joisan? Why did they turn their destruction against their own men?"

"That was not done by the invaders; it was Dame Math. She used the Power."

For a moment he was silent and then he demanded, "But how can such a thing be? She was a Dame—a Dame of Norstead Abbey."

"It seemed that before she swore to the Flame she had other knowledge. It was her choice to call upon that in the end. Do you not think we can move now, Toross?" I was shivering in my wet clothing, trying hard to control the shaking of my body. Though it was late summer, this eve brought with it the foretaste of autumn.

"They will be waiting." He was on his knees, peering back to the river.

"The enemy—have they already climbed so high in the dale?" It appeared our small gift of fortune was fast-dwindling.

"No—Angarl, Rudo." Toross named the armsmen who had come with him out of the south. "My mother sent them back, and they were to press me into going into the hills. Had I not seen you in the hands of our enemies, the Hounds of Alizon, I might have yielded to them."

That we were not alone, if we could reach his men, gave me a spark of comfort, though both men were old, sour and dour. Rudo was one-eyed, and Angarl had lost a hand many years before.

So we began a stealthy withdrawal. I could not honestly understand why we were not sighted, though we took to all the cover the rough ground afforded. That there had come no outcry on my escape was also a mystery. I had expected them early on my trail—unless they believed I had perished in the river.

We found a narrow track winding upward, and Toross pushed the pace here. I would not admit that I found the going increasingly difficult, but strained my energy to the utmost to keep up. That he had laid me under debt to him weighed on me also. I was grateful, as anyone would be grateful for their life given back to them. Yet that Toross was the giver could cause future difficulties. But there was no reason to look forward to those—what mattered now was that we continued to claw our way through the dark.

Though I had lived in the dale all my life, I had only a general idea of where we might be heading. We needed to get west, but to do so and pass any enemy patrol, we must first head south. My wet boots became a torture to my feet. Twice I stopped and wrung out my skirt as best I could. Now it was plastered to my legs, chafing my skin.

Toross headed on and up with confidence, as if he knew exactly where he was bound, and I could only follow and trust in him.

We struck another track, faint, but at least easier footing than the way we had climbed, and this angled west. If the enemy had not combed this high, then we were heading around them. Once we heard more screams out of the night from the opposite bank of the river. Again I tried to close my ears to what I could in no way help. Toross did not falter in stride as those sounds reached us, but padded on. If they moved him to anger I did not know it. We did not talk as we went, saving all our breath for our exertions.

In spite of every effort, we could not move silently. There were scrapes of footfall on rock, the crack of a branch underfoot, the swish of our passing through brush. And after each of those small betrayals we froze to wait and listen.

Still our fortune held. The moon was rising—a full moon like a great lantern in the sky. It could show us the pitfalls before us, but it could also display us to a hunter. Toross halted. Now he caught my arm and drew me close to whisper in my ear. "We must cross the river at the traders' ford. It is the only way to reach the hill-paths."

He was right, of course, but to me that was our death blow. There was no way we could cross that well-known ford without being sighted. Even if by some miracle we could get across—why, then we had a long distance through open fields to traverse.

"We cannot try the ford; they will see us."

"Have you a better plan then, Joisan?"

"None save that we keep west on this side of the river. It is all sheep pasturage and steep hillsides where they cannot ride us down without warning."

"Ride us down!" He made a bitter sound that was not laughter. "They need only point one of their weapons at us from afar and we die. I have seen what I have seen!"

"Better such a death than to fall into their hands. The ford is too great a risk."

"Yes," he agreed. "But I do not know this way. If you do, Joisan, it will be you who will lead us."

What I knew of this upper dale was little enough, and I tried hard to call it to mind. My hope was a wooded section that was like a cloak. This had none too good a reputation with the dalesmen and was seldom entered, mainly because it had been rumored to cover some ruin of the Old Ones. Such tales were enough to ward off intruders, and, had we been fleeing any dales pursuit, to gain the edge of that wood would have given us freedom. But the invaders had no such traditions to stay them. Now I said nothing of the legend, only that I thought it would give us shelter. And if we could make our way through it, we might then continue about the rim of the dale and straight northwest to join our kin.

As we went, the effort slowed our pace. I fought the great weariness of my body, made bone and muscle answer my will alone. How it was with Toross I did not know, but he was not hurrying as we stumbled on.

The fires of the enemy camp were well behind us. Twice we lay face-down, hardly breathing, on the hillside, while men moved below, hoping we could so blend in with the earth. And each time, while my heart beat wildly, I heard them move on.

So we came to the edge of the wood, and there our luck failed us just when hope was the strongest. For there was a shout behind and a harsh crack of noise. Toross cried out and swept me on before him, pushing me into the underbrush of the ill-omened place. I felt him sag and fall, and turned to catch him by the shoulders, half-dragging, half-leading him on with me.

He stumbled forward, almost his whole weight resting on me. In that moment I though of Dame Math. Oh, that I had her wand in my hand, the Power strong in me so that I could blast those behind.

Fire burned on my breast, so hot and fierce a flame, I staggered and loosed my grip on Toross so that he fell heavily to the ground moaning. I tore at the lacings of my mail shirt to bring out what was causing that torment.

The gryphon globe in my hand was burning hot. I would have hurled it from me, but I could not. Before me as I stood came the sounds of men running, calling out. The glow of the globe; that would reveal us in an instant! Yet I could not throw or drop it. I could only stand and hold it so, a lamp to draw death to us.

Still the running feet did not come. Rather they bore away, downhill along the fringe of the wood. I heard an excited shout or two from the lower slope—almost as if they harried some quarry. But how could they when we were here with the globe as a beacon?

My ears reported that they were indeed drawing off. I could hardly believe that was the truth. With the globe as a battle torch this thin screen of brush could not conceal us. But we were free, with the chase going away.

Toross moaned faintly, and I bent over him. There was a growing stain on his shirt, a thread of blood trickling from his half-open mouth. What could I do? We must not stay here—I was sure that at any moment they would return.

I dropped the globe to my breast, where it lay blazing.

There were no burns on my flesh where I had cupped that orb against my will, though in those moments when I had held it I might have been grasping a red-hot coal.

"Toross!" To move him might do his wound great harm; to leave him here certainly meant his death. I had no choice. I must get him on his feet and moving!

The blaze of the globe lit his crumpled body. As I bent over him, setting my hands in his armpits, he stirred, opened his eyes and stared straight up, not seeming to see me at all.

As my hands tightened on him, I had a curious sensation such as I had never experienced before. Spreading out from that blazing crystal on my breast came waves of energy. They coursed and rippled down my arms, through my fingers—

Toross moaned again and coughed, spewing forth blood and froth. But he wavered upward at my pull. When he was on his feet I set my shoulder under his, drew his arm about me, and staggered on. His feet moved clumsily, and most of the weight of his body rested on me, but I managed to keep him moving.

What saved us was that, though a screen of brush ringed the wood, there was comparatively little undergrowth beneath the trees, so we tottered along, heading away from the dangers in the open. I did not know how far I could maange to half-carry Toross, but I would keep going as long as I could.

I am not sure when I noticed that we were following a road—or at least a walk of stones that gave us almost level footing. In the light of the globe, for it continued to blaze, I could see the pavement, moss-grown, but quite straight. Toross coughed again with blood following. And we came out under the moon's rays, the woods a dark wall as we stood in a paved place into which that white-silver radiance poured with unnatural force, as if it were focused directly on us with all the strength the moon could ever have.

Kerovan:

On the hill-slope I, Kerovan of Ulmsdale, faced the wayfarer in trader's clothing, who was no trader, as I knew when his staff beckoned me out of hiding against my will. I put my hand to sword hilt as I came, but he smiled, gently, tolerantly, as one might upon a frightened child.

"Lord Kerovan, no unfriend faces you." He dropped the point of the staff.

Instantly I was freed from that compulsion. But I had no desire to dodge back and away again, for there was that in his face which promised truth.

"Who are you?" Perhaps I demanded that more abruptly than courtesy allowed.

"What is a name?" he returned. The point of his wand now touched the ground and shifted here and there, though he did not watch it, as if he wrote runes in the dust. "A traveler may have many names. Let it suffice for now that in these dales I am called Neevor."

I thought he gave me a quick, searching look, as if to see if I knew that name. But my want of understanding must have been plain to read. I thought he sighed, as if regretting something lost.

"I have known Ulmsdale in the past," he continued. "And to the House of Ulric I have been no unfriend—nor do I stand aside when one of his blood needs aid. Where do you go, Lord Kerovan?"

I began to suspect who—or what—he might be. And I was awed. But because he stood in the guise he did I felt no fear

"I go to the forest lodge, seeking Riwal."

"Riwal—he was a seeker of roads, worshiping knowledge above all things. Though he never entered the wide door, he stood on its threshold, and those I serve did not deny him."

"You say of him 'was.' Where is he now?"

Again that wand-tip, which had come to rest, scrabbled across the earth.

"There are roads amany. Understand only that the one he had taken hence is not yours to follow."

I snatched at what might lie behind that evasion, believing the worst, because of all I had seen and heard, not only this night but in the months in the south.

"You mean he is dead! And by whose hand?" Once more that cold anger possessed me. Had Hlymer also taken this friend from me?

"The hand that dealt the blow was but an instrument—a tool. Riwal sought certain forces, and there were those who stood in opposition. Thus he was removed."

Neevor apparently did not believe in open speech, but was fond of involvements that veiled the question rather than revealed it.

"He turned to the Light, not Dark!" I spoke for my friend.

"Would I be here otherwise, Lord Kerovan? I am a messenger of those forces he sought, to which he was guiding you before the war horns sounded. Listen well. You are one poised upon a mountain peak with before you two paths. Both are dark with danger; both may lead you to what those of your blood speak of as death. It is in your fate that you can turn to either from this night onward. You have it in you to become as your kin-blood, for you were born in the Shrine of—" Did he utter some name then? I believe that he did. Yet it was one not meant to be spoken by man. I cowered, putting my hands to my ears to shut out the awful echoes from the sky above.

He watched me closely, as if to make sure of my reaction. Now his wand-staff swung up, pointing to me, and down its length came a puff of radiance that floated from its tip through the air and broke against my face before I could dodge the touch, though I felt nothing.

"Kinsman," he said, in his gentle voice, losing that majesty of tone he had held a moment earlier.

"Kinsman?"

"It seems that when the Lady Tephana wrought her bargain, she did not understand what she achieved. However, she sensed it; yes, she sensed it. You were a changeling, Kerovan, but not for her purposes. In that she read aright. She had set to fashion an encasement of blood, bone, and flesh for her use. Only the spirit it enclosed was not of her calling. It does not advantage one to take liberties with Gunnora. I do not know who looks through your eyes. I think that he yet sleeps, or only half-wakes. But the time will come when you shall remember, at least in part, and then your heritage shall be yours. No, not Ulmsdale—for the dales will no longer hold you—you shall seek and you shall find. But before that you must play out what lies here, for you are half dalesman."

I was trying to understand. Did he mean that the Lady Tephana had worked with some Power before my birth, to make my body a vessel into which to pour some manifestation of the Dark? If so my hoofed feet might be the mark. But —what *was* I?

"Not what you fear in this moment, Kerovan," he answered my unspoken thought swiftly. "Halfling you are, and your father's son, though he was under ensorcellment when he begot you. But where that seeker of Dark Knowledge strove to make a weapon to be used for her own purposes, she gave entry to another instead. I cannot read the rune for you. The discovery of what you truly are, and can be, you must make for yourself. You can return now, ally yourself with them, and find she cannot stand against you. Or—"

His wand indicated the barren hillside. "Or you can walk into a world where the Dark and what you call death will sniff at your heels, ever seeking a way for which there is no guide. The choice is yours."

"They speak of calling wind and wave to defeat the invader," I said. "Is this good or ill for Ulmsdale?"

"To loose any Power carries great risk, and those who strive to follow the old ways but are not of the blood, risk double."

"Can I prevent them then?"

He drew back. I thought his voice colder as he answered, "If you so wish."

"Perhaps there is a third way." I had thought of it once or twice as I climbed these slopes. "I can claim kin-right from Ithkrypt and gain a force to retake Ulmsdale before the enemy comes." But even as I spoke, I knew how thin a chance I had. Lord Cyart was fighting in the south and must have stripped his dale of forces, save for a handful of defenders. There would be none there to be spared, even if I went as a beggar.

"The choice is yours," Neevor repeated. And I knew he would give no advice.

My duty in Ulmsdale was part of my training. If I turned my back now upon my father's land, made no attempt to save those dwelling in it from disaster, either by enemy hand or the spells of that witch and her brood, then I would be traitor to all bred in me.

"I am my father's heir. I cannot turn my back upon his people. Nor do I take part in their witchery. There may be those to follow me—"

He shook his head. "Try not to build a wall out of shifting sand, Kerovan. That Dark biding within the walls of Ulmskeep has spread. No armsman will rise to your summons."

I did not doubt that he knew exactly what he said. There was that about Neevor which carried full belief. So—it must be Ithkrypt after all. At least I would find shelter there from which to gather men and support. Also I must send a message to Lord Imgry.

Neevor thrust his wand-staff through his belt. Then he turned to his led pony, tumbling from its back the small pack that had been lashed there.

"Hiku is no battle charger, but he is sure-footed in the hills. Take him, Kerovan, with the Fourth Blessing." Once more he reached for his wand and with it he tapped me lightly on the forehead, right shoulder, left, and over my heart.

Straightway then, I had the feeling my decision had pleased him. Yet I also knew that I could not be sure it was the right one. For it was laid upon me that I must choose my own road for myself and not by the advice of another.

I had forgotten my bare hoofs, but now as I moved toward the pony, my boots swung against my thigh and I caught at them. As I loosened them from my belt, ready to draw them on again, I had a strong revulsion against hiding my deformity —or was it so? It was a difference, yes, but what I had seen in my father's chamber this night, a deformity of spirit, seemed to me the greater evil.

No, I was done with hiding. If Joisan and her kind turned from me in disgust, then I was free of them. I hurled the boots from me, holding to that sense of freedom I had had since I shed them.

"Well done," Neevor said. "Be yourself, Kerovan, not ruled by the belief that one man must be like another. I have hopes for you after all."

Deliberately he urged the second pony on a few paces and then, standing with one hand on its shoulder, he drew a circle on the earth around the animal and himself. Following the point of his wand there sprang up a thin, bluish haze. As he completed the encirclement, it thickened to hide both man and beast. As I watched, it faded, but I was not surprised to see that its going disclosed emptiness—that the trader and his mount were gone.

I had guessed that he was one of the Old Ones. And that he had come to me was not by any chance. But he left me much to think on. Half-blood was I then, having kinship to the mysterious forelords in this land? I was a tool of my mother's desiring, though not to her purpose—yes, so much he told me fitted with the facts I knew and answered many questions.

I clung to the human part of me now: the fact that I was in truth Ulric's son, no matter what that sorceress had done to set it awry. That thought I cherished. For in death my father had come closer and dearer to me than ever he had been in life. Ulmsdale had been his. Therefore I would do what I could to see it safe, which meant I must ride for Ithkrypt.

I could not even be sure that the pony was of the natural order of beasts, seeing by whose hand he had come to me. But he seemed to be exactly like any other of his breed. He was sure-footed. Still there were stretches where I must go afoot and lead him.

By dawn I was well into the heights. As I made a rough camp, I lifted off my gift-mount something Neevor had not removed along with the pack, a stout hide bag. In it was a water bottle of lamantine wood. But it did not contain water, rather a white drink that was more refreshing and warming than any wine I had ever tasted. There was also a round box of the same wood with a tightly fitting cover. I worked this off, to find inside journey cakes that had been so protected by their container they seemed fresh from the griddle. Nor were they the common sort, but had embedded in them bits of dried fruit and cured meat. One of them satisfied my hunger, as great as that now was, and the rest I kept for the future.

Though sleep tugged at my eyelids and my body demanded rest, I sat for a while in a niche between two rock teeth, thinking on all that had happened to me this night. My hoofed feet stretched before me. I studied them, trying to put myself in the place of one sighting them without warning. Perhaps I had been foolish to cast away my boots. No, in the same instant as that thought entered my mind, I rejected it. This I would do and so I would go—Joisan and her people must see me as I was and accept or deny me. There must be between us no untruths or half-truths, such as had filled my father's house with a web of dark deceit and clung there now as a foul shadow.

I unlatched my belt-purse and for the first time in months brought out that case, deliberately opened it, and slid into my hand Joisan's picture. A girl's face, and one painted nearly two years ago. In that time we had both grown older, changed. What was she like, this maid with large eyes and hair the color of autumn leaves? Was she some subdued daughter-of-the-house, well-lessoned in the ways of women but ignorant of the world outside Ithkrypt's stout walls? For the first time I began to think of her as a person, apart from the fact that by custom she was as much my possession as the sword at my belt, the mail on my back.

My knowledge of women was small. In the south I had listened to the boasting tales men tell around the campfires of any army. But I had added no experience of my own. I thought now that perhaps my mixed blood, my inheritance from the Old Ones, had marked me with more than hoofs; that it had set upon my needs and desires some barrier against the dale maids. If that was so, what would become of my union with Joisan?

I could break bride-oath, but to do such would be to lay a stain on her, and such a trick would be as evil as if I stood up before her assembled House and defamed her. That I could not do. But perhaps when we at last met face to face she would look upon me and make such a repudiation, and I would not gainsay it. Nor would I allow thereafter any dale-feud to come from my dismissal.

Yet at this moment when I looked upon her face in the dawn light, I wanted to see her, and I did not relish her breaking bride-oath with me. Why had I sent her the englobed gryphon? Almost during the past months I had forgotten that—but my interrupted journey to see Riwal brought it back to mind. What had lain so heavily on me then that I had sent that wonder to her, as if such a gift was necessary? I tried to picture it in my mind now—the crystal ball with its gryphon within, a warning claw raised—

But—

I was no longer looking at the dale below. I could no longer see the pony grazing. Rather I saw—her!

She was before me so clearly at that moment that I might have reached out and touched her skirt where she crouched. Her russet hair was in wild disorder over her shoulders, and through its straying strands I could see the gleam of mail. On her breast hung the gryphon, and it blazed with light. Her face was bruised, and there was fear in her eyes. Against her knee rested the head of a young man. His eyes were closed, and across his lips bubbled the froth of blood that marked a wound from which there was no healing. Her hand touched his forehead gently, and she watched him with a tenseness that meant his life or death had meaning for her.

Perhaps this was farseeing, though I had only once had such a gift or curse set upon me before. I knew that the face of the dying man was not mine, and her sorrow was for another. Perhaps therein lay my answer. Nor could I fault her if it was. For we were naught to each other but names. I had not even sent her the picture that had been her own asking from me.

That the gryphon blazed so clearly puzzled me a little after I had schooled myself to accept the meaning of what I saw. It was as if life had poured into that globe. So—perhaps now I knew the reason why I had been so strangely moved to send it to her. Though I had been the finder and had treasured it, it was not mine to have and hold, but was meant rather to lie where it now rested, and was truly hers and not mine. I must accept that also.

How long did that farsight or vision last? I did not know. I knew only that it was true. The strange youth was dying, or would die, and she would mourn him thereafter.

But such a death argued that Ithkrypt was not the refuge I had looked to find. It was not usual for a daleswoman to wear mail like a warrior, but we did not live in ordinary times. She was armored, and her comrade was dying; to that there could be only one explanation. Ithkrypt was either attacked or soon would be. Still that knowledge did not deter me. Rather it drew me—for I had a duty also to Joisan, whether or no she would ever now turn to me happily. If she were in danger, there was even more reason I should cross the ridges to her.

Ulmsdale, once my father's and now under the hands of those I knew to be of ill intent; Ithkrypt perhaps overrun—I was traveling from one danger to another. Death was surely sniffing at my heels, ready to lay claw-hand on my shoulder. But this road was mine, and I could take no other.

The vision was gone, and with its going my weariness settled so heavily upon me that I could not fight it. I slept the day away in my hole, for when I roused it was already dusk.

I wakened to the pony nudging against my shoulder, as if the beast were a sentry on guard.

Dusk—yes—and more. There was a gathering of thick clouds, such as I had seldom seen. So dark and heavy was that massing that I could not now sight the Giant's Fist! And the pony crowded in against me as I scrambled to my feet.

The beast was sweating; the smell of it was rank. He pushed his head against my shoulder, and I gentled him with neck-stroking. This was fear the like of which I had seldom seen before in any animal. Emotion gripped me also: a vast apprehension, as if some force beyond understanding gathered, a force that was inimical to all my kind and could, if it would, sweep us like grains of dust from its path.

I backed against the rock wall, my hands still on the pony, waiting. I did not know for what, except I feared it as I never had feared anything before in my life.

There was no wind, no sound. That terrible stillness added to my fear. The dale, the world, cowered and waited.

From the east there was a sudden flash of light. Not the usual lightning, but rather a wide swath across all the heavens. Eastward—over the sea—

Power of wind and wave they had spoken of—were they about to summon that? Then the invaders' ships must lie near to Ulmsport, and they had had little time to ready their plans. What would happen?

The pony uttered a strange sound such as I had never heard from any mount before. It was almost a whimper. And that oppression increased until it seemed that the very air about us was kept from our lungs and we could not breathe freely. Still there came no wind, but sheet lightning flashed seaward. Now came a long roll—as if a thousand war drums beat together.

Above the clouds was a night of such darkness I could see no more than if I were blindfolded. Surely this was no ordinary storm, at least like none I had seen before in my lifetime. My lifetime. Deep in me a thread of memory stirred—but it could not be memory—for it was not of this life but another.

But that was foolishness! A man had but one lifetime and the memories of that—one lifetime—

My skin, where it was exposed to the air, itched and burned as if the atmosphere were poisoned. Then I saw light —but not in the sky—rather auras about rocks as if they were palely burning lanterns, their light a foggy discharge.

For the third time, sheet lightning blanketed the east, and after it came the drum roll. Then followed the wind—

Wind, but such wind as I swear the dale had never felt before. I crouched between the rocks, my face buried in the trembling pony's rough mane, the smell of the beast's sweat in my nostrils. He was steaming wet under my hands. There was no way I could shut out the sound of that wind. And surely we would be scooped out of our small refuge by its force, whirled out to be beaten to death in the open.

I braced my hoofs deep in the ground, used the rock at my back and side as best I could to anchor me, and felt the pony, iron-tense in my hold, doing likewise. If the poor beast whimpered now, I could no longer hear him, for the sound of the elements was deafening. The drum beat had become a roar to which there was no end.

I could not think; I could only cower in dull hope of escaping the full fury. But as it continued I grew somewhat accustomed to it, as one can when the first sharp edge of any fear is dulled by a continuation of its source. I realized then that the wind blew from east to west, and its power must be directed from the sea upon Ulmsport.

What such a storm might do along the coast I could not imagine, save that it would utterly devastate everything within its hammer blows. If there had been an enemy fleet drawing to port, that must be completely overwhelmed. But the innocent would suffer with the invader. What of the port and those who dwelt there? If this storm was born of the Power those in the keep thought to summon, then they had either lost control of it or had indeed drawn hither something greater than they had planned.

How long did it last? I lost all track of time. There was no night, no day—only black dark and the roaring—and the fear of something that was not of normal nature. What of the keep? It seemed to me that this fury could well shake even those great stones one from the other, splitting open the firm old building as if it were a ripe fruit.

There was no slacking off as would occur in a true storm. One moment the deafening roar, the fury—then silence, complete, dead. I thought at first that the continued noise, the pressure, had deafened me. Then I heard a soft sound from the pony. He pushed against me, backing into the open.

Above, it was once more dawn. The dark clouds, tattered as my father's death banner, faded into nothingness. Had it been so long we had been pent there? I stumbled after the pony into the quiet open.

The air no longer held that acridness which had tortured our breathing, but was fresh and cool. And there was a curious—I could only define it as emptiness—in it.

I must see what had happened below. That thought drove me. Leading Hiku along the narrow rim of the dale, I headed back toward the Giant's Fist. These heights had been scoured. Vast areas of trees and brush had been simply torn away, leaving scars in the earth to mark their former rooting.

So obvious were these signs of destruction, I was prepared in part for what I did sight at the foot of the heights. Yet it was far worse than I expected.

Part of the keep still stood, though its outline was not that of a complete building any longer. About it was water —a great sheet of water on the surface of which floated a covering of wreckage, perhaps part of it ships, part the houses of Ulmsport, but too tangled to be identified with any surety. And that water came from the east—the sea had claimed most of Ulmsdale.

Had those below escaped? I could see no signs of life. The village was under water save for a roof or two. So the disaster those below had wantonly summoned had fallen.

Were they caught up in the maelstrom of the force they could not control? That I hoped. But that Ulmsdale as I had known it was dead, was manifest. No man could have a future here. For I believed that what the sea had won, it would not surrender. If the invaders thought to use this as a foothold, they were defeated.

I turned my face from that lump which had been the keep, and so from the past. In a way, I still had a duty laid upon me—I must learn how it fared with Joisan. And then— there lay the south and the long, long battles to come.

Thus I tramped away from the Fist with no desire to look again at the ruin in the dale, and my heart was sore, not for any loss of mine, for I had never truly felt that it was my holding, but for the wreckage of all my father had cherished and sought by every means he knew to protect. And I think I cursed as I went, though silently, those who had done this thing.

As we stood under the moon in that secret place of stone, the gryphon blazing on my breast, Toross slipped from my hold to the ground. I knelt beside him, drawing the garment from his chest that I might see his hurt. His head lay against my knee, and from his lips a stream of blood trickled. That he had come this far was a thing hardly to be believed when I saw the wound exposed. Enough of Dame Math's healing knowledge was mine to know that it was indeed a death blow, though I slit my underlinen with his knife and made a pad to halt the seepage.

I gentled his head against me. In so very little could I ease the passing of this man who had given his life that I might live. In the light of the gryphon and the moon I could well see his face.

What twisting of fate had brought us two together? Had I allowed myself, I might have wanted to joyfully welcome Toross for my lord. Why had I not?

In the library of the Abbey I had found many curious pieces of lore not generally taught, perhaps considered mysteries of the Flame. And one such roll of runes I now remembered—that a man—or woman—does not live a single life, but rather returns to this world at another time for the purpose of paying some debt that he or she owes to another. Therefore in each life one is bound to some other by ties that are not of this life and time, but reach far back into a past no seer can delve. Toross had been drawn to me from the first, so much so that he had nearly dimmed the honor of his House to seek me out, to urge upon me a similar feeling.

Though I had held fast against him, yet he had come here to die in my arms, because my life meant more to him than his own. What debt had he owed me, if that old belief were true? Or had he now laid some debt upon me that must be paid in turn?

His head moved in my hold. I leaned close to hear his whisper:

"Water—"

Water! I had none. To my knowledge the closest lay in the river a long distance from us. I took up my skirt, still heavily dampened, and wiped his face, wishing bitterly that I could give him such a little thing. Then I saw in the dead-white radiance, which seemed so intense in this place, that plants grew about the paved space. Tall as my shoulder they stood, with great, fleshy leaves outspread in the moonlight. And on those were drops of silver. I recognized a plant Dame Math had used. Yet hers had been very small compared to these. These plants had the art of condensing water on their leaves with the coming of night's cool.

Gently I laid Toross down and went to gather this un-expected boon, tearing off the largest leaves with care, lest I spill their precious cargo. And I brought them to wet his lips, eased a few drops into his mouth. So little it was that I despaired, but perhaps the leaves had some healing quality they imparted to those droplets, for these seemed to satisfy his thirst.

I took him up again, and as I settled his head against me, his eyes opened and he knew me. He smiled.

"My—lady—"

I would have hushed him, not for what he said, but that it wasted his strength, and of that he had so little left. But he would not have it so.

"I—knew—my—lady—from—the—first—I saw you." His voice grew stronger as he talked, instead of weaker. "You are very fair, Joisan, very wise, very—desirable. But it—" He coughed, and more blood came, which I wiped away quickly with the wet leaves. "Not for me," he ended clearly.

He did not try to speak again for a while, and then,

"Not for the lordship, not ever, Joisan. You—must—believe that. I—would—have—come wooing if you had no dowry at all. Not the lordship—though they said it was the way to make sure of that. I wanted—you!"

"I know," I assured him. That was true. His kin might have urged him to wed with me for Ithkrypt, but Toross had wanted me more than any keep. The great pity of it was that all I could feel for him was friendship, and such love as one might give a brother—nothing more.

"Had you not wedded—" He gasped and choked. Now speech was beyond him.

At the last I gave what I had to offer to ease him—a lie that I spoke with all the ring of truth I could muster.

"I would have welcomed you, Toross."

He smiled then, such a smile as was a crossbow's bolt in my heart. And I knew that my lie had been well said. Then he turned his head a little, resting his stained lips against my breast, and his eyes closed as if he would sleep. But it was not sleep that came as I held him so. After a space I laid him down and wavered to my feet, looking about me, unable for that moment to look upon him.

I set myself rather to view this place. That we had come to some site of the Old Ones I had realized. But then its shape had been of no importance, merely that it was the end to which I could bring Toross. Now, sharply defined in the moonlight, I could see all of it.

There were no walls, no remains of such, just the pavement, dazzling in the moonlight. For the first time I was aware that some of the light came from the ancient stones themselves, similar to the glow of the globe.

Still those stones, in spite of their gleam, appeared to be little different from the rocks that formed the walls of Ithkrypt. Only the light pulsated a little as if it came and went like the breathing of some great animal.

Not only the glow but the shape of the pavement astonished me. It was laid in the form of a five-pointed star. As I stood there, swaying a little, it seemed to force its form upon my eyes as if it had a meaning that was necessary for me to see and understand. But my knowledge of the Old Ones and their ways was so fragmentary that I could not guess into what we had intruded, save it had never been fashioned to serve a Dark Power, but Light, and that it had indeed been a place of forces, some remnants of which still clung.

Had I only known how to use those! Perhaps I could have saved Toross, saved the dalespeople who would now look to me for leadership. If I only knew more! I think I cried out then in my desolation of spirit, for the loss of something I had never had, but which might have meant so much.

There was something here—Suddenly I threw back my head and gazed upward, stretched wide my arms. It was as if I were trying to open some long-closed door within me, to welcome into starved darkness a filling of light. There was a need in me, and if I asked I would be given. Yet I did not know what I was to ask for, and so in the end my arms fell to my sides and I was still empty. I was gnawed also by the knowing that I had been offered something wondrous which I was too ignorant to take. The thought of my own failure was the bitterest of all.

With this loss still upon me I turned about to face Toross. He lay as if asleep, and the glow of the stone was all about him. There was no way I could entomb him after the manner of the dales, with his armor upon him, his hands folded on the hilt of his sword to show that he had fallen valiantly in battle. Even this I could not do for his honor. Yet in this place such seemed unnecessary, for he rested in such glory and peace as I did not think any of our tomb chambers held. And he slept.

So I knelt and took up his hands, crossing them, though not on any sword hilt. And, last of all, I kissed him as he slept, for he had desired and served me to the utmost, even if I could not be to him as he wished.

Then I went forth from the star place and I broke off ferns and sweet-smelling herbs which grew here as if in a Wisewoman's garden. These I brought, and with them I covered Toross, save for his face, which I left open to the night. And I petitioned whatever Power lingered in this place that he indeed rest in peace. Then I turned and left him, knowing within my heart that with Toross now all was well, no matter what lay elsewhere in this war-riven and tormented land.

Beyond the edge of the star I hesitated. Should I retrace my way or strive to travel on, using the wood for cover, hoping beyond that to find some trail my people had taken? In the end I chose the latter.

Here the trees stood thicker and there was no path, nor could I be sure that I headed straight. I was no woodsman and I might be wandering. But I did my best.

When I came at last to that screen of thick brush which was the outer ring of the wood, my mouth was dry with thirst. I wavered as I walked from weariness, being faint with hunger. But before me was the narrowing end of the dale and the heights over which the refugees from Ithkrypt must have fled.

The light of pre-dawn was in the sky, my only lamp, for the glow had gone from the globe. It was dead, and I was alone, and the burden of a heavy heart weighed upon me as much as my weariness.

I reached a spur of rock behind which there was a hollow, and I knew I could go no farther. Around it grew sparse patches of berries, some of the fruit ripe. It was tart, mouth-twisting, what one would not usually eat without meat, for which it would be a relish. But it was food, and I stripped the ground-hugging bushes quickly, stuffing the fruit into my mouth as ravenously as anyone who knows bitter hunger.

That I could go on without rest I doubted; nor did I think I could find a better hiding place than this hollow. But before I crept within, I used Toross' knife to change my clothing for this wilderness scrambling. My skirt was divided for riding, but the folds were so thick and long they had nearly proved my undoing. Now I slashed away, tearing off long strips. These I used to bind down the "legs" of my shortened skirt, narrowing the folds and anchoring them as tightly as I could above my boots. The garment was far more bulky than a man's breeches, but I had greater freedom of movement than before.

Having done this, I huddled back into the hollow, sure my whirling thoughts would not let me sleep, no matter how deep my fatigue. My hands went to my breast, closing about the globe, without my willing.

It had no warmth now, yet there was something about the smooth feel of it that was comforting. And so, clasping it, I did fall asleep.

All men dream, and usually upon waking one remembers such dreams only in fragments—which may be of terror and darkness or, at long intervals, of such pleasure that one longs to hold on to them even as they fast fade. Yet what I experienced now was unlike any dream I had ever known.

I was in a small place, and outside swept storm winds—but winds of far more than normal fury. There was someone with me in that place. I caught a suggestion of a shoulder outline, a head turned from me, and there was a strong need that I know who this was. But I could not see a face or name a name. I could only cower as those racking winds beat by the opening of the crack in which we sheltered. As it had been in the place of the star, so was it here, the knowledge that had I only the gift, the ability, I could gain what I needed and that good would come of it. Yet I had it not, and the dream was gone—or else I could not remember more of it then or ever.

When I roused, the sun was almost down, and the shadows long about me. I sat up, still weary, still thirsty and longing for even as much water as I had shaken from the leaves in the wood. There was a dull ache in my middle, perhaps from the berries, perhaps from lack of food. I got to my knees and peered down-slope for any sign of the enemy.

Thus it was I spied those two making their way along as scouts do. My hand was at knife hilt in an instant. But in a moment I saw these were dalesmen. I whistled softly that call that we had learned for just such a use as this.

They flattened themselves instantly to the earth, then their heads rose a little at my second whistle. Seeing me, it took them only a few moments to join me, and I knew them for Toross' armsmen.

"Rudo, Angarl!" They could have been my brother-kin, so rejoiced was I to see them.

"My Lady! Then the Lord Toross brought you forth!" Rudo exclaimed.

"He did indeed. Great honor he cast upon his House."

The armsman looked beyond me into the hollow, and I saw that he guessed what dire report I must make now.

"The invaders have a weapon that can slay from a distance. As we ran, the Lord Toross was struck. He died in the safety to which he brought me. Honor to his name forever!" Did it help that at this moment I could use the formal words of a warrior's last farewell?

Both these men were well past middle age. What Toross might have been to them, or what ties—perhaps of almost kin-friendship—he might have had with them, I did not know. They bowed their heads at my words and repeated harshly after me, "Honor to his name forever!"

Then Angarl spoke. "Where is he, Lady? We must see to him—"

"He lies in a holy place of the Old Ones. To that we were guided, and there he died. And the peace of that place shall be his forever."

They glanced from one to the other. I could see their sense of custom warred in them with awe. And I added, "That which abides there welcomed him, yes, and gave him to drink in his final hour, and offered sweet herbs for his bedding. He rests as becomes a proud warrior, and on this you have my oath."

That they believed. For we all know that while there are places of the Dark Power to be shunned, there are others that offer peace and comfort, even to interlopers. And if such a place welcomed and held Toross now, he was indeed laid to rest with honor.

"It is well, Lady," Rudo answered me heavily, and I could see that indeed Toross had meant much to these two.

"You have come from the dalespeople?" I asked in turn.

"And have you aught to eat—or drink?" My pride departed, and I wanted badly what they might carry.

"Oh—of a certainty, Lady." Angarl used his good hand to unstrap a bag from his belt, and in it was a bottle of water and tough journey cakes. I had to use all my control to drink sparingly and eat in small bites, lest my stomach rebel.

"We are of the band that went with the Forester Borsal. My lady and her daughter were also with us. But they turned back to see Lord Toross. We have been hunting him, since he did not join us by moonrise—"

"You are on this side of the river then—"

"Those demons hunt over the dale. If our lord had lived, this would have been the only free way," Rudo said simply.

"They are in all the dale now?"

Angarl nodded. "Yes. Two bands of our people were captured because they moved too slowly. Also, few of the flocks and herds got away. The beasts refused the climb to the pass, and the herders and shepherds could not force them to it. Those who tried too long—" He made a small gesture to signal their fate.

"You can find your way back?"

"Yes, Lady. But we had best be on our way quickly. There are parts that are hard going in the dark. Were it not summer and the dusk later in coming, we could not do it."

Their food heartened me, and their company even more. Also I found that the precautions I had taken to turn my skirt into breeches aided my going, so I was able to set out at a pace I could not have held the night before. Before I went, I returned the gryphon into hiding under my mail, for to me it was a private thing.

Our way was rough, and even my guides had to pause and cast around at times to find landmarks by which they could sight their way, for here there was not even a sheep track for a road. We climbed as the night grew darker. It was colder here, and I shivered when the wind struck full on. We talked very little, they no more than giving me a word of guidance when the occasion arose. My weariness was returning. But I made no complaint and did the best I could, asking nothing from them. In this hour their companionship was enough.

We could not take the last climb through the pass in the dead of night, so once more I sheltered among rocks, this time with Rudo on my right, Angarl on my left. I must have slept, for I do not remember anything after our settling there until Rudo stirred and spoke.

"Best be on now, Lady Joisan. There is the dawn, and we do not know how high those murderers range in their search for blood on their swords."

The light was gray, hardly better than twilight. I sighted gathering clouds. Perhaps we were to face rain—though we should welcome what washed away our tracks.

It did begin to rain with steady persistence. There was not even tree cover as we slipped and slid down from the pass into the valley beyond. I knew this country only vaguely. At the level of the dale, if one traveled through the lower pass, there was a road—heading toward Norstead. Though the lords cared for it after a fashion (mainly by chopping back any undergrowth for three spear lengths on either side so that the opening might deter ambushes by outlaws), it was not a smooth track.

The river was too wide and shallow hereabouts to provide for any craft save when the spring floods were in spate. And this part of the country lacked settlers. It was grazing ground, and in winter the grasses on the lower lands helped to feed the stock. But no one lived here, save seasonally.

Our people are few in the western dales. And dalesmen cling to company. Those who do turn hunter, forester, or trader are misfits who do not rub well against their fellows and are usually looked upon as being but a grade or two above the outlaws, since they are wandering, rootless men of whom anything may be expected. Thus we largely keep to the richer lands and within arrow flight of our dales. Our peopled dales are scattered. Norsdale, perhaps five days' journey westward by horse, more on foot, was the nearest settlement of which I knew.

But we did not descend to the road to Norsdale, being warned by fire smoke on the valley floor. Our people would not light such. Again we kept to the upper slopes, angling south. So we came near to being the targets of crossbow bolts from our own kin.

There was a sharp challenge from a screen of bush; then a woman came into the open to face us. I knew her for Nalda, whose husband had been miller at Ithkrypt, a tall woman of great strength in which she took pride, sometimes in her way seeming more man than woman when compared to the chattering gossips in the village. She held her bow at ready, the bolt laid on, and did not lower it as we came up. But on seeing me, her rough face lightened.

"My Lady, well come, oh, well come!" Her greeting warmed my long-chilled heart.

"Well come in truth, Nalda. Who is with you?"

She reached forth to touch my arm, as if she needed that to assure herself I did indeed stand there.

"There be ten of us—the Lady Islaugha and the Lady Yngilda, my lad Timon and—but, Lady Joisan, what of Stark, my man?"

I remembered that red slaughter by the river. She must have read it in my face. Her own grew hard and fierce in an instant.

"So be it," she said then, "so be it! He was a good man, Lady, and he died well—"

"He died well," I assured her speedily. I would never tell any daleswoman the manner of dying I had seen. For the dead were our heroes, and that is all we needed to know to hold them in honor.

"But what do I think of! Come quickly—those demons are in the valley below. We would have moved on, but the Lady Islaugha, she would not go, and we could not leave her. She waits for the Lord Toross."

"Who will not come now. And if the invaders are already hereabouts we must move on quickly. Ten of you—what men?"

"Rudo and Angarl." She nodded to my companions. "Insfar, who was shepherd in the Fourth Section. He escaped over the rocks with a hole in his shoulder, for these thrice-damned hunters of honest men have that which kills at a distance. The rest are women and two children. We have four cross-bows, two long bows, our belt knives and Insfar's wolf spear. And among us food for mayhap three days, if we eat light and make one mouthful do the work of three."

And Norsdale was far away—

"Mounts?"

"None, my Lady. We took to the upper pass and could not bring them. That was where we lost the rest Borstal guided—they went ahead in the night. There are sheep, perhaps a cow or two running wild—but whether we can hunt them—" She shrugged.

So much for all our plans of escape. I only hoped that some other parties of our people had gotten away sooner, been better equipped, and could get through to Norsdale. Whether they could rouse any there to come to our rescue, I doubted. In spite of my own need I could understand that those there would think a second time before venturing forth on such a search. They would be better occupied making ready their defenses against the invaders.

Thus escorted by Nalda, who seemed to have taken command of this small band, I came into their camp, though there was little about it of any camp. Seeing me, the Lady Islaugha was on her feet instantly.

"Toross?" Her cry was a demand. In her pale face her eyes glowed as the gryphon globe had glowed, as if within her was a fire.

My control was shaken. As I tried to find the right words, she came to me, her hands on my shoulders, and she shook me as if so to bring my answer.

"Where is Toross?"

"He—he was slain—" How could I clothe it in any soothing words? She wanted only the truth, and no one could soften that for her.

"Dead—dead!" She dropped her hold on me and stepped back. Now first there was horror in her expression, as if in me she saw one of the invaders bloody-handed from slaughter, and then a hardening of feature, a mask of hate so bitter it was a blow.

"He died for you—who would not look to him. Would not look to him who could have had any maid, yes, and wife, too, if he only lifted his finger and beckoned once! What had you to catch his eye, hold him? If he gained Ithkrypt with you, yes, that I could accept. But to die—and you stand here alive—"

I had no words. I could only face her storm. For in her twisted way of thinking she was right. That I had given Toross no encouragement meant nothing to her. What mattered was that he had wanted me and I had stood aloof, and he had died to save me.

She paused, and now her mouth worked and she spat, the spittle landing at my feet.

"Very well, take my curse also. And with it the oath of bearing and forebearing, for that you owe to me—and to Yngilda also. You have taken our kin-lord—therefore you stand in his place."

She invoked the old custom of our people, laying upon me the burden of her life as a blood-price, which in her eyes it was. From this time forth I must care for her—and Yngilda —protect them and smooth their way as best I could, even as if I were Toross himself.

Kerovan:

Once more I stood on heights and looked down to death and destruction. Wind and wave had brought death to Ulmsdale, but here destruction had been wrought by the malice of men. It had taken me ten days to reach the point from which I spied on Ithkrypt, or what remained of it. One whole day of that time had been spent in reaching this pinnacle from which I could see a keep battered into dust.

Oddly enough there were no signs of the crawling monsters that breached walls in this fashion. Yet there were few stones of the keep still stacked one upon the other. And it was plain an enemy force was encamped here.

They had come upriver by boats, and these were drawn up on the opposite shore of the river.

My duty was divided. This landing must be reported, yet Joisan was much on my mind. No wonder I had sighted her in that vision clad in mail and gentle with a dying man.

Was she captive or dead? Back in the trackless wilderness through which I had come, I had crossed trails of small groups moving westward, refugees by all evidence. Perhaps she had so fled. But where in all those leagues of wild land could I find her?

Lord Imgry had set me a duty that was plain. Once more I was torn between two demands, and I had one thin hope. There were signal posts in the heights. Messages could be flashed from peak to peak—in the sun by reflection from well-burnished shields; at night by torches held before the same backing. I knew the northern one of those, which could not be too far from Ithkrypt. If that had not been overrun and taken, Imgry would have his warning, and I would be free to hunt for Joisan.

Using scout skill I slipped away from the vantage point that had shown me Ithkrypt. There were parties of invaders out, and they went brashly, with the arrogance of conquerors who had nothing to fear. Some drove footsore cattle and bleating sheep back to slaughter in their camp; others worked to the west, seeking fugitives perhaps, or making out trails to lead an army inland even as Imgry had feared, that they might come down on us to crush our beleaguered force between two of theirs.

I found Hiku an excellent mount for my purposes. The pony seemed to follow by his own choice that country into which he could merge so that only one alerted to our presence there could have been aware of our passing. Also he appeared tireless, able to keep going when a stable-bred mount might have given out, footsore and blowing.

That these dales had their natural landmarks was a boon, for I could so check my direction. But I came across evidence that the invaders were spreading out from Ithkrypt. And I knew that I would not be a moment too soon. Perhaps I was already a day or so too late in sounding the alarm.

I found the crest on which the signal niche was located and there studied with dismay the traces of those come before me. For it was the order of such posts that there be no trail pointing to them; yet here men, more than two or three, had passed openly, taking no trouble to cover their tracks.

With bare steel in my fist, my war hood laced, I climbed to the space where I should have found a three-man squad of signal-men. But death had been before me, as the splashes of clotted blood testified. There was the socket in which the shield had been set so it could be readied to either catch the sun or frame the light of a torch—there was even a broken torch flung to earth and trampled. I looked south, able to make out the next peak on which one of our outposts was stationed. Had those attacked here been able to give the alarm?

Now I applied my forest knowledge to the evidence and decided that battle had been done in mid-morning. It was now mid-afternoon. Had they wings, perhaps the invaders could have flown from this height to the one I could see, but men, mounted or on foot, could not have already won to that second point in such time. If no warning had gone forth, I must in some manner give it.

The shield had been wrenched away. I carried none myself, for my activities as scout had made me discard all such equipment. Signal—how could I signal without the means?

I chewed a knuckle and tried to think. I had a sword, a long forester's knife, and a rope worn as a belt about my middle. My mail was not shining, but coated over on purpose with a greenish sap which helped to conceal me.

Going forth from the spy niche I looked around—hoping against hope that the shield might have been tossed away. But that was rating the enemy too low. There was only one thing I might do, and in the doing I coud bring them back on me as if I had purposefully lashed a nest of Anda wasps—set a fire. The smoke would not convey any precise message, as did the wink of reflection from the shield, but it would warn those ahead.

I searched the ground for wood, carrying it back to the signal post. My last armful was not culled from the ground under the gnarled slope trees, but selected from leaves on those same trees.

I used my strike light and the fire caught, held well. Into it then I fed, handful by handful, the leaves I had gathered. Billows of yellowish smoke appeared, along with fumes that drove me coughing from the fireside, my eyes streaming tears. But as those cleared I could see a column of smoke reaching well into the sky, such a mark as no one could miss.

There was little or no wind, even here on the upper slopes, and the smoke was a well-rounded pillar. This gave me another idea—to interrupt the smoke and then let it flow again would add emphasis to the warning. I unstrapped my cloak, and with it in hand went back to the fire.

It was a chancy business, but, though I was awkward, I managed to so break the column that no one could mistake it was meant for a signal. A moment or two later there came a flash from the other peak that I could read. They had accepted the warning and would now swing their shield and pass it on. Lord Imgry might not have exact news from the north, but he would know that the enemy had reached this point.

My duty done, I must be on my way with all speed—heading westward. To seek Joisan I could do no more than try to find the trail of one of those bands of refugees and discover from them what might have happened to my lady.

If so far fortune had favored me, now that was not true. For I learned shortly that the pursuit was up, and such pursuit as made my heart beat fast and dried my mouth as I urged Hiku on. They had out their hounds!

We speak of those of Alizon as Hounds, naming them so for their hunters on four legs, which are unlike our own dogs of the chase. They have gray-white coats, and they are very thin, though large and long of leg; their heads are narrow, moving with the fluid ease of a serpent, their eyes yellow.

Few of them were with the invaders, but those we had seen in the south were deadly, trained to hunt and kill, and with something about them wholly evil.

As I rode from where that smoke still curled, I heard the sound of a horn as I had heard it twice before in the south. It was the summoning of a hound master. I knew that once set on my trail, those gray-white, flitting ghosts, which had no true kinship with our guardian dogs of the dale keeps, would ferret me out.

So I set to every trick I knew for covering and confusing my trail. Yet after each attempt at concealment, a distant yapping told me I had not escaped. At last Hiku, again of his own accord, as if no beast brain lay within his skull but some other more powerful one, tugged loose from my controlling rein and struck to the north. He half slid, half leaped down a crumbling bank into a stream, and up that, against the current, he splashed his way.

I loosed all rein hold, letting him pick his own path, for he had found a road which could lead us to freedom. It was plain he knew exactly what he was doing.

The stream was not river-sized, but perhaps a tributary to the river that ran through Ithkrypt. The water was very clear. One could look down to see not only the stones and gravel that floored it, but also those finned and crawling things to which it was home.

Suddenly Hiku came to a full stop, the water washing about his knees. So sudden was that halt that I was nearly shaken from my seat. The pony swung his head back and forth, lowering it to the water's edge. Then he whinnied and turned his head as if addressing me in his own language.

So odd were his actions I knew this was no light matter. As he lowered his head once more to the stream I believed he was striving to call my attention to something therein and was growing impatient at my not understanding some plain message.

I leaned forward to peer into the water ahead. It was impressed upon me now that Hiku's actions were not unlike those of someone facing an unsprung trap. Was there some water dweller formidable enough to threaten the pony?

Easing sword out of sheath, I made ready for attack. The pony held his head stiffly, as if to guide my attention to a certain point. I took my bearing from him in my search.

Stones, gravel—then—yes! There was something, hardly

o be distinguished from the natural objects among which it ay.

I dropped from Hiku's back, planting my hoofs securely n the stream bed against the wash of the current. Then I vorked forward until I could see better.

There was a loop, not of stone, or at least of any stone I had ever seen, blue-green in color. And it stood upright, seemingly wedged between two rocks. With infinite care I lowered sword point into the flood, worked it within that oop, and then raised it.

Though it had looked firmly wedged, it gave to my pull so easily I was near overbalanced by the release. And I snapped the blade up in reflex, so that what it held could not slide back into the water.

Instead it slipped down the length of the blade to clang against the hilt, touch my fingers. I almost dropped it, or even flung it from me, for there was an instant flow of energy from the loop into my flesh.

Gingerly I shook it a little down my sword, away from my fingers, and then held it closer to my eyes. What ringed my steel was a wristlet, or even an archer's bow guard, about two fingers's wide in span. The material was perhaps metal, though like no metal I knew. Out of the water it glowed, to draw the eye. Though the overall color was blue-green, now that I saw it close, I made out a very intricate pattern woven and interwoven of threads of red-gold. And some of these, I was sure, formed runes.

That this had belonged to the Old Ones I had not the least doubt, and that it was a thing of power I was sure from Hiku's action. For we dalesmen know that the instincts of beasts about some of the ancient remains are more to be relied upon than our own. Yet when I brought the armlet closer to the pony, he did not display any of the signs of alarm that I knew would come if this was the thing of a Dark One. Rather he stretched forth his head as if he sniffed some pleasing odor rising from it.

Emboldened by his reaction, I touched it with fingertip. Again I felt that surge of power. At length I conquered my awe and closed my fingers on it, drawing it off the blade.

Either the flow of energy lessened, or I had become accustomed to it. Now it was no more than a gentle warmth. And I was reminded of that other relic—the crystal-enclosed gryphon.

Without thinking I slipped the band over my hand, and it

settled and clung about my wrist snugly, as if it had been made for my wearing alone. As I held it at eye level, the entwined design appeared to flow, to move. Quickly I dropped my hand. For the space of a breath or two I had seen—what? Now that I no longer looked, I could not say—save that it was very strange, and I was more than a little in awe of it. Yet I had no desire to take off this find. In fact, when I glanced at my wrist as I remounted, I had an odd thought that sometime—somewhere—I had worn such before. But how could that be? For I would take blood oath I had never seen its like. But then who can untangle the mysteries of the Old Ones?

Hiku went on briskly, and I listened ever for the sound of the hound horn, the yap of the pack. Once I thought I did hear it, very faint and far away, and that heartened me. It would seem that Hiku had indeed chosen his road well.

As yet he made no move to leave the stream, but continued to plow through the water steady-footed. I did not urge him, willing to leave such a choice to him.

The stream curved, and a screen of well-leafed bushes gave way to show me what lay ahead. Hiku now sought the bank of a sand bar to the right. But I gazed ahead in amazement. Here was a lake not uncommon in the dales, but it was what man—or thinking beings—had set upon it that surprised me.

The water was bridged completely across the widest part. However, that crossway was not meant for a roadway, but rather gave access to a building, not unlike a small keep, erected in the middle of the water. It presented no windows on the bridge level, but the next story and two towers, each forming a gate to the bridge, had narrow slits on the lower levels, wider as they rose in the towers.

From the shore where we were, the whole structure seemed untouched by time. But the far end of the bridge, reaching toward the opposite side of the lake, was gone. The other bridgehead was not far from us and, strange as the keep appeared (it was clearly of the Old Ones' time), I thought it offered the best shelter for the coming night.

Hiku was in no way reluctant to venture onto the bridge, but went on bravely enough, the ring of his hoofs sounding a hollow beat-beat which somehow set me to listening, as if I expected a response from the building ahead.

I saw that I had chosen well, for there was a section of the bridge meant to be pulled back toward the tower, leaving a defensive gap between land and keep. Whether that could still be moved was my first concern. Having crossed, I made fast the end of my rope to rings there provided.

Hiku pulled valiantly and, dismounted, I lent my strength to his. At first I thought the movable bridge section too deeply rooted by time to yield. But after picking with sword point, digging at free soil and wind-blown leaves, I tried again. This time, with a shudder, it gave, not to the extent its makers had intended, but enough to leave a sizable gap between bridge and tower.

The gate of the keep yawned before me darkly. I blamed myself for not bringing the makings of a torch with me. Once more I relied on the pony's senses. When I released him from the drag rope, he gave a great sigh and footed slowly forward, unled or urged, his head hanging a little. I followed after, sure we had come to a place where old dreams might cluster, but that was empty of threat for us now.

Over us arched the bulk of the tower, but there was light beyond, and we came into a courtyard into which opened the main rooms of the structure. If it had been built on a natural island, there was no trace of that, for the walls went straight down on the outer side to the water. In the courtyard a balcony, reached by a flight of stairs on either side, ran from one gate tower to the other, both right and left.

In the center of the open space there were growing things. Grass, bushes, even a couple of small trees, shared crowded space. Hiku fell to grazing as if he had known all along that this particular pasture awaited him. I wondered if he did; if Neevor had come this way.

I dropped my journey bag and went on, passing through the other tower gate out to the matching bridge. It was firm, uneroded. I thought of the wide differences among the Old Ones' ruins. For some may be as ill-treated by time as those Riwal and I had found along the Waste road, and others stand as sturdy as if their makers had moved out only yesterday.

When I came to the cutoff end of the bridge, I found—not as I had half-expected now, a section pulled back—but that the bridge material was fused into glassy slag. I stretched my hand to touch that surface and felt a sharp throb of pain. On my wrist the band was glowing, and I accepted what I believed to be a warning. I retreated to the courtyard.

Wood I found in the garden, if garden it had been. But I did not hasten to make a torch. I had no desire now to enter the balcony rooms to explore in the upper reaches of the towers. Instead I scraped up dried grass of an earlier season, and with my cloak, which still reeked of the signal smoke, I made a bed. In my exploration I found water running from a pipe that ended in a curious head, the stream pouring from both mouth and eyes into a trough and then away along a runnel. Hiku drank there without hesitation, and I washed my smut-streaked face and hands and drank my fill.

I ate one of my cakes, crumbled another, and spread it on wide leaves for Hiku. He relished that and only went back to grazing when he had caught up the last possible crumb with his tongue. Settling back on my cloak bed, my battle hood unlaced, and as comfortable as any scout can be in the field, I lay looking up at the stars as the night closed down.

One could hear the wash of water outside the walls, the buzz of an insect, and, a little later, the call of some night hunter on wings. The upper reaches of the tower could well house both owls and nighthawks. But for the rest there was a great quiet that matched an emptiness in this place.

I was heartened by what seemed to be the good fortune of this day—the fact that my signal had been read, the finding of the talisman—

Talisman? Why had my thoughts so named the armlet? I sought it now with the fingers of my other hand. It was slightly warm to the touch; it fitted my wrist so snugly, it did not turn as I rubbed it, yet I was aware of no punishing constriction. I felt, under my fingertips, that the designs upon it were in slight relief, and I found that I was trying to follow this line or that by touch alone. I was still doing it as sleep overcame me.

That sleep was deep, dreamless, and I awoke from it refreshed and with confidence. It seemed to me that I could face without fears all this day might bring, and I was eager to be gone.

Hiku stood by the trough, shaking his head, the water flying in drops from his muzzle. I hailed him happily as if he could answer me in human speech. He nickered as though he found this a morning to make one feel joyfully alive.

Even though I had daylight as an aid, I had no wish to explore. The driving need to know what had happened to Joisan was part of me. I waited only to eat, and then I readied to leave.

Whether the portion of the bridge that had moved at our urging last night could now be replaced, I began to wonder.

When we came to the portion lying on top of the other surface, I examined it with care. In the bright light of day I saw,
jutting up on the north side of the parapet, a rod as thick as
my forearm.

This was too short to have been a support for anything
overhead, but it must have a purpose, and I hoped it dealt
with the controls on the bridge. In test I bore down on it with
all my strength, and nothing happened. From steady pressure
I turned to quick, sharp jerks. There was a hard grating, it
loosened, and once more I applied pressure.

The bridge section we had worked with such infinite labor
to drag back trembled and began, with screeches of protest,
to edge forward. It did not quite complete the span again, but
lacked only perhaps a foot of locking together. The gap was
not enough to prison us.

Back on shore, before I mounted Hiku, I gazed back at the
lake keep. It was so strongly built a fortress, so easily de-
fended, that I marked it down to serve at some future
time. With the bridge drawn back, even the crawling monsters of the invaders could not reach it. And its lower walls
without breaks could safely hide a third of the army in the
south. Yes, this was a fortress that we might make good use
of.

Now as I turned Hiku north, planning to cut across refugee
trails heading west, I saw that the land about this portion of
the lake must once have been under plow. There were even
patches of stunted grain still growing. I passed an orchard of
trees with ripening fruit. This land must have fed the lake
dwellers once. I would have liked to explore, but Joisan's
plight did not allow that.

A day it took me to cross that countryside to the next rise
of hills. I saw animals in plenty, deer grazing, which meant
no hunters. Among them, as I neared the hills, were some
gaunt and wild-eyed cattle which I believed had been lost
from some herd harried by the invaders. Those sighting me
snorted and galloped away clumsily.

As I re-entered the hills, I found the cattle's trail marked
by hoof prints and droppings. It angled through a rift, and
I followed it warily, hoping for an easy passage, but also
aware that the cattle might be hunted.

Yet I met no enemy. At length, a day later, I chanced directly on what I sought, tracks left by a small band who
were not forest-trained enough to hide their going. There
were only three horses, and most of the traces had been left

by women and children. These must be fugitives from Ithdale, and though there was one chance in perhaps a thousand of Joisan being among them, I might learn something of her.

The tracks were several days old. They tried to head west, but the nature of the rough ground kept pushing them south instead. And this was wild country.

On the morning of the fourth day of trailing, I came to the top of a ridge and, smelling smoke, I crept up to make sure this was the party I sought and not a band of enemy scouts.

The valley was wider here, with a stream in its middle. By the banks of that were shelters of hacked branches covered with other branches and grass. A woman bent over a fire, feeding it one stick at a time. As I watched a second figure crept from one of those lean-tos and straightened to full height.

Morning light caught the glitter of mail that the newcomer was now pulling on. Her head was bare, her hair tied back in a red-brown rope falling between her shoulders. Fortune had favored me once again—that this was indeed Joisan, though I was too far to see her face, I was somehow sure.

My purpose was now clear. I must front her as soon as possible. And when she moved purposefully away from the fire and set off along the river, I was glad. I wanted to meet her alone, not under the staring eyes of her people.

If she were to turn from me in disgust at the sight of my hoofs, any relationship would end before it was begun. I must know that without witnesses. I slipped down-slope to intercept her, using the same caution I would have had she been the enemy.

Joisan:

In our struggle westward during the flight from Ithdale, we had had a little luck in the finding of three strayed ponies, upon the backs of which our weaker ones could ride in turn. This I ordered—that all was share and share alike, with no deference to rank. Yngilda glowered at me, though the Lady Islaugha, after her first violent outburst, went silent as if I did not exist. I thankfully accepted that.

That there was no easy road to Norsdale, we learned within the second day of our journey. The invaders, either in pursuit of fugitives or animals, quartered the land, and we were driven far off our course.

Food was our great need, for luckily, this being summer, we could shelter in the open. But though our animals could graze, we could not live on grasses. And the distance we covered in a day became less and less, since we must also hunt to fill our bellies.

Insfar, who had been a shepherd and had knowledge of wild berries and edible plants, was our guide here. There were mushrooms, and every stream or pool was an invitation to try fishing.

Our arrows and bolts were too few to waste on hunting unless we could make very sure of the shot, and I forbade their being thrown away. Rudo, in spite of being one-eyed, had luck with a slingshot and carried it ever with him, along with a store of pebbles. Four times he added rabbits to the pot. But there was less than a mouthful of meat apiece when that was served out.

We had a second problem, one which had slowed this band of fugitives from the first. Martine, who had been wedded only last fall to the son of the village headman, was heavy with child, her time near upon her. I knew we must find, and shortly, a place wherein we could not only camp for a space, but also have food. Yet nowhere in this rugged land did there seem any welcome.

On the fifth day of our frighteningly slow travel, Rudo and Timon, scouting ahead, returned with brighter faces. We had not cut across any invader trail now for more than a day and so we had a faint ray of hope we had gotten beyond their ranging. What our scouts offered us was a camping ground. And none too soon, I believed, for Nalda, who had kept an eye on Martine, looked very sober.

If we turned a little south, Rudo reported, we would find a valley with not only water but game. He had also discovered a thicket of pla-plums fully ripe. And there was no sign of any visitors.

"Best foot it there, Lady Joisan." Nalda spoke with her usual frankness. "That one"—she nodded at Martine, who sat on the nearest pony, her head dropping, her hands pressed to her swelling belly—"is nigh her time. I do not think she is going to get through this day before her pains come."

We came into the valley. As Rudo promised, it had many advantages. And the men, though Insfar could use only one arm and Angarl one hand, set about hacking down saplings and setting up lean-tos—the first of which Nalda took for Martine.

She had foreseen rightly. By moonrise our party had gathered a new member, squalling lustily, and named Alwin for his dead father. Thus also our staying here for some time was ordered.

It was the next morning I set my will against Yngilda's. If we were to survive, we must gather all the food we might find, keeping ourselves on spare rations while we dried or otherwise prepared the rest for the trail ahead.

I was learned in the provisioning of a keep, but here where there was no salt, no utensils with which to work—nothing but hands, my memory, and what I could improvise—it seemed I faced an impossible task. Yet it was one I must master.

The village women made no murmur, and even the two children did as they were bid at their mother's side. It made me hot with anger when Yngilda did not bestir herself from the lean-to or make any move to join our foraging party.

I went to her, a bag roughly woven from grass and small vines in my hand. Coaxing would not stir her, that I was sure. This was a case for the rough of one's tongue, and that, exasperated and driven as I was, I could easily give.

"On your feet, girl! You will go with Nalda and take heed of what she says—"

She looked at me stony-eyed. "You are bondswoman to us,

Joisan. If you would grub in the dirt with fieldwomen, that is your choice. I do not forget my blood—"

"Then live upon it!" I bade her. "Who hunts not food does not eat by another's labor. And I am no bondswoman."

I threw the bag to her, and she spurned it with her foot. So I turned and tramped away to join the others. But I swore that I would hold to my promise. She was able-bodied and young—I would share with the Lady Islaugha, but not with her.

Of the Lady Islaugha I thought now impatiently. She had sunk into herself: for no better way could I descibe her appearance since I had reported Toross' death. As with Dame Math at the last, age had settled upon her in a single day; so, though she was still in middle years by reckoning, she was to all eyes an aged woman.

She had retreated into her own thoughts, and sometimes we could not rouse her, even to eat what was put into her hand, without a great effort. Now and then she muttered in whispers of which I could not catch more than a word or so, and from these I guessed that she spoke with those I could not see and who, perhaps, were long gone from this world.

I hoped that this was a temporary state born of shock and that in time she would be herself. But of that I could not be sure. If I could only get her to Norstead Abbey where the Dames were learned in nursing, perhaps she might be brought back to the world. But Norsdale seemed farther from us each day.

Yngilda had no such excuse, and she must take upon herself a share of our hardships. The sooner she learned that fact, the better! It was with no pleasant feelings that I went out to hunt.

I had a long bow and three arrows. At Ithkrypt in practice shooting I had proven myself marksman. But shooting at a target and at living prey were, I knew, two different matters, and I must not waste any more of those arrows. So my greater hope this morning was fixed on the river.

With patience and care I had worked at the edge of my mail shirt and broken off a couple of links, shaping them roughly into hooks, raveling my cloak hem and twisting together fibers for a cord. It was poor equipment for a fisherman, but the best I had. And as the foragers separated, the men heading for the grassland where rabbits might be found, the women for the plum thicket, I kept on along the river bank.

Only necessity made it possible for me to bait the first hook with a living insect. I had always shrunk from hurting any creature, and this use of a small life was to me another horror to be added to those of the immediate past.

I found a place where I could wade out to a square rock around which the water washed. There were trees here, and it was cool, shadowed from the sun. But it was still so warm that I shed my mail and the padded jacket under that, keeping on only my undershift, but wishing I might drop that also and slide into the water to wash clean, not only from the dust and sweat of our journeying, but from memory also.

The gryphon swung free, but it held none of the life it had shown the night when Toross and I fled together. I studied it now. It was marvelously wrought. Where had it come from? Overseas—a fairing bought from some Sulcar trader? Or—was it a talisman of the Old Ones?

Talisman—my mind played with that thought. Had it served us as a guide on our flight from Ithkrypt to the star place in the wood? That had been of the Old Ones, and this—could it be, I speculated, that such baubles as this had connection with remains of the Old Ones?

It was an interesting thought, but not one to produce food. I had best attend to the reason for my being here. I dropped my baited line into the water.

Twice I had a strike, but the fish got away. And the second time it took my hook. I had never possessed great patience, but that morning I forced myself to cultivate it as I never had before.

I gained two fish with the second hook. But neither was large. And I feared that unless luck changed, this was no way to replenish our supplies. Leaving my rock, I trudged farther along the stream and, to my joy, found in a side eddy a bed of watercress I plundered.

As the sun turned westward, I turned back to camp. I had eaten some berries and chewed on a handful of my watercress. But I ached with hunger as I went, hoping that the rest had had better luck. When I struck away from the river, I came across the first piece of real fortune I had had all day.

There was a snarl and a deeper answer. Dropping my bag of fish and watercress, I put arrow to bow string and stole forward past a screen of brush.

On the body of a fresh-killed cow crouched a half-grown

snow cat, its ears flattened to its skull, its teeth bared in a death-promising grin. Facing it was a broc-boar.

These grim scavengers were meat eaters, but this one must have either been wild with some private fury, or ravening with hunger, or it would not have challenged the cat over its own kill. And it would seem that the cat was wary of the boar, as if it sensed that the other's challenge had a double element of danger.

The boar was digging its tusks into the earth already softened by its pawing forefeet, tossing bits of sod into the air and squealing in a rising crescendo of sound.

Side by side on the ground the boar would outweigh the cat, I thought. I had seen only two broc-boars in my life, and both had been well under the weight and shoulder height of this monster.

The cat screamed in fury as it sprang, not at the boar, but back from the prey it had cut down. And the boar moved after it with a nimbleness I would not have guessed possible. With another protest of feline rage, the snow cat leaped to a crag and up, soon gaining the heights. From there I could hear its hissing and growling growing fainter as it left the field to the boar who stood, its head cocked, listening.

Almost without planning, I moved then. It was dangerous. Wound that tight package of porcine fury, and I might be horribly dead. But as yet the boar had not winded me, and I saw in it such a promise of food as I could not, in my hunger, resist. Also it was standing now in just the position where I could get a telling shot.

I loosed my arrow and a second later threw myself backward into such hiding as the brush gave me. I heard a terrible squeal and a thudding, but I dared not wait. If I had failed, that four-footed death would be after me. So I ran.

Before I reached camp I sighted Rudo and Insfar and gasped out my story.

"If the boar did not follow you, Lady, it was because it could not," Insfar said. "They are devils for attack. But it may well be your shot was lucky—"

"It was folly," Rudo commented sourly and directly. "It might well have slain you."

He had the truth of it. My hunger had betrayed me into the rankest folly. I accepted his words humbly, knowing that I might now be lying dead.

We returned together, scouting the terrain as if we expected an attack from ambush. We had circled, going up-slope. When we finally reached the scene, there lay the cow and, beyond, on bloodstained ground torn by hoofs and tusks, the boar also. My arrow had sunk behind its shoulders and into the heart.

I found this stroke of fortune earned me awe from the rest of the party. Such a happening was so rare that it might be deemed an act dictated by the Power. I believe that from that hour my people held that some of Dame Math's knowledge and skills were also mine. Though they did not say it to my face, I saw them send favor signs in my direction, and they paid heed to all I said, as if what I uttered were farseeings.

Yngilda remained my thorn-in-the-flesh. I kept to my resolve that first night, and when the flesh was roasting on spits above the fire, so that the savor of it brought juices flowing into the mouth, I spoke aloud so all could hear.

The able-bodied who did not labor equally to supply us all would not share in the fruits of our seeking. So I said, after I had given full praise for the results of that day's harvesting. I saw that all shared that night—save Yngilda. But her I refused openly, that all might note I did not accept rank as an excuse for idleness.

She flung at me that I was under blood-curse to her family. But I said as firmly that I accepted the Lady Islaugha as my charge, and her I would serve. To that these assembled could bear witness. However, Yngilda was young, of strong body, and therefore she would find none here to wait upon her—it would be equal sharing.

I think she would have liked to fly at me, to rake my face and eyes with her fingers. But in that company she stood alone, measured for what she was, and she knew it. So at last she turned from us and crawled back into her lean-to, and I heard her crying, but such weeping as comes from anger and not from sorrow. I had no pity for her. But I also realized that I had made an enemy who would remain an unfriend.

However, it seemed as one day followed another Yngilda had reconsidered her position and thought the better of her obstinacy. She did not do her share of the work graciously, but work she did, even to the odorous business of helping to spread the strips of beef to sun-dry after we butchered the cow that had fallen to the snow cat.

We were frugal, even making use of the bones of both slaughtered animals, their hides (though these could only be rough-cured), and the tusks of the boar. Martine regained her strength, so I had hopes that before the warm weather was past we could fight our way to Norsdale and I could at last lay down my burden of leadership.

Lady Islaugha took to wandering away, in search, perhaps, of Toross. One of our number had to guard her ever, since while so driven to this wandering, her strength seemed the greater and she would set off briskly, often struggling with her guardian if he tried to thwart her, only to falter later when she tired. Then her guardian would lead her back.

Timon fashioned some better fishhooks, and I continued to try my luck along the river. I think out of stubbornness, determined to win a victory here as I had with the boar. But, judging by my continued failures, my luck did not hold in water as it had on land. So clear was that water that ofttimes I sighted the shadows of what were indeed giants compared to the unwary fish I managed to pull out. But either there was some trick of baiting I did not understand, or else these were warier than most fish.

It was during the third day when I followed the river that there came upon me the strong sensation of being watched. So acute did this grow that my hand went to Toross' knife in my belt. From time to time I halted to look around, certain that if I turned quickly enough I could sight some face framed in the grass or in a bush.

I grew so uneasy that I decided to return to camp and alert my people. Some scout of the invaders might have found our backtrail. If so, we might be already doomed, unless we could find and slay him before he reported to his force.

As I turned, the bush parted and one stepped into the open. I had drawn steel in the same instant, ready to defend myself.

He held up empty hands as if he knew what passed in my mind. At the same time, seeing him in full, I knew he was no invader. His battle hood was loosened to lie back on his shoulders. And he wore no over-jerkin or tabard with arms emblazoned on it. Rather did his mail and leather look dulled and dingy, as if purposefully darkened.

But—As my eyes swept down his slim body I stiffened. He wore no boots, his leather breeches were in-fastened at his ankles with straps and his feet—but he had no feet! He stood upon hoofs like one of the cows.

From that impossibility I swiftly looked to his face again, half-expecting to find it monstrous also in some way. But it was not. A man's face truly, browned by sun and wind, the cheeks a little hollowed, the mouth firm-set. He was not as handsome as Toross and—my eyes met his, and in spite of my control I took a step or so back. For those eyes, like the hoofed feet, were not of human man.

They were the color of that amber known to us as "butter," a deep yellow, and in them the pupil was more slit than circle. Not a man's eyes—

When I drew back there was a change in his face, or did I only imagine that? And now I remembered Dame Math's teaching (had she ever in the past, before she had joined Norsdale, met such a one?), so between us in the air I drew a certain sign.

He smiled, but it seemed that smile was a wry, almost twisted one, as if in some manner he regretted that I knew him for what he was—one of the Old Ones. For the first time he spoke:

"Greetings, Lady."

"And to you—" I hesitated, for by what honorific should an Old One be courteously addressed? That had not been in my training. Thus I gave him what I would grant one of my rank in the dales. "Lord, greeting."

"I do not hear you add 'fair meeting,' " he said then. "Do you deem me without testing unfriend?"

"I deem you beyond my measuring," I answered frankly, for I believed that to be true, and perhaps he could read my mind. Such was child's play for one of *them*.

He looked puzzled. "Who think you that I am, Lady?"

"One of those who held dominion here before my blood came to High Hallack."

"An Old One—but—" His wry smile came again. "So be it, Lady. I shall say you neither aye nor nay, since you have named me so. But you and your folk yonder seem in a sorry case. It may be that I can be of some assistance to you."

I knew so little—there were those among the Old Ones who were said to be favorable to men, who had on occasion given them assistance. There were others of the Dark whose malice meant great peril. Trust is a precious gift. If I chose wrong now, we would all suffer. Yet there was that about him which argued that he was not of the Dark.

"What have you to offer? We would reach Norsdale if we can, but the way—"

He interrupted me. "If you seek to go westward there are

many perils. But I can bring you to a shelter that will serve you better than here. There is fruit and game there also—"

I gazed into those golden eyes, troubled. When he spoke so, I wanted to believe. But I was not alone; there were these people of mine. And to trust an Old One—

His smile went as I hesitated. There was a coldness in his face, as if he had held out his hand and been rebuffed. My unease grew. Perhaps he was one disposed to aid my kind, but would take offense if that aid were refused, thus bringing on us his displeasure.

"You must forgive me." I sought for words to assuage the ire I feared might be rising in him. "I have had no meeting with—with your people heretofore. If I do not comport myself as I should, it comes from ignorance alone and not from any wish to offend. Among the dales you appear only in our legends. Some of those are favorable; some deal with the Dark Ones who give us hate instead of friendship. Thus we walk warily in your presence."

"Because the Old Ones have what you call the Power," he said. "Well, that may be so. But I mean you nothing but good, Lady. Look upon what you wear there on your breast—hold it out that I may touch it with my fingertip—you will see that this is so."

I looked to the crystal gryphon. Though there was bright sun on us, not moonlight, I could perceive that it was glowing; almost it appeared as if the creature within the ball was about to give tongue and speak for this stranger, so oddly knowing did the carving look. I did then as he suggested, took the chain from about my neck and held the globe in my hand, stretching it forth to him.

He touched it with fingertip only, and the globe flashed into such radiant glory that I near dropped it. In that moment I knew that all he said was the truth, and that here had come one out of the unknown past of this land to do us service. So my heart lightened, though my awe of him was greater.

"Lord." I bowed my head before him, giving homage to that which he was. "In all things behold one whom you can bid—"

Again he interrupted me, this time speaking with such sharpness that it was a rebuke.

"I am no lord of yours, Lady, nor are you under my bidding. You are to make you choice freely. I can offer you and your people a strong shelter and what aid a single man can give—and I am not ignorant of the ways of war. But

more than your friendship—if you can find it in you sometime when we are better acquainted to offer me that—I do
not claim!" There was such authority in his tone as he spoke,
as if it were very necessary that he make this plain to me
(though I was not sure of his meaning), that I was abashed.
But I knew I must abide by his wishes.

He came back with me to my people, and they were also
in awe of him, shrinking away. I watched him and saw the
bitterness in his face, and there came into my mind that he
was hurt at this effect he had upon people, so in turn I felt
something of his pain—though how I knew all this I could not
tell.

But he being who he was, his orders were obeyed without
question. He whistled, and there came down from the hills
in answer a mountain pony sure-footed and steady. And on
this he mounted Martine. On our other horses we packed
what we had harvested here and we went under his guidance.

In the end he brought us to a place that was indeed a
greater wonder in its way than any keep of the dales, for it
was built upon lake. To it led two bridges, though one was
broken off and useless. But the other, as he showed us, could
have a section moved in it, leaving a defensive gap across
which no foeman could come.

Best of all, this land had once been under cultivation. There
was fruit and stunted, wild-growing grain to be harvested.

With this promise against famine we knew we could remain
here for as long as we needed to give our people strength and
gather more food for the journey. And my trust in him was
secure.

He gave us no name. Perhaps with him it was as it is with
the Wisewomen who believe that if one knows their name one
can then establish domination over them. In my mind I called
him Lord Amber, because of his eyes.

Five days he stayed with us, seeing all was well. Then he
said that he would go on scout, making sure those of Alizon
had not struck inland far enough to trouble us.

"You speak as if the Hounds are also your enemies," I
said, curious. "Yet your people have not been attacked—it is
my kin they sweep away."

"The land is mine," he answered. "I have already fought
these elsewhere. I shall fight again, until they are driven back
into the sea from which they came."

I knew a thrill of excitement. What would it mean to my
poor, beleaguered people if there were others such as he, pos-

sessors of the Power who would aid us in this death struggle? I longed to ask him if there were, and again it was as if he read my thoughts.

"You think the Power could be used to vanquish these?" There was brooding sadness in his face. "Be not wishful for that, Lady Joisan. He or she who summons such cannot always control it. Best not to call so. But this I will tell you: I believe this place to be as safe as any now in the hills. If you choose well, you will abide here until I return."

I nodded eagerly. "Be assured we shall, Lord." In that moment I had a queer desire to stretch forth my hand, perhaps touch his arm—as if some touch of mine could lighten that burden I thought rested ever on him. Such a fancy had no meaning in it, and of course I did not follow that odd whim.

I saw the shrinking in her eyes and knew that there could be naught between us. But it was only in my losing that I came to learn how much I had held in my heart the thought that, to at least one, I would be no monster but a man. How right had been that instinct that had kept me from obeying her wish and sending her my portrait. For she would never know now that I was Kerovan.

That Joisan took me to be one of the Old Ones was a two-way matter. On the one hand it kept her from asking questions that I must either struggle to evade or to which I must give answers. On the other hand she would expect from me some evidences of the "Power." For that lack, I would also need to find excuses. But for a few days I could set actions before words.

The poor camp was a refuge for a pitiful band. There were but four who might be termed—very loosely indeed—fighting men. Two were past middle age, one lacked a hand, the other an eye. There was a green boy who I suspected had never drawn steel, and a hill shepherd who was wounded. The rest were women and children, though of that number there were some who could stand shoulder to shoulder with any armsman if there be need.

Mostly they were villagers, but there were two other ladies—one old, one young. The older was in a state of shock and had to be watched lest she wander off. Joisan confided in me that her son had been slain and that she now refused to accept that, but wished to search for him.

Of Ithdale itself she had a strange tale, almost as strange as the blasting of Ulmskeep. It seemed that one of her own House had called down some manifestation of the Power on the keep, catching thereby a goodly number of the Hounds. But before that there had been some warning, and she hoped many of her people had managed to flee westward. Their goal was Norsdale, but now they had no guide. Also there was one of the women who had recently given birth and could not travel long or hard.

It was then I thought of that fortress in the lake and how it could be a shelter for this band until they recovered strength. That much I could do for my lady, bring her and hers to a roof over their heads and a small measure of safety.

That she wore my gift was no matter of pride for me, for I was certain she did not wear it because of any attachment for its giver, but rather because she delighted in it for itself. Now and then I saw her hand seek and caress it, almost as if from such fondling she received strength.

The younger of the two ladies, Yngilda, who was kinsman to Joisan, I did not like. She watched my lady from under downcast lids with a sly hatred, though Joisan showed no ill will toward her. What lay between them in the past I had no inkling, but this Yngilda I would noways trust.

Of Joisan herself—but those thoughts I battled, summoning always in answer to them the memory of her expression when she had seen my unbooted feet. How wise I had been in my choice to bare that deformity to the world. Had I continued to hide it, made myself known to Joisan, found her welcoming and then—No, it was far better to eat bitterness early than to have it twist one doubly by following on the sweet.

That Joisan was such a lady as one might treasure, that I learned in those few days when, under my guidance, they made their way to the keep in the lake. Though many times she must have been weary and downhearted, yet she was ready to shoulder duty's burdens without complaint. And her courage was as great as her heart. Had I only been as other men—

Now I chewed upon the sourness of that memory-vision in which she had supported a dying man in grief. Did that lie in the past or the future? I had no right to question her, for I had surrendered that with my claim upon her.

Somehow, if it was in my power, I would get them to what safety Norsdale promised. Then—well, I was now a landless man. It would be easy to drop out of reckoning. I could join some lord's menie. Or I could go into the Waste, where those who were outcast from the dales carried their shame or despair. However, I would see Joisan safe before I said farewell.

When those from Ithdale had settled into the keep and had mastered the defensive use of the sliding bridge, I sought Joisan and told her that I must scout for the invaders. That was in part the truth, but with that need there was another, that I go forth and do battle with myself, for there were times when she seemed to reach to me. Not with hand, or invitation of voice. But she would look at me when she thought my attention elsewhere, and there was a vague questioning in her face, as if she sensed that there was a bond between us.

Because there was a weakness in me that yearned toward making myself known, trading on any familiarity that had grown, I was determined that I must get away until I could build such an inner control as would never yield. In her eyes at first sighting I had been a monster. Because she now believed me an Old One with whom the human standards of form did not hold, she accepted me fully. But as a man—I was flawed.

On leaving the lake keep, I circled out to the north and west. This was wild country, though it did not have the desolation of the Waste. Nor did I come upon any other Old Ones' ruins, as I expected to with the impressive lake structure so near.

Three days I quested in the direction I thought we must follow to Norsdale. Though I did not know any trail, I had a good idea of the general direction. The way was rough; the wider dalelands of the east changed here to a series of knife-narrow valleys walled by sharp ridges, weary path for foot travelers. Also they would not be able to go fast. And I began to wonder as I struck more westerly whether they would not be better placed to wait within the lake keep for spring.

On the fourth day I cut across a fresh trail. It was of a small party, not more than four. They were mounted, but their animals were plainly not the heavier beasts the Hounds favored, the tracks being those of unshod hill ponies. More fugitives? Perhaps—but in times of war no man accepts an untested assumption.

Joisan had told me her people had been widely scattered when they fled. These could be more from Ithdale. I had a duty to make sure, to guide them if they were.

Yet I took no chances and followed with a scout's wiles. The trail was, I believed, several days old. Twice I came to where they had camped, or rather sheltered, for there were no signs of fires. Also—their going spoke of more than flight —it was as if they knew exactly where they were going, driven more by purpose than fear.

Their direction, making allowances for natural obstacles, led directly to the lake keep. Noting that, I was more than a little uneasy. Four men did not make a formidable force, but four men, armed and ready, could take Joisan's people by surprise. And these might be outlaws drawn out of the Waste by the bait of loot.

I might have held their trail had it not been for the storm. It came with the evening of the same day. Though it was a summer shower compared to the fury I had seen unleashed in Ulmsdale, yet it was not an easy torrent of rain or force of wind to face. With darkness added, I was made to seek cover and wait it out.

As I waited, my mind fastened on one evil chance after another. I could not rid myself of the belief that these I followed were unfriends. And I had lived on the edge of the Waste too many years not to know what outlaws would do to the helpless. Now I could only hold to self-control, try to believe that Joisan had followed my last orders and taken up the bridge section and that they would not admit strangers to the keep. Ithkrypt had not known such raiders. They could accept any dalesman as friend.

By morning the storm had cleared, but it had washed away the trail. I was too concerned to cast about hunting it. The need to return to the lake, discover what chanced there, rode me strong.

But I had two days yet on the way, even though I pushed myself and Hiku to the limit of endurance. When I came into the lake valley and saw the keep, I had worked myself into such a state of foreboding as prepared me to find a bloody massacre.

There was a hail from one of the largely overgrown fields that brought me up short. Nalda and two of the other women waved from a peaceful scene. They were engaged in harvesting the thin stand of stunted grain, gleaning every stalk and heaping it on two outspread cloaks.

"Fair news, my Lord!" Nalda's voice rang loud in my ears as she crossed the field to reach me. "My lady's lord has come at last! He heard of her distress and rode to her service!"

I stared at her unbelieving. Then common sense made it all clear—she did not mean Joisan, of course. She spoke of the lord wed to Yngilda—though I had thought he was supposed to have died when his keep was overrun in the south.

"The Lady Yngilda must be giving praise to Gunnora at this hour," I had wit enough to answer.

Nalda stared at me as strangely as perhaps I had at her a moment earlier.

"That one—she is widowed, not wed! No, it is the Lord

Kerovan, he who has been so long wed to our dear lady! He rode in three days since—to rejoice our hearts. Lord, my lady has asked all to watch for you, to urge you to hasten to the keep—"

"Be sure that I shall!" I said between set teeth. Who this false Kerovan was, I had no idea, but that I must see him, must save Joisan from any danger. Someone who knew of our marriage, who perhaps thought me dead, was taking advantage of the situation. And the thought that he could be with Joisan now was like a sword through me. That she might in time turn to another I had tried to endure, but that another had come to her in false guise—that I would not countenance.

For now I could call on my repute as an Old One of unknown but awesome powers. I could proclaim Kerovan dead, unmask this intruder, and she would believe me. Thus I had only to reach the keep, confront the impostor.

I urged my weary Hiku to a trot, though I longed to fling myself from his back, go pounding ahead into the keep, to call out this thief of another man's name and slay him out of hand —not because he had taken my name, but because he had boldly used it as a cloak to reach Joisan. In that moment how I wished I was truly what she thought me, one who could summon forces beyond the understanding of men.

Angarl, the one-handed, was on sentry duty and gave me a greeting I forced myself to answer. Very shortly I was in the courtyard. The deserted emptiness which had restrained me on my first visit here from too detailed exploration was gone. Life had returned to the hold, and it was now a place for humans.

Two men loitered by the water-trough, chaffing with one of the village girls, their deeper laughter banishing even more the atmosphere of the alien. They wore House badges adorned with my gryphon on their over-jerkins.

Before they looked up, I studied them. Neither was familiar —I had begun to wonder if survivors from Ulmsdale might have been drawn into this. However, the fact I did not recognize them meant little, for I had been away from Ulmskeep for months before my father's death, and he might have hired newcomers to augment his forces, taking the places of those who rode south with me.

That they wore such badges meant this was no hastily improvised scheme on the part of someone who had heard a rumor or two. Here was careful preparation—but why? Had

Joisan still had Ithkrypt with men and arms, then I could have understood such a move. The false Kerovan would have ruled in Ithdale. But she was a landless, homeless fugitive. Why then?

One of the men glanced up, saw me, and nudged his fellow. Their laughter was gone; they eyed me warily. But I did not approach them. Rather I slid from Hiku's back and walked, stiff with the weariness of the trail, toward that tower room Joisan had made her own.

"You—!" The call was harsh, arrogant.

I swung around to see the two armsmen striding toward me. It was not until they fronted me that they seemed to realize I differed from their kind. I faced them calmly, bringing into my bearing the stiffness of one who has been approached by those beneath him in rank in a manner highly unbecoming.

"You—" the leader began again, but he was now uncertain. I saw his comrade nudge him in the ribs. It was the second man who now pushed a little to the fore.

"Your pardon, Lord," he said, his eyes searching me up and down. "Whom do you seek?"

His assumption of a steward's duties here fed my anger.

"Not you, fellow." I turned away.

Perhaps they would have liked to have intercepted me, but they did not quite dare. And I did not look to them again as I came to the tower doorway, now curtained with a horse blanket.

"Good fortune to the house!" I raised my voice.

"Lord Amber!" The blanket was thrust aside and Joisan stood before me.

There was that in her face at that moment which hurt. So he had won this already, this radiance! So ill had I played my part I had thrown away all. All? Another part of me questioned it. I had already decided that this was not for me. How could I then question her happiness if one she believed to be her lord had come to serve her in the depths of her need? That he was an imposter was all I must think on, that she must not be deceived.

"Lord Amber, you have come!" She put forth her hand, but did not quite touch mine, which I had raised against my will. Having spoken so, she stood looking at me. I could not understand—

"Who comes, my fair one?"

I knew that voice from the dusk of the room behind her. Knowing it, my hate near broke bounds so that I thirsted to draw steel and press him into combat. Rogear here—but why?

"Lord Amber, have you heard? My lord has come—hearing of our troubles he has come—"

She spoke hurriedly and there was that in her voice which made me watch her closely. I had seen Joisan afraid. I had seen her rise above fear and pain of heart and mind, be strong for others to lean upon. But at this moment I thought that it was not joy that colored her tone. Outwardly she might present this smiling face, inwardly—no—

Her lord had not brought her happiness! Excitement stirred in me at that which I thought no guess but honest truth. She had not found in Rogear what she sought.

She retreated a step or two, though she had not answered his question. I followed, to stand facing my mother's kin. He wore a war tabard over his mail, with that gryphon to which he had no right worked on it. Above that his face was handsome, his mouth curved in that small secret smile, until he saw me—

In that instant the smile was wiped from his lips. His eyes narrowed, and there was about him watchfulness as if we both held swords in hand and were set against one another.

"My Lord." Joisan spoke hurriedly, as if she sensed what lay between us and wished to avoid battle. But she addressed me first as the higher in rank. "This is my promised Lord, Kerovan who is heir to Ulmsdale."

"Lord—Kerovan?" I made a question of that. I could denounce Rogear at once. But so could he me. Or could he? That which had been my bane, my deformity—would not Joisan continue to think it proved me alien? At any rate, Rogear must not be allowed to play any dark game here—whether it meant Joisan turning from me in disgust or not.

"I think not!" My words fell into the silence like blows.

In that moment Rogear's hand came up, something flashing in it—the crystal gryphon. From it struck a ray of light straight at my head. Pain burst behind my eyes, I was both blind and in such agony that I could not think, only feel. I staggered back against the wall, fighting to keep my feet. My arm was upflung in a futile effort to counter this stroke I was unprepared to face. I heard Joisan scream, and hard upon that cry another of rage and pain. Still blind, I was thrust aside and fell to the floor.

Joisan screamed again, and I heard sounds of a struggle.

But I could not *see!* Not trying to rise, I threw myself toward the sounds.

"No! No!" Joisan's voice. "Loose me!"

Rogear had Joisan! A foot stamped upon my hand, giving me a second thrust of agony so great I could not stand it, yet I must! If he had Joisan, could drag her out—

I flung out my sound arm, touched a body, embraced kicking legs, and threw the weight of my shoulder against him, bearing him under me to the floor.

"Joisan—run!" I cried. I could not fight when I could not see; I could only hold on, taking his blows, trying to keep him so she could escape.

"No!" Her voice again, and with a cold note in it that I had never heard before. "Lie you very still, my Lord."

"Lord Amber," she said now, "I hold a knife blade to his throat. You may loose him."

He did indeed lie as one who would offer no more fight. I backed away a little.

"You say," she continued in that same tone, "this is not Kerovan. Why, my Lord?"

I made my choice. "Kerovan is dead, my Lady. Dead in an ambush laid by this Rogear above his father's keep. This Rogear has knowledge of the Old Ones—from the Dark Path—"

I heard a quickly drawn breath. "Dead? And this one dares to wear my lord's name to deceive me?"

Rogear spoke up then. "Tell her your name—"

"As you know, we do not give our names to mankind," I improvised.

"Mankind? And what are—"

"Lord Kerovan." My head jerked toward that new voice. "What do you—" It was one of the armsmen from the courtyard.

"Lord *Kerovan* does nothing," Joisan answered. "As for this one, take him and ride."

"Shall we take her, Lord?" asked the armsman.

I had gotten to my feet, faced toward that voice, though I could not see.

"Let the wench go. She is of no importance now." By his tone Rogear had regained his full confidence.

"And him, Lord?" Someone was moving toward me. My crushed hand hung useless. In any event I could not see him.

"No!" Rogear's answer was the exact opposite of what I expected to hear. In that moment a single thrust from a sword would have finished it all in his favor, and he could have had his will of Joisan. "Touch him on your peril!"

"We ride," he added. "I have what I came for—"

"No! Not that! Give me the gryphon!" Joisan's cry ended in the thud of a blow, and her slight body struck against mine. She would have slipped to the floor, but I flung my arm about her. They were gone, though I cried out for any in the courtyard to stop them.

"Joisan!" I held her close against me. She was a slack weight—if I could only *see!* What had that devil done to her? "Joisan!" Had he killed her?

But Joisan was not dead, only struck senseless, as those who came running told me. As for Rogear and his men, they were away. I sat by Joisan's bed, holding her hand in mine. About my useless eyes was bound a cloth wet in water in which herbs had been steeped. Only in that hour did I begin to face the fact that perhaps my sight was gone from me. Just as I had not been able to save Joisan from that last blow, so I would never again be able to step between her and any other harm. That was the black hour in which I learned how much she had come to be a part of me. The pain I had known earlier as I stood aside from making myself known was as nothing to what I now felt.

"Lord—" Joisan's voice, weak and thin, but still her voice.

"Joisan!"

"He took—he took my lord's gift—the gryphon." She was sobbing now.

Fumbling, I drew her into my arms, so she wept upon my shoulder.

"It was the truth you spoke; he is not Kerovan?"

"The truth. It is as I said, Kerovan died in ambush at Ulmsdale. Rogear is betrothed to Kerovan's sister."

"And I never saw my lord. But his gift—that one shall not have it! By the Nine Words of Min, he shall not! It is a wondrous thing, and his hands besmirch it. And he used it as a weapon, Lord—he used it to burn your eyes!"

That flash from the globe—

"But also, Lord, your own power answered, from this band on your wrist. If you had only held that sooner as a shield." Her fingers were feather-light on my arm above the armlet. "Lord, they say those of you people are mighty in healcraft. If you have not that talent yourself, can we not take you to them? It is in my service this grievous hurt came to you. I owe you a blood-debt—"

"No. There is no debt between us," I denied quickly. "This Rogear has always been my unfriend. Had we met anywhere he would have sought to kill me." And, I thought bleakly then, perhaps I would be better dead now of a wound, than alive with this cloth about my head marking my loss.

"I have something of healcraft, and so has Nalda. Perhaps the sight will come again. Oh, my Lord, I do not know why he sought me here. I have no longer lands or fortune—save that which he took with him. Know you of this gryphon? It was sent me by my lord. Was it then such a great treasure of his House that this Rogear would risk so much to get it into his hands?"

Her query drew my thoughts away from my own darkness to consider why Rogear had come. The crystal gryphon—that it had strange powers was entirely possible. He was learned in the lore of the Old Ones—the Dark Old Ones. I had heard enough from Riwal to know that when one went some distance down the path of alien knowledge, things of power, both light and dark, could make themselves known to the initiate.

I had been with Riwal when I first found it. Neevor had said Riwal was dead, but he had evaded giving a description of how my friend had died. Supposing Rogear, already practiced in the Old Ones' learning, had somehow ferreted out Riwal, learned from him about the gryphon, traced it thereafter to my lady? That would mean it was such a talisman as could cause great troubles. In Rogear's hand its use would be a danger to the world I knew. Joisan was right, we must strive to get it back. But how—? I put my hand to my bandaged eyes with a sigh. Could it ever be done?

I was in the eastern watchtower when my lord came to us. Though there was no alarm gong hung there, yet in the uppermost room we had found a metal plate set into the wall. A sword hilt laid vigorously to that brought forth a carrying sound. After Lord Amber rode out, we kept a sentry there by day—secure at night with the bridge drawn against any shoreside visitor.

So was I alert to the riders and beat out an alarm before I saw that they rode at a quiet amble and that Timon came afoot with them. He was under no restraint, but spoke with their leader in a friendly fashion. For a moment or two I was excited by the belief that some of our men might have escaped the slaughter by the river and been able to trace us. Then I saw that their battle tabards were not red but green.

They could be scouts of some other dale, and from them we could claim escort to Norsdale, though that thought made me a little unhappy. I wanted to reach Norsdale with my people. There the Lady Islaugha would find the proper tending, and the others for whom I was responsible would find new homes. Though the Lord Amber had indeed provided us with such a refuge as I had never hoped to find in this wilderness, we could not stay here forever.

I did not know why I had been so content here, as I had not been since that long-ago time before Lord Cyart had ridden south at the beginning of our time of trouble.

Now, even as the sound died away, I sped down the stair, eager to see who these newcomers might be. Yet I ordered my pace as I reached the courtyard, for chance had made me ruler in this place, and I must carry myself with proper dignity.

When I saw what was emblazoned on the tabard of he who led that very small company I was shaken. So well did I know that rearing gryphon! These were my lord's people. Or even—perhaps—

"My dear Lady!" He swung from his saddle and held out his hands to me in greeting, his voice warm.

160

Though I wore no skirt now, I swept him the curtsy of greeting. However, I was glad he attempted no warmer salute than voice and hand.

"My Lord Kerovan?" I made that more question than recognition.

"I so stand before you." He continued to smile. Yet—

So this was my wedded lord? Well, he had not Toross' regularity of feature, but neither was he unpleasing to look upon. For a dalesman his hair was very dark—a ruddy darkness—and his face less broad across the jaw—more oval. Despite those ugly rumors that Yngilda had first loosed for me, there was certainly nothing uncanny in him. Now Lord Amber was plainly of alien stock, but my Lord was as any dalesman.

That was our first meeting, and it was a constrained and uneasy one with many eyes watching. But how else could it be in this time and place when we two so bound together were strangers to one another?

I was grateful that he treated me with courtesy and deference, as one yet to be won, not a possession already in his hand. And he was both kind and gentle in his manner. Still—

Why did I feel that I wanted nothing more of him, that I regretted that he had come? He spoke me fair, always in that voice which was so pleasing, telling me that he, too, was now homeless—that Ulmskeep had fallen to the invaders. He and his men had been in flight from there, striving to reach Ithdale, when he had crossed the path of some of our people. Learning how it had been with us, he then pushed on to search for me.

"We were told you were with the army in the south, my Lord," I said, more to make conversation than to demand any explanation.

"That I was, for my father. But when he became ill he sent for me. Alas, I arrived too late. Lord Ulric was already dead, and the invaders so close to our gates that our last battle was forced upon me in great haste. But we were favored in that there was a storm from the sea, and so those of Alizon took nothing. In the end they were totally destroyed."

"But you said that your keep had fallen."

"Not to the Hounds. It was the sea that brought down our walls: wind and wave swept in, taking the land. Ulmsport"— he gestured—"now all lies under water."

"However," he continued briskly, "the lad who brought us here says you seek Norsdale—"

I told him our tale and of how I was curse-bound to the Lady Islaugha and must see her to safety.

He was grave-faced now, hearing me through without question, nodding now and then in agreement to something I said.

"You are well south of your proper trail," he replied, with the authority of one who knew exactly where he was. "And your fortune has been great to find such shelter as this."

"The finding was not ours, but Lord Amber's."

"Lord Amber? Who bears such an unusual name?"

I flushed. "He does not speak his name—that is mine for him, since every man must have a name. He—he is one of the Old Ones—one well disposed toward us."

I was not too ill at ease at that moment to miss noting his reaction to my words. He stiffened, his face now a mask behind which thoughts might race without sign. I have seen a fox stand so still as it listened for a distant hunter. A moment later that alert was gone, or else he concealed it.

"One of the Old Ones, my Lady? But they have been long gone. Perhaps this fellow seeks to deceive you for some purpose. How can you be sure he is such? Did he proclaim it so?"

"He had no need, as you will see when he returns. No man would be like him." I was a little irked at the note in his voice, as if he believed me some silly maid to whom any tale can be told. And since I had led my people I had become one to make decisions, to stand firm. I had no liking to be pressed again into the old position of a daleswoman, that only my lord or another man could see the truth in any question and then decide what was best for me. Before I was Kerovan's lady I was myself!

"So he returns? Where is he now?"

"He went some days ago to scout for the invaders," I replied shortly. "Yes, he will return."

"Well enough." My lord nodded again. "But there are different kinds of Old Ones, as our people learned long ago, to their sorrow. Some would be friends, after a distant fashion; some ignore us unless we infringe upon their secrets; and others follow the Dark Path."

"As well I know," I answered. "But Amber can touch your gift, and it blazes as it did when it saved me from the Hounds."

"My gift—?"

Did I hear aright now? Had there been surprise in his tone? But no, I schooled my thoughts, I must not react so to everything he said as if we were unfriends and not life comrades, as we must learn to be.

He was smiling once more. "Yes, my gift. Then it has been of good use to you, dear one?"

"The best!" My hand went to my breast, where the gryphon lay safe as I ever kept it so. "My Lord, I am not wrong then in believing it is a treasure of the Old Ones?"

He leaned forward across the stone-slab table between us, where he had broken his fast on the best we had to offer. There was eagerness in his eyes, even if emotion did not show elsewhere on his countenance.

"You are not wrong! And since it has served you so well, I am doubly glad that it was in your hands. Let me look upon it once again."

I loosed the lacing of my jerkin, pulled at the chain to draw it forth. Yet something kept me from slipping it off and putting it into the hand he laid palm up on the table as if to receive it.

"It does not leave me, as you see, night or day." I made excuse. "Can you say the same for my return gift to you, my lord?" I tried to make that question light, the teasing of a maid with her wooer.

"Of course." Had he touched his own breast swiftly? Yet he made no move to show me the picture I had sent him.

"Still you did not follow my wishes sent with it." I pursued the matter. I do not know why, but my uneasiness was growing. There was nothing I had seen in him or his manner to make me unhappy yet, but there was a shadow here that I could sense and that vaguely alarmed me. I found that I was restoring the gryphon to its hiding place hastily, almost as if I feared he might take his own gift from me by force. What lay between us that I should feel this way?

"There was no time, nor trusted messenger," he was saying. However, I was sure he watched the globe as long as it was in sight with greater interest than he had for my face above it.

"You are forgiven, Lord." I kept to the light voice, molding my manner on that of the maids I had seen in Trevamper in that long-ago time before all this evil had broken upon the dales. "And now—I must be back to my duties. You and your men must have lodging, though you will find it somewhat bare. None of us sleep soft here."

"You sleep safe, which in these days is much to say." He arose with me. "Where do you quarter us?"

"In the west tower," I answered, and drew a breath of relief that he had not asserted his right and demanded my compliance. What was the matter with me? In all ways he had shown consideration and courtesy, and in the days that followed it was the same.

He spoke of our efforts to harvest the stunted grain from the old fields and pick and dry the fruit. He praised our forelooking. He was quick to say that such a band as ours— of the old, the very young, and the ailing—would be extra long on the road and would need all the food we could gather. His armsmen took over sentry duty, leaving us free to work in field and orchard.

Nor did he press for my company, which eased my feeling of constraint. Only I was haunted by an uneasiness I could not account for. He was kind; he strove to make himself pleasing to me in thought and word. And yet—the longer he stayed, the more unhappy I was. Also I was a little frightened at the prospect to come of the time when he would be my lord in truth.

Sometimes he rode forth to scout along the hills, assuring us added protection. I would not see him from dawn until sunset, when we drew in that movable part of the bridge. However, twice in the dusk I saw him in conversation with Yngilda, whom he treated with the same courtesy he showed to me and Lady Islaugha, though the latter seemed hardly aware of his presence.

I do not believe he sought out my kinswoman. Their meetings must have been of her contrivance. She watched him hungrily. At the time I believed I knew what lay in her mind —her lord was dead; she had naught to look forward to save a dragging life at Norsdale. Yet I, whom she hated—yes, hated, for I no longer disguised from myself that her dislike of me had crystallized through envy to something deeper and blacker—had Kerovan, eager to serve me. That she might make trouble between us, well, that, too, was possible. But I did not think so, for I could see no way that even a spiteful tongue could disturb the relationship we now had, it being so shallow a one.

Had my heart followed my hand, that would have been a different matter. Undoubtedly I would have resented meddling. As it was, no action of hers disturbed me.

On the fifth day after his arrival, Kerovan did not stay so late in the hills, but came back in mid-afternoon. I had been in the fields, for another pair of hands was needed. One of the children had run a thorn into her foot, so I brought her back to wash and bind it with healing herbs we had found.

Her tears soothed, her hurt tended, she went running back to her mother, leaving me to put away our small supply of medicants. While I was so busied, my lord came to me.

"My fair one, will you give into my hand that gift I sent you? There is perhaps the chance that it can serve you even better than it has, for I have some of the old learning and have added to it since I sent you this. There are things of power which, rightfully used, are better than any weapons known to our kind. If we indeed have such a one, we can count on an easier journey to Norsdale."

My hand went to what I wore. In no way did I wish to yield to his request. Still, I had no excuse. I did not understand myself, why I shrank from letting it go out of my hands. Most reluctantly I loosed lacings and drew it forth. Still I held it cupped for a long moment while his hand was held forth to take it. He smiled at me as one who would encourage a timid child.

At length, with an inner sigh, I gave it to him. He took a step into the light of the slit window, held it at eye level as if he were fronting the tiny gryphon in some silent communication.

It was at that moment that I heard from without the traveler's greeting, "Good fortune to his house."

I did not have to see the speaker. I knew at once and was past Kerovan into the open.

"Lord Amber!" I did not understand the emotion awakened in me at the sound of his voice. It was as if all the uneasiness of the past few days was gone, that safety stood here on hoofed feet, gazing at me with golden eyes.

"You have come!" I put forth my hand, eager to clasp his. But that reserve which was always a part of him kept me from completing that gesture.

"Who comes, my fair one?" Kerovan's voice broke through the wonderful feeling of release, of security. I had to find other words.

"Lord Amber, have you heard? My lord has come—hearing of our troubles he has come."

I retreated a little, chilled by a loss I could not define. The Old One followed. I did not look to my lord, only still into those golden eyes.

"My Lord, this is my promised lord, Kerovan, who is heir to Ulmsdale."

His face was secret, close, as I had seen it other times.

"Lord Kerovan?" He repeated it as if he asked a question. And then he added with the force of one bringing down a sword in a swift, lashing stroke, "I think not!"

Kerovan's hand came up, the globe clasped tight in his fingers. From that shot a piercing ray of light, striking full into Lord Amber's eyes. He flung up one hand as he staggered back. On the wrist of that hand I saw an answering glow, as if a blue mist spread to raise a curtain about him.

I screamed and struck at Kerovan, striving to snatch the crystal from him. But he beat me off, and in his face I read that which changed my uneasiness to fear.

Kerovan caught me in a strong hold and dragged me toward the door. Lord Amber, one hand to his eyes, was on his hands and knees, his head moving as if he strove to find us by sound alone, as if he were *blind!*

I beat at Kerovan, twisting in his hold. "No! Loose me!"

Lord Amber lurched toward us. I saw Kerovan raise his boot, stamp, and grind one of those groping hands against the floor. But with his other arm Lord Amber caught Kerovan about the knees and bore him down by the weight of his body.

"Joisan, run!" he cried.

I was free of Kerovan, but run I would not. Not while Lord Amber took the vicious blows Kerovan was dealing.

"No!" my belt knife, Toross' legacy, was in my hands. I crouched above the struggling men, caught Kerovan's hair, and jerked his head back, putting the edge of that blade to his throat. "Lie you very still, my lord," I ordered. He must have read my purpose in my face, for he obeyed.

Not taking my eyes from him, I said then, "Lord Amber, I hold knife-edge to his throat. Loose him."

He believed me and edged away.

"You say," I continued, "this is not Kerovan. Why?

He was rising to his feet one hand still to his eyes. "Kerovan is dead, my Lady." His voice sounded very weary. "Dead in an ambush laid by this Rogear above his father's keep. This Rogear has knowledge of the Old Ones—from the Dark side."

My breath hissed between my teeth. So much was made plain to me now. "Dead? And this one dared to wear my lord's name to deceive me?"

Rogear spoke up then. "Tell her your name—"

Lord Amber answered him. "As you know, we give not our names to mankind."

"Mankind? And what are—"

"Lord Kerovan!" I was so startled by that voice from the door I jerked away from my guard post. "What do you—?" One of his armsmen stood there.

I spoke quickly. "Lord *Kerovan* does nothing! As for this one—take him and ride!"

There was a second man behind him, with the bolt on his crossbow, which was aimed not at me but at Lord Amber. And in his face a horrible eagerness, as if he would joy in loosing death.

"Shall we take her, Lord?" asked the first man.

Lord Amber was moving toward him, his hands empty. And the man held ready steel.

Rogear had rolled away from me. "Let the wench go. She is of no importance now."

"And him, Lord?"

"No! Touch him not, on your peril!"

I had thought he would order Lord Amber's death, if one of the Old Ones can be so killed.

"We ride," he added. "I have what I came for." He was putting the gryphon into the inner pocket of his tabard.

That roused me to action. "No. Not that!" I sprang at him. "Give me the gryphon!"

He aimed a blow at my head with his other hand, and I did not dodge in time. A burst of pain drove me into darkness.

When I awoke I lay on my bed-place, and the dusk was deep. But I saw that Lord Amber was beside me, and my hand lay in his. There was a bandage bound about his head, covering his eyes.

"Lord—"

He turned his head instantly to me. "Joisan!"

"He took the gryphon!" For I had brought out of the dark that memory, strong enough to urge me into action.

Lord Amber drew me gently to him, and I wept as I had not in all those days of danger and sorrow that lay behind me. Between my sobs I asked, "It was the truth you spoke? He was not Kerovan?"

"It was the truth. It is as I said. Kerovan died in Ulmsdale. Rogear, who is betrothed to Kerovan's sister, arranged the ambush."

"And I never saw my lord," I said then in sad wonder. "But his gift, that one shall not have it!" Anger brought me strength. "By the Nine Words of Min, he shall not! It is a wondrous thing and his hands besmirch it! He used it as a weapon, Lord—he used it to burn your eyes. It was what rested on your wrist that defeated him. If you had only used it sooner as a shield!" I put my fingers to his wrist a little above that armlet. "Lord," I continued, "they say those of your people are mighty in healcraft. If you cannot aid yourself, can we not take you to them? It is in my service that this grievous hurt was done you, I owe this as a blood-debt—"

But he denied that with force and quickly. "No! There is no debt between us. Had we met elsewhere he would have sought to kill me."

"I have something of healcraft," I said then, "and Nalda." But in my heart I knew how limited we were, and that gave birth to fear. "Perhaps the sight will return. Oh, my Lord, I do not know why he sought me here—I have no longer lands nor fortune—save what he took with him. Know you of the gryphon? It was sent to me by Kerovan. Was it then such a great treasure of his House that this Rogear would risk much to get it into his hands?"

"No. It is no treasure out of Ulmsdale. Kerovan himself found it. But it is a thing of power and Rogear has enough of the Dark knowledge to use such. To leave it in his hands now—"

I could reach his thoughts as well as if he put them into words—to leave such a weapon with one of the Dark Ones was something we were bound in honor not to allow. But Rogear—not only did he ride with armsmen prepared to slay, but he had already shown he could harness the gryphon to his service too.

"My Lord, what can we do then to gain it once more?" I asked simply. For in this man (if man one might call him), I centered now all my trust.

"For the present"—weariness was deep in his voice—"I fear very little. Perhaps Rudo or Angarl can follow his trail a little, mark his path from here. But we cannot follow—yet—"

Again I believed that I knew his thoughts. He must nurse some hope that his sight would return. Or else he had some power of his own he could summon to aid. In this thing he must ride as marshal, I as an armsman. For I knew that the quest, or coming battle, was as much mine as his. It was my folly that had delievered the gryphon to Rogear. Thus my hand must have a part in its return.

My head ached cruelly, and Nalda brought a bowl of herb tea that she said I must drink. I suspected that it would make me sleep, and I would have refused. But Lord Amber urged me to it, and I could not set my will against his.

Then Nalda said she had a new ointment for his eyes, something she had used on burns, and that she would dress them again. I do not think he believed it would help, but he allowed her to take his hand and guide him forth.

I was only on the edge of drowsiness when Yngilda came to me, standing above my bed and staring down as if I had, in the space of hours, taken on a new face.

"So your lord is dead, Joisan" she said. I detected satisfaction in her words. That I did not prosper over her meant much.

"He is dead." I felt nothing. Kerovan had been a name for eight years—little more. To me he was still a name. How can one sorrow for a name? Instead it was a matter for rejoicing that I had that strange, instinctive dislike for the impostor. Rogear was not my lord; I need feel no discomfort or guilt because I did not like or trust him. My lord was dead, having never really lived for me.

"You do not weep." She watched me with that sly malice with which she so often favored me.

"How can I weep for one I never knew?" I asked.

She shrugged. "One shows proper feeling—" she accused.

We were no longer bound by keep custom, not here, not with our world swept away by the red tide of war. Were I back at Ithkrypt, yes, I would have kept the terms of conventional mourning as would be expected of me. Here there was no reason for form alone. I was sorry that a good man had died, and by the treachery of his kin, but mourn more than that I could not.

She drew from an inner pocket a strip of cloth made into a bag. I caught a whiff of scent from it and knew it for one of the herb bags put under pillows for those with aching heads.

"My mother's, but she does not need it this night." Yngilda spoke brusquely, as if she believed I might refuse her offering.

I was surprised, yes, but not unduly so. Perhaps now that we were equal before the world, Yngilda would no longer think me the more fortunate. So I thanked her and allowed her to slip the scented bag beneath my head where the warmth of my body could release the odor to soothe me.

The herb broth was doing its work also. I found it hard to keep my eyes open. I remember seeing Yngilda turn away toward the door, and then—I must have slept.

"It is Nalda?" I turned my head, though I could not see.

"Yes, Lord." She spoke briskly, and I silently thanked her for her way toward me. There was no pity in her manner, only the confidence of one who had nursed hurts and expected healing to come from her service.

"Lady Joisan?"

"She sleeps, Lord. And truly she has taken little hurt, save that the blow was a hard one. But there be no bones broken or other injury."

"Have the men reported in yet?"

"No, you shall see them at once when they come. Now here is some soup, Lord. A man must keep his belly filled if he would hold his strength. Open your mouth—"

She spooned it into me as if I were a baby. Nor could I then say her "no." But in me was a rage against what had happened and a dark feeling of misery that there was naught I could do for myself.

Nalda guided me to my bed, and I stretched thereupon. But sleep, even rest, was far from me, wearied from the trail as I was. I lay rigid, as one who expects any moment to be called to arms, though I might never be again.

I thought of Joisan—of her need to regain the gryphon. I knew that she was right; that it must be taken from Rogear. He had not been caught in the doom of wind and wave. Had then those others escaped also—Hlymer who was no true brother, the Lady Tephana, Lisana—?

Now I raised my hands to explore the bandage over my eyes. It was still damp, and I was sure it was of no use to me.

Rogear—if he had come after the gryphon—how could he have known of it save through Riwal, and from Jago, that it had passed to Joisan? What *was* it that he had come to seize? I knew so little at a time when knowledge was so essential.

I rested my arm across my forehead, the back of my wrist upon that bandage. How long was it before my thoughts were shaken out of the drear path they followed, and I realized something was in progress?

The wrist band! Joisan had said it defeated the ray from the crystal. From it now—I sat up and tore away the bandage. A warmth spread from the wristlet where it touched my flesh. Perhaps instinct, perhaps "memory" guided me now, for I held that band of strange metal first against my right eye and then against my left, pressing upon the closed lids. I did not try to see as yet. What I did was simple. Why I did it I did not know, save there came from that act a sense of well-being, a renewed confidence in life.

I dropped my hand and opened my eyes.

Dark! I could have cried my vast despair aloud. I had thought—hoped—

Then I turned my head a little and—light! Limited—but there. And I realized that I sat within a darkened room with light marking the doorway. Hastily I arose and went to it.

Night, yes, but no darker than any night I had seen before. When I had raised my head to look heavenward—stars! Stars glittering more brightly than I could remember. I could see!

Joisan! Instantly in my joy I knew I must share this with her. And that was mainly instinct too. I looked around the courtyard to get my bearings and headed to her room.

The doorway curtain was down and made me pause. Nalda had said she had given her lady a sleeping draught and that she would rest until morning. But even if I could not tell her of this miracle, I could at least look upon her dear face. There was a faint glimmer of light behind the curtain. They must have left one of the rush lamps with her.

So I entered, wishing to shout aloud my tidings, yet walking softly, trying to control even my breathing lest I disturb her rest.

Only, there was no one on her bed! The light cloak that must have been her night covering was tossed aside; the couch of leaves, grass, and brush was empty.

Empty save for something that lay in the hollow where her head must have rested. It caught my eye and I scooped it up. I held a bag, lumpily stuffed with herbs, which gave forth a strong odor. Among the leaves and roots there was a harder knot.

I gasped and the bag fell to the floor. About the band on my wrist coiled a thin blue haze, as if the metal had given forth a puff of smoke. I needed no instruction as to the nature of what was in that bag. Black evil shouted aloud in my mind.

Stooping, I caught up the bag by the point of my knife and dropped it on the stone table, close to the rush light. Without laying finger on it I slit the cloth, using the knife point to dig and probe until I brought into sight a thing about the size and shape of a Sulcar trading coin. It was dull black, yet also veined in red, and those veins—No, they were not veins after all, but some runic pattern as involved as those on my wristlet.

This was a thing of Power, that I knew. But of the Dark Power. Anyone touching it—

Joisan! How had this evil thing come into her bed? In that moment such a fear rent me that I shouted, calling on Nalda who should certainly be near at hand. The fury of my voice echoed hollowly out into the courtyard. I called again, heard other voices upraised—

"My Lord," Nalda stood in the doorway, "what—"

I pointed to the bed. "Where is my lady?"

She exclaimed, hurried forward, stark surprise on her face.

"But—where else could she be, Lord? She was sleeping, as the drink would make her. I would take Gunnora's Three Oaths that she could not stir until morning—"

"Did you leave this in her bed?" I had controlled my fear, outwardly at least. Now I used the knife to indicate the torn bag and its contents.

She leaned close, sniffing. "My lord, this is a soothing bag such as we make for the Lady Islaugha when she is restless. One of these beneath her pillow, and she is not so led by her fancies. It is of good herbs—"

"Do you also add this?" My knife point was close to the evil symbol.

She bent her head again. When she raised it and her eyes met mine, she looked stricken.

"Lord, I know not what that thing is, but—it is wrong!" Then something else burst upon her. "Lord—your eyes—you can see!"

I brushed that aside. Once that relief had filled my world, but of greater concern now was what had happened to Joisan. That she had been exposed to this thing of the Dark was agony to think on.

"Yes," I answered shortly. "But my lady slept with this by her, and she is gone. I know not what deviltry has been wrought here—but we must find her soon!"

So the aroused company searched from sentry towers to bridge ends. As the one that worked was pulled up for the night, I could see no way Joisan could have gone ashore. Yet it was plain she was not hidden in any of the rooms we explored.

In the end I had to accept that Joisan was nowhere in the keep. There remained—the lake! I stood at the bridge gap looking into the water, holding my torch to be reflected from its surface. Rogear—there was only one who would have done this thing! But he had been well away when Joisan had been laid on her bed. Someone in this place had been his servant in the matter. And from that servant I would have the truth!

I summoned them all, men, women, children, into the courtyard, and on a stone there I placed that ominous thing which had been a weapon aimed at my lady. I no longer felt the heat of first anger in me. For there had crept a cold along my bones, and my mind fastened on one thing alone—there would be such a blood-price for Joisan as these dales had never seen.

"Your lady has been taken from you by treachery." I spoke slowly, simply, so that the youngest there might understand. "While she was weak of body this evil thing was put into her bed, and so she was driven forth, perhaps to her death." Now I ventured onto ground of which I was not sure, depending heavily on what I had learned from Riwal. "Those who meddle with such a thing as this carry the taint of it upon them. For it is an essence of evil as to soil beyond cleansing. Therefore you shall each and every one of you display your hands and—"

There was a swirl among the women, a cry. Nalda had seized upon one who stood beside her, held fast a screaming girl. I was with them in an instant.

The Lady Yngilda—I might have expected it.

I spoke to Nalda. "Bring her! Do you need help?"

"Not so!" She was a strong wench and she held the whimpering girl easily.

I spoke then to the others. "I shall settle this matter. And I lay upon you—let no one touch, for his spirit's sake, what lies here."

They did not move from the courtyard, and none followed us as we returned to Joisan's chamber.

I thrust my torch into one of the wall rings, thus giving us more light. Nalda had twisted Yngilda's arms behind her back, prisoning her wrists in a grip I think even few men could have broken. She swung her captive around to face me. The girl was blubbering, still jerking futilely to loose herself.

Catching her by the chin, I forced her head up to meet me eye to eye.

"This was of your doing." I made that an accusation, no question.

She wailed, looking half out of her wits. But she could not escape me so.

"Who set you to this? Rogear?"

She wailed again, and Nalda gave her a vigorous shake. "Answer!" she hissed into her ear.

Yngilda gulped. "Her lord—he said she must come to him—that would bring her—"

I believed that she spoke the truth of what Rogear had told her. But that Yngilda had been moved by any goodwill toward Joisan in the doing of this I knew was not so. That Rogear had left such a trap out of malice I could also believe.

"Bring her to her death," I said softly. "You stand there with her blood on your hands, Yngilda, as surely as if you had used your kife!"

"No!" she cried. "She is not dead, not dead! I tell you she went—"

"Into the lake," I finished grimly.

"Yes, but she swam—I watched—I did, I tell you!"

Again I believed she spoke truthfully, and that cold ice in me cracked a little. If Joisan had gone ashore, if she were under some ensorcellment—then I still had a chance to save her.

"It is a long swim—"

"She climbed ashore; I saw!" She screamed back at me in a frenzy of terror, as if what she read in my face near broke her wits.

I turned to the door. "Insfar, Angarl." I summoned those two who had proven best at tracking. "Go ashore and look for any sign that someone came out of the lake!"

They were on their way at once. I came back to Nalda and her charge.

"I can do no more for you and your people now," I told Nalda. "If my lady has been ensorcelled—"

"She is bespelled," Nalda broke in. "Lord, bring her back safe from that!"

"What I can do, be sure that I will." I said that as sol-

emnly as any oath one could make with blood before kinsmen. "I must follow my lady. You will be safe here—at least
for a time."

"My Lord, think not of us. But rather fasten your thoughts
upon my lady. We shall be safe. Now—what of this one?"
She looked to Yngilda, who was weeping noisily.

I shrugged. Now that I had what I wanted from her, the
girl was nothing to me. "Do as you will. But I lay upon you
that she should be well watched. She has dealt with a Dark
One and obeyed him. Through her more evil may come."

"We shall see to her." There was such a promise in Nalda's
voice that I thought Yngilda might well shiver.

I went back to the courtyard and took up the coin of evil
on the point of my knife and carried it down the bridge that
had been broken. There I threw it into the water. I would
not bury it in the ground lest the unknowing chance upon it.

Dawn was breaking when I rode forth on Hiku with fresh
provisions for the trail. Yngilda had spoken the truth; a
swimmer had come ashore, crushing lake reeds and leaving
a trace that could not be mistaken. Beginning there I must
follow my lady.

What manner of sorcery had been used on her I did not
know, but that she was drawn against her will I had no
doubts. I tracked her to the valley rim. There she was met by
those who were mounted, and I knew that Rogear and his
armsmen had lurked there waiting for her.

Four they were, and with perhaps such weapons as I could
not imagine, my lady probably well bound so I could not
entice her in any way from their company. I might only follow, trusting fortune to give me a chance, ready to help fortune when it did.

The trail led west and north, as I thought it might. It was
my belief that Rogear intended to return to his own keep.
He had come to Ulmsdale to obtain power. Perhaps now with
the gryphon he had it.

They did not often halt, and for all my pushing they kept
ever ahead. On the second day I found traces that told me
their party had been augmented by three more riders. Also
there were led horses, so that they could change mounts when
theirs wearied. Whereas I had only Hiku, who was already
worn.

Still the rough-coated pony never failed me, and I thought
that any mount supplied by Neevor might be more than he
seemed in outward appearance. It was after I snatched the

rest I must have on the third night and headed on in the morning that I realized we were skirting lands I knew, coming into the forested fringe which had been my boyhood roving place.

There could be only one goal for those I followed. They were heading for the Waste. Well, what else could I expect—they dabbled in forbidden knowledge; surely they would turn to some possible source of the Power they wooed. But why had they taken my lady? To spite me? No, Rogear would have no interest in that. To his mind I was maimed, not to be considered an enemy any longer. And he had the gryphon—why must he have Joisan also? I kept thinking of this as I went, trying this explanantion and that, yet none seemed to fit.

On the morning of the fifth day I reached the edge of the Waste, near, I realized upon checking landmarks, to that road which ran to the naked cliff. And I was not greatly surprised to discover the trail I followed led in that direction.

Once more I rode on that ancient pavement. But it was difficult to remember that time, as if what had happened to me before had been the actions of another Kerovan who was not I, or even close kin. How I wished now for Riwal. He would have known so much more, though he was no Old One. But the safeguards he had had were not mine, and those I trailed were far more learned, I feared, than Riwal.

One night I camped along the road, scanting my rest, on my way before dawn. Here were the hills where those carvings stood out on the cliff faces. I found in my going curling runes resembling those on my wristlet. From time to time, viewing them, I felt a quickening excitement, as if I were on the very verge of understanding their meaning, yet I never did.

As before, I believed I was dogged by something that spied upon me. Though it might not have been dangerous in itself, what it might serve was another matter. I reached again the place of the great face. And before it I found evidence of those I hunted.

Set out on a rock before that great countenance was a bowl and, flanking it, two holders of incense. The bowl still held a film of oily liquid, and the incense holders had been recently used. All were of a black metal or stone I did not know. But I would not have set fingertip to them for my life's sake. Around my wrist once more that blue warning arose. What I did I was moved to by revulsion. I hunted about for stones and, with the largest of these, I smashed all that was set out. There came a shrill noise as they were powdered into fragments. Almost one could believe that the things had life of their own. But I did not leave them behind me as a ready focus for any remnant of the Dark that might linger here.

When I came to that great star, which had so awed Riwal, I found no similar signs of any ceremony, only marks in the earth to show that here they had left the narrowed road on the far side, squeezed by as if they wished to be as distant from that carving in passing as they could get. This, then, they feared. I paused for a moment to study it. But it held no heartening message save that—they had feared it.

Ahead lay only the cliff wall; they could go no farther. I had come to my journey's end, and I had no better plan in my head than to front boldly what waited me there. So I dismounted and spoke to Hiku:

"Friend, you have served me well; return now to him who gave you." I stripped away bridle and riding pad, dropping them to the road, because I believed that what lay before me was death. It would not be their choice of death, however, for my lady and me, but mine. If need be she would die by my hand, clean of the evil they might try to lay on her.

My fingers went to the band on my wrist, seeking the pattern there. It was a thing of power, I knew. Only I had not the key of its use. However, touching it so, I stared upon the star and longed to know what would defeat the Dark Ones ahead.

It was at that moment Neevor's words returned to me:

"You shall seek and you shall find. Your own heritage shall be yours. The discovery of what you are and can be you must make for yourself."

Brave words—said only to hearten? Or were they prophecy? Riwal said that to call upon a name in this place would unlock some force. But I knew no names; I was only human —of mixed blood perhaps—but human—

It seemed to me in that moment that I had spoken that word aloud; that it echoed back to me from the walls.

I flung up my arm before the star, and I made my plea, but not aloud. If there was any power here that might be drawn upon, let it come to me. Even if it blasted me, let me hold it long enough to free my lady, to deal with Rogear who sought to bring to this land that which was better lost. Let—it—fill— me—

It was as if something within me moved, slowly, grudgingly, as might a long-locked door. There was a flow from behind that door, one I did not understand. With it came such a maze of shadow memories as nearly overbore me. But I fought to remember who I was and why I stood there. And the memories were but shadows after all; my will was the sun to banish them.

But I *knew*! The shadows left behind that much. I had a weapon. Whether it would stand against what those others might marshal I could not tell until I put it to the final test. And the time was now!

I trotted ahead, urgency driving me. A sound broke the silence, a chanting that rose and fell as waves pound a coast. I rounded the bend and came upon those I sought. But of me they took no notice. They were too intent on what they would do here.

Upon the ground was a star enclosed in a circle. And that circle had been drawn in blood, blood that smoked and stank and had been drained from the armsmen who lay dead at one side like so much refuse.

On each point of the star was a spear of darkness, of oily smoke, that struck up into the sky, adding its stench to that of the blood. And before each of the points stood one of their party, four facing inward, the fifth placed before the wall to stare blank-eyed at it.

Hlymer, Rogear, Lisana, the Lady Tephana and, with her face to the wall, my Joisan. The four chanted, but she stood as one who walked through nightmares and could not help herself. Her hands were at her breast, and between them she held the gryphon.

It was if they shouted their purpose aloud, for I knew it. They were before a door, and Joisan held the key. By some fate she alone could use it, and so they had brought her for that task. What lay behind that door to which this road ran —who knew. But that I would let them open it—no!

Still they did not see me, for they were so intent upon what they did that the world beyond their star-in-circle had ceased to have real existence for them. Now I perceived something else around that line of smoking: blood-edged creatures as wispy as shadows. Now and then some dreadful snout sniffed at that barrier or dabbled in it. Fresh blood drew these remnants of ancient evil, but they were worn by centuries to such poor things they were shadows only. Of them I had no fear.

Some sighted me and came padding in my direction, their

eyes glinting like bits of devilish fire. Without my willing it consciously, my arm swung up and they cowered away, their eyes upon my wrist band. So I came to the circle of blood. There the smoke made me sick to the center of my being, but against that body weakness I held firm.

Now I raised my voice and I named names, slowly, distinctly. And my words cut through the spell their chanting raised.

"Tephana, Rogear, Lisana, Hlymer—" As I spoke each, I faced a little toward the one I so named. There was a shadow flicker in my mind. Yes, this was the right of it! This had I done once before in another place and time.

All four of them started as if they had been quick-awakened from sleep. Their eyes no longer centered on Joisan's back; they turned to me. I saw black rage flare in Rogear's, and perhaps in those of Lisana and Hlymer. But the Lady Tephana smiled.

"Welcome, Kerovan. So, after all, you prove the blood runs true." Her voice was sweeter than I had ever heard it, as she counterfeited what should have bound us together and never would. But if she thought me so poor a thing that I could be so deceived, she reckoned little of what she had once wrought.

Again that shadow knowledge moved in my mind, and I made her no answer. Instead I raised my hand, and from my wristlet a beam of blue light shot to touch the back of Joisan's head.

I saw her sway, and she gave a piteous cry. Still that which controlled me kept me to the attack, if attack it was. Slowly she turned around, seeming to shrink under a blow she could not ward off. Now she was away from the wall, facing me across the star-in-circle. Her eyes were no longer empty of what was Joisan. There was intelligence and life in them again, as she looked about her.

I heard a beast's growl from Hlymer. He would have leaped for my throat, but the Lady Tephana gestured, and he was silent and quiet in his place. Her hands moved back and forth in an odd manner as if she wove something between them. But I had little time to watch, for Rogear had moved also. He had Joisan in his hold, keeping her between us as a shield.

"The game is still ours, Kerovan, and it is to the death," he said. We might have been facing each other across a gaming board in a keep hall.

"To the death—but to yours, not mine, Rogear." With my upheld hand I sketched a sign, a star without a circle. Between us in the air that star not only glowed blue-green, but it traveled through the space between us until it was close to him at face level.

I saw his face go gaunt, old. But he did not lose his belief in himself. Only he dropped his hold on Joisan and stepped forward saying, "So be it!"

"No!" The Lady Tephana raised her eyes from what she wove without substance. "There is no need. He is—"

"There is every need," Rogear told her. "He is much more than we deemed him. He must be finished, or we shall be finished too. Spin no more small spells, Lady. You had the fashioning of him flesh and bone, if not spirit. Lend me your full will now."

I saw for the first time uncertainty in her face. She glanced at me and then away swiftly, as if she could not bear to look upon me.

"Tell me," Rogear pressed, "do you stand with me in this? Those two"—he motioned to Hlymer and Lisana—"can be counted as nothing now. It is us against what you sought to make and failed in the doing."

"I—" she began, and then hesitated. But at last the agreement he wished came from her. "I stand with you, Rogear."

And I thought—so be it. From this last battle there would be no escape, nor did I wish it.

Joisan:

I dreamed and could not wake, and the dream was dark with fear at its core. For me there was no escape, for in this dream I walked as one without will of my own. He who gave the order was Rogear.

First there was the calling, a need so laid upon me that I left the keep, trusted myself to the waters about it, swam for the shore. Then I must have traveled yet farther across those deserted fields until Rogear was there and he horsed me before him to ride.

There were parts I could not remember. Food was put in my hands and I ate, yet I tasted nothing. I drank and was aware of neither thirst nor the quenching of it. We were joined by others, and I saw them only as shadows.

On we rode into strange places, but these were the places of dreams, never clearly seen. At last we came to the end of that journey. There was—no! I do not wish to remember that part of the dream. But afterward, I held my lord's gift in my hands and it was laid upon me, as much as if I were in bonds, that I must stand, and when orders came I must obey. But what I was to do—and why—?

Before me was a cliff rising up and up, and behind me I heard a sound, a sound that lashed at me. I wanted to run— yet as in all ill dreams I could not move, only stand and look upon the rock and wait—

Then—

There was pain bursting in my head, like fire come to devour my mind, burn out all thought. But what vanished in those flames was that which held me prisoner to another's will. Weakly I turned away from the cliff to look upon those who held me captive.

Lord Amber!

Not as I had seen him last with bandaged eyes, fumbling in blindness, but as a warrior now, ready for battle, though his sword was sheathed and he had no knife-of-honor ready. Still, that he warred in another way, I knew.

There were four others. And I saw then there was a star

drawn in the earth and that I stood in the point that fronted the cliff, those others to my right and left in the other points.

One was Rogear, two were women, the fourth another man. He made a move in the direction of Lord Amber, but the woman to my right stayed him with a gesture. Rogear sprang before I could move and held me like a battle shield.

"The game is still ours, Kerovan," he said, "and it is to the death."

Kerovan! What did he mean? My lord was dead.

Lord Amber—it was Lord Amber who answered him. "To the death, but to yours, not mine, Rogear." I saw him draw a sign in the air, and there was a blue star that traveled to hang before Rogear's eyes.

He loosed me and stepped away, saying, "So be it."

"No!" The woman to my right spoke: "There is no need. He is—"

Rogear interrupted her. "There is every need. He is much more than we deemed him. And he must be finished, or we shall be finished too. Spin no more small spells, Lady. You had the fashioning of him, flesh and bone, if not spirit. Lend me your full will now!"

She glanced swiftly then at Lord Amber; then away. I saw her lips tighten. In that moment she was far older than she had seemed earlier, as if age settled on her with the thoughts in her mind.

"Tell me," Rogear continued, "do you stand with me in this? Those two"—he motioned toward the other man, the girl—"can be counted as nothing now. It is us against what you sought to make and failed in the doing."

I saw her bite her lip. It was plain she was in two minds. But at last she gave him what he desired. "I stand with you, Rogear."

"Kerovan," Rogear had called him, this man I would have taken blood-oath was one of the Old Ones. At that moment, all those sly whispers and rumors flooded back in my mind—that my lord was of tainted blood, becursed, that his own mother could not bear to look upon him. His own mother! Could it be—? Rogear said this woman had the fashioning of him, flesh and bone, but not spirit. Not spirit!

I looked upon Lord Amber and knew the truth, several truths. But this was not the time for the speaking of truth, nor the asking of whys and wherefores. He faced those who were deadly enemies, for there be no more deadly enemies then those of close blood-kin when evil works. And they were four against his one!

His one—! I looked about me wildly. I had no weapons—not even Toross' knife. But a stone—even my bare hands if need be—Only this was not fighting as I had known it. This was a matter of Power—Power such as Math had loosed at her death hour. And I had no gift of such. I tried to clench my fist. A chain looped about my fingers and cut my flesh. The gryphon—I still had the gryphon! I remember how Rogear had used it before—could not Lord Amber do likewise? If I could throw it to him—But Rogear was between; he need only turn, wrest it from me, use it as he had before—

With this in mind, I wrapped my two hands tight about the globe, saying to myself that Rogear would not take it from me to use against my lord, not while I had life to defend it!

My lord—Kerovan? I did not know the rights of that—whether Lord Amber had lied to me. But had he, my heart told me, then it had been with good reason. For just as I had shrunk from Rogear when he played Kerovan to entrap me, so did I now range myself with this other in time of battle. Old One or no, Kerovan or no, whether he wished it or no, in that instant of time I knew that we were tied together in such a way no axe bond or Cup and Flame ceremony could add to. That I welcomed this I could not have said, only it was as inevitable as death itself.

This being so, I must stand to his aid. Though how I could—

Almost I cried aloud with pain. My hands—! I looked down. My shrinking flesh could not hide the glow I held. The gryphon was coming to life, growing hotter and hotter. Might I then use it as Rogear had—to strike out in flame? But I could not hold it—the pain was too intense now.

If I grasped it by the chain alone—? I loosed it a little to dangle. It was as if all the lamps that had once burned in Ithkrypt's shattered hall were gathered into one!

"Look to her!" The girl on my left leaped at me, her hand outstretched to strike the gryphon from my hold.

By its chain I swung it at her and she cowered away, her hands to her face, falling to the ground with a scream.

So I had learned how to use what I held! Having so learned, I prepared to put it into further practice. A small black ball fell at my feet, thrown by the other woman. It broke, and from it curled an oily black snake, to wreathe about my ankles with the speed of a striking serpent, holding me as fast as if those coils were chains of steel.

I had been so occupied by my discovery concerning the gryphon that I had not seen what chanced with my lord. But now, fast captive, unable to swing my globe far enough, I watched in despair.

The other man held forth his right hand, and Rogear clasped it. Just so was he hand-linked to the woman, and the three faced my lord as one. Now the woman took into her other hand, from where it was set in her girdle as a sword might be, a rod of black along which red lines moved as if they were crawling things. She pointed this at my lord and began to chant, outlining his body with her wand—head to loins and up again to head.

I saw him tremble, waver, as if a rain of blows battered him. He held his arm ever before him, striving to move it so that the blue band about his wrist was before the point of the rod. Yet that he was hard set it was plain to see, and I wrestled with the smoky tangle about my feet, striving to reach those evil three with the globe.

"Unmade, I will it!" The woman's voice rolled like thunder. "As I made, so shall it be unmade!"

My lord—by the Flame, I swear it! I saw his body shaken, thin, becoming more shadow than substance. And out of nowhere came a wind to whirl and buffet that shadow, tearing at it.

I feared to loose the gryphon, but this must be stopped— the wind, that roll of chant-thunder—the rod that moved, erasing my lord as if he had never been! Shadow though he was, torn as he was, still he stood, and it seemed to me the black rod moved more slowly. Was she tiring?

I saw Rogear's face. His eyes were closed, and there was such a look of intense concentration there I guessed his will was backing hers. Did I dare loose my only weapon now?

Hoping I had not made the wrong choice, I hurled the gryphon at Rogear. It struck his shoulder, fell to the ground, rolled across the point of the star, stopped just within the circle. But the hand with which Rogear had gripped that of the woman fell from her grasp, limply to his side. He went to his knees, dragging with him the other man, who fell forward and lay still. While along Rogear's body, spreading outward from where the gryphon had struck, played lines of blue like small hungry flames, and he rocked back and forth, jerking with his other hand to free himself from the hold on the prone man. Yet it appeared he could not loose that finger locking.

The lines of fire ran down his arm swiftly, crossing to the body of the other man. Now Rogear did not strive to break that hold, and I guessed that he was willing the fire to pass from him into the other, who was now writhing feebly and moaning.

While he fought thus with his will, the woman stood alone. And her wand was held in a hand plainly failing. My lord was no longer a shadow, and the wind was dying. He looked to the woman steadily and without fear. In his eyes was something I could not read. Now he did not trouble to move his hand to ward off the rod. Rather, he held the wristlet level between them at heart height and he spoke, his words cutting through her chant.

"Do you know me at last, Tephana. I am—" He uttered a sound which might be a name, yet was unlike any name I had ever heard.

She raised her rod like a lash, as if she would beat him across the face in a rage too great to be borne.

"No!"

"Yes and yes and yes! I am awake—at long last!"

She twirled the rod at shoulder height, as I have seen a man ready a throwing spear. And throw it she did, as if she believed its point would reach his heart.

But, though he stood so close, it did not touch him, passing over his shoulder to strike against a rock and shatter with a ringing sound.

Her hands went to her ears, as if that sound were more than she could bear to hear. She wavered, but she did not fall. Now Rogear dragged himself up to his feet, moved beside her. His one hand still hung limply by his side, the other he raised swiftly, and let it fall on her shoulder. His face was white, stricken, yet I saw his eyes and knew that his will and his hate were blazingly alive.

"Fool!" His lips moved as if his face had stiffened into a mask. "Fight! You have the Power. Would you let that which you marred in the making triumph over you now?"

Lord Amber laughed! It was joyful laughter, as if he had no cares in the world.

"Ah, Rogear, you would-be opener of gates, ambitious for what, if you knew all, you would not dare to face. Do you not yet understand the truth? You seek to reach that which is beyond you: not only to reach it, but to put to use that which is not for your small mind—to Dark use—"

It was as if each word was a lash laid across Rogear's face, and I saw such anger mirrored there as I thought no human features could contain. His mouth worked, and there was spittle on his lips. Then he spoke.

I cannot put into words what rang then in my head. I know that I sank to the ground, as though a great hand were pressing me flat. Above Rogear's head stood a column of black flame, not red like honest fire but—*black!* Its tip inclined toward Lord Amber. But he did not start away. He stood watching as if this did not concern him.

Though I cried a warning, I did not hear my own words. The flame leaned and leaned, out across the star, the circle which enclosed it, poised over Lord Amber's head. Yet he did not even raise his eyes to see its threat, only watched Rogear.

About Rogear and the woman he held to him, the flame leaped and thickened as if it fed upon their bodies. It grew darker than ever, until they were hidden. And the tip of the flame moved as if trying to reach Lord Amber. Still it did not.

Slowly it began to die, fall back upon itself, growing less and less. And as it went it did not disclose Rogear or the woman. Finally it was but a glowering spark on the pavement—and nothing! They, too, were gone.

I put my hands to my eyes. To see that ending—it gave me such fear as I had never known, even though it did not threaten me. Then—there was silence!

I waited for my lord to speak—opening my eyes when he did not. And I cried out, forgetting all else. For no longer did he stand confidently upright to face his foes. He lay as crumpled beyond the circle as those who left within it—and as still.

About my feet the serpent no longer coiled. I staggered toward him, stopping only to pick up the gryphon. That was plain crystal again, its warmth and life gone.

As I had once held Toross against the coming of death, so did I now cradle my lord's head against me. His eyes were closed. I could not see their strange yellow fires. At first I thought he was dead. But under my questing fingers his heart still beat, if slowly. In so much he had won, he was still alive. And if I could only keep him so—

"He will live."

I turned my head, startled, fierce in my protection of the one I held. From whence had this one come? He stood with his back to the wall of the cliff, leaning a little on a staff carven with runes. His face seemed to shift queerly when I looked upon him, now appearing that of a man in late middle life, again that of a young warrior. But his clothing was gray as the stone behind him and could have been that of a trader.

"Who——?" I began.

He shook his head, looking at me gently as one who soothes a child. "What is a name? Well, you may call me Neevor, which is as good a name as any and once of some service to me—— and others."

Now he stood away from the cliff and came into the circle. But as he came he used his staff to gesture right and left. The evil outer circle was gone; the star also. Then he pointed to the girl, the other man, to all other evidences of those who had striven to call the Power here. And they were also gone, as if they were part of a dream from which I had now awakened.

At last he neared me and my lord, and he was smiling. Putting out the staff again, he touched my forehead and, secondly, touched my lord on the breast. I was no longer afraid, but filled with a vast happiness and courage, so that in that moment I could have stood even against the full army of invaders. Yet this was better than battle courage, for it reached for life and not death.

Neevor nodded to me. "Just so," he said, as if pleased. "Look to your key, Joisan, for it will turn only for you, as that one who dabbled in what was far beyond him knew."

"Key?" I was bemused by his order.

"Ah, child, what wear you now upon your breast? Freely given to you it was with goodwill, by one who found the lost ——and not by chance. Patterns are set in one time, to be followed to the end of all years to come. Woven in, woven out——"

The tip of his staff moved across the ground back and forth. I watched it, feeling that I could understand its meaning if I only made some effort, knew more.

I heard him laugh. "You shall, Joisan, you shall——all in good time."

My lord opened his eyes, and there was life and recognition in his expression, but also puzzlement. He stirred as if to leave my hold, but I tightened that.

"I am——" he said slowly.

Neevor stood beside us, regarding us with the warmth of a smile.

"In this time and place you are Kerovan. Perhaps a little less than you once were, but with the way before you to return if you wish. Did I not name you 'kinsman'?"

"But I—I was—"

Neevor's staff touched him once more on the forehead. "You were a part, not the whole. As you now are, you could not long contain what came to remind you of what you were and can be. Just as those poor fools could not contain the evil they called down, which consumed them in the end. Be content, Kerovan, yet seek—for those who seek find." He turned a little and pointed with his staff to the blankness of the cliff. "There lies the gate; open it when you wish, there is much beyond to interest you."

With that he was gone!

"My Lord!"

He struggled up, breaking my hold. Not to put me aside as I feared he now would, but rather to take me in his arms.

"Joisan!" He said only my name, but that was enough. This was the oneness I had ever sought, without knowing, and finding it was all the riches of the world spread before me for the taking.

Kerovan:

I held Joisan in my arms. I was Kerovan, surely I was Kerovan. Still—

Because that memory of the other one, the one who had worn my body for a space as I have worn mail, clung, so did I also cling to Joisan, who was human, who was living as I knew life and not—

Then the full sense of who and what I was as Kerovan returned. Gently I loosed my hold of her. Standing, I drew her to her feet. Then I was aware that the happiness of her face was fading and she watched me with troubled eyes.

"You—you are going away!" She clutched my forearms with her hands, would not let me turn from her. "I can feel it—you are going from me because you wish to!" Now her words had an angry ring.

I could remember our first meeting and how she had looked upon me then—I who was not wholly human, part something else that I did not yet know or understand.

"I am not an Old One," I told her straightly. "I am indeed Kerovan, who was born thus!" I shook off her hold to step back and show her one of those hoofed feet, thrust stiffly out that she might see it plain. "I was born by sorcery, to become a tool for one who aspired to the Power. You watched her try to destroy what she had created, and instead she herself was destroyed."

Joisan glanced to where the flame had eaten up those two.

"Twice-cursed was I from the beginning: by my father's line and by my mother's desire. Do you understand? No fit mate for any human woman am I. I have said—Kerovan is dead. That is the truth, just as Ulmsdale is destroyed, and with it all the House of Ulm. . . ."

"You are my promised, wedded lord, call yourself what you desire."

How could I break that tie she pulled so tight between us? Half of me, no, more than half, wanted to yield, to be as other men. But the fact that I had been a vessel into which something else had poured, even though that was gone again

190

—How could I be sure it would not return, with force enough to reach out to Joisan? I could not—tainted, cursed, deformed —give me that name best-suited. I was no lord for her.

Once more I retreated, edging away, lest her hand meet mine once again and I could not control the desire of that part of me human-rooted. Yet I could not turn and go from her, leave her alone in the Waste. And if I went with her, back to her people, could I continue to hold to my resolve?

"Did you not listen to Neevor?" She did not follow me; rather she stood, her hands clasped on her breast over the englobed gryphon. "Did you not listen then?" Still there was anger in her voice, and she regarded me as one who is exasperated by stupidity.

"He called you kinsman—therefore you are more than you deem yourself. You are you—no tool for any one, Kerovan. And you are my dear Lord. If you strive to say me 'no,' then you shall discover I have no pride. I shall follow wherever you go, and in the face of all shall I claim you. Do you believe me?"

I did, and believing could see that now I could not deal otherwise than seem to agree.

"Yes," I made simple answer.

"Good enough. And if in the future you try to walk away from me again, never shall you find that easy." It was not a warning or a promise, but a statement of fact. Having seemingly settled that to her satisfaction, she looked once more to the cliff.

"Neevor spoke of a door and a key which I hold. Someday I shall put that to the test."

"Someday?" Yes, I could remember Neevor's words better now that I had my emotions under control.

"Yes. We—we are not ready—I think—I feel—" Joisan nodded. "It is something we must do together, remember that, Kerovan—*together!*"

"Where to, then? Back to your people?" I felt rootless, lost in these dales. I would leave the choice to her, since all my ties were gone save one.

"That is best," she answered briskly. "I have promised them what measure of safety can be found nowadays. When they have won to that, then we shall be free!"

Joisan flung wide her arms, as if the taste of that freedom was already hers. But could it be freedom if she held to that other tie? I would walk her road for now because I had no choice. But never would I let her be the loser because she looked at me and saw a Kerovan to whom she was oath-tied.

My poor lord, how bitter must have been his hurts in the past! I wish that I could run back down the years and rub out the memory of each, one by one. He has been named monster until he believes it—but if he could only look upon himself through my eyes—

We shall walk together, and I shall build a mirror that he may see himself as he is, and, so seeing, be free from all the sorrow the Dark Ones laid upon him. Yes, we shall return to my people—though they are not truly mine anymore—for I feel as one who has taken another road and can look back only a little way. We shall make sure that they reach Norsdale. For the rest—

So I thought in that hour, and wise was that thought. For sometimes wisdom comes not altogether through age and experience, but suddenly like an arrow flight. I nursed my key within my hand—that bride gift which had been first my bane and then my salvation. I put my other hand within my lord's, so we went together, turning away for a space from the gate Neevor promised us, knowing within my heart that we would return and that it would open upon—But what mattered what lay beyond if we went together to see?